NEVER SOMEWHERE ELSE

Alex Gray was born and educated in Glasgow. She has worked as a folk singer, a visiting officer in the DSS and an English teacher. She has been awarded the Scottish Association of Writers Constable and Pitlochry trophies for her crime writing. Married with a son and a daughter, she now writes full time. *Never Somewhere Else* is her first novel.

NEVER SOMEWHERE ELSE

ALEX GRAY

First published in Great Britain in 2002 by Canongate Crime,
an imprint of Canongate Books Ltd, 14 High Street,
Edinburgh EH1 1TE

10 9 8 7 6 5 4 3 2 1

Epigraph on page vii is from Norman MacCaig: *Collected Poems*,
published by Chatto & Windus.
Reprinted by permission of The Random House Group Ltd

British Library Cataloguing-in-Publication Data
A catalogue record for this book is available on
request from the British Library

ISBN 1 84195 218 4

Typeset by Palimpsest Book Production Limited,
Polmont, Stirlingshire
Printed and bound by Creative Print and Design,
Ebbw Vale, Wales

www.canongate.net

To D.D.
with love

The frontier is never
Somewhere else. And no stockades
Can keep the midnight out.

Norman MacCaig: from 'Hotel Room, 12th floor'

Prologue

'See you tomorrow!'

'Sure. See you!'

Donna Henderson turned into the narrow cobbled lane that was a short cut to the taxi rank. Her friends continued down the street, chattering like sparrows, their much brighter plumage a vivid splash against the drab city night. The older girls were heading off to yet another club, but Donna was on a strict curfew. Protestations about being nearly old enough to vote had cut no ice. Still, it wasn't long till her birthday. Then she'd go clubbing all night if she felt like it.

Her mouth relaxed into a smile as she thought about tomorrow. Tomorrow she would be working with that new stylist, Mark. In her mind she saw them together. She would be all attentiveness while he would surely reward her efforts with one of his gorgeous smiles. The fantasy continued on down the lane, past the back doors of restaurants and the cinema, past the chained-off squares of car parks belonging to the darkened offices above. There was a street light halfway down, an ornate structure dating from the earlier part of the twentieth century. Its weird elongated shapes, which were now a hallmark of this city, drew the eye upwards.

Donna, looking up at the lantern's black outline against the sodium glow of the sky, did not see the movement from the shadows until it was too late.

The silver bicycle chain swept upwards in a graceful arc then two leather-clad fists yanked it tight. Donna's hands scrabbled towards her neck for a moment.

As she fell, the lamp swung overhead, scattering shards of light. Then unseen hands put out the light for good. Donna never heard the thud as her body hit the cobbles.

The shadowy figure bent over her body and smoothed her hair from the now distorted face. Fingers traced the brow line in a slow caress. From the depth of its shadow, the figure breathed a long sigh over the dead girl. Under the lamplight a blade flashed out and there was a frenzy of activity as flesh and hair were hacked away.

For a moment only the sound of traffic could be heard passing by the mouth of the lane then the black figure laughed softly, holding up a blood-soaked scalp.

Donna Henderson's body lay in the narrow lane, arms flung out as if in protest, blood shining like a pool of patent leather over the cobbles.

It was over so quickly. All her dreams of tomorrow crushed in that swift and brutal act.

Hilary Fleming strode through the knee-length grasses, her hands stuck into the pockets of her waxed jacket. The wind which blew her blonde hair over her eyes flattened the grasses around her. For a moment she lost sight of Toby then, pushing back her hair, she saw his feathery tail thrashing through the thicker undergrowth ahead. Hilary smiled as she raised her face to the morning sun. What a perfect way to begin the day!

Suddenly Toby broke into a paroxysm of barking, darting backwards and forwards at an overgrown laurel bush. Squirrels, thought Hilary. Stupid dog. She quickened her pace, the grasses swishing against her green wellingtons.

Then she stopped abruptly, the smile freezing on her lips.

From under the bright green laurel leaves a white arm protruded. White, bloodless and certainly dead.

Hilary's gorge rose and she was aware of Toby's concerned whines mingling with a strange high noise which became her own scream.

1

The tall man in the raincoat stood a little apart from the activity surrounding the body. He had seen enough to fill in his report, had asked the pathologist all the relevant questions, but he lingered still, regarding the section of the park that was cordoned off by police tape. This was the third young woman to be found in St Mungo's Park and it was the business of the man in the raincoat to find answers to the questions of who had killed them and why.

As he stared at the scene of this latest crime a worried blackbird flapped out of the laurel bushes, breaking into his reverie.

They would have to close the park now, for sure. Round the clock surveillance would put an even greater strain on their limited resources but something drastic had to be done to stop the killer revisiting the scene of his crimes. The Press wanted to know if it was the work of a serial killer. He hadn't confirmed that yet, but the corpses certainly bore the hallmarks of that type of murder.

His gaze returned to the girl's body. It was out of sight now, its grisly contents concealed in the body bag. He wondered at the mentality behind such a vicious act and, as ever, how on earth he was going to find words that sought to explain this to a grieving mother and father.

'No, I've told them to wait for the forensic report. No. We'll discuss it later.'

Chief Inspector Lorimer put down the phone and glared at it. He sat for a few moments, fists clenched on the desk in front of him, face set in grim, determined lines.

It was a face which could never have been called handsome, but there was something which made you look twice. Craggy features and a strong jawline might have indicated a well-weathered sportsman.

In fact he had been a rugby player in his younger days. The mouth was thin, downturned and looked incapable of smiling. It didn't have much practice in this line of work. What really made a person stop and look again, though, were the pale blue eyes. A dreamer or a poet might have been gazing out of them. Combined with Lorimer's sterner features, they came as a disconcerting surprise. Hardened criminals had broken under these strange staring eyes.

Lorimer had his blue eyes to thank for his career as a policeman. He had never considered the police force as a way of earning his living when he had left school. University had been the obvious choice and he soon immersed himself in a variety of Arts subjects, favouring Art History as his principal discipline. In a decade when job choices had been plentiful, Lorimer had not been overly concerned about what career lay ahead of him on graduation. One with prospects, he'd assured himself vaguely, except that it would never be banking. That decision had been taken one week into his first summer job in a city bank. The tedium and office small talk was only just bearable for a few weeks; certainly not for a lifetime.

Ironically the job in the bank was the catalyst which brought about an abrupt end to Lorimer's student days.

On the day that was to mark such a radical change in his lifestyle, Lorimer had been summoned to his manager's office where two uniformed police officers stood, eyeing him with interest. The manager had been terse in explaining the situation and the student had found himself being driven off discreetly to the local police station to be put into a line up.

'A man with penetrating blue eyes' fitting Lorimer's description was sought in connection with a spate of robberies from branches of his own bank, he was told. Youthful indignation had given way to curiosity after the identity parade had eliminated him as the culprit. Lorimer had lingered in the station with the officers, drinking tea and asking questions, in no hurry to return to his flinty-faced bank manager who clearly had him tried and sentenced already.

With the alarming experience of being a suspect, for however short a time, had come the realisation that villains were very much a part of everyday society; a realisation quickly confirmed by chatting to the officers in charge. There was an allure about this kind of job which sought out and found criminals who might look just like himself.

Now, several decades later, Lorimer was the Detective Chief Inspector in his Divisional Headquarters. Years of experience in and out of uniform lay behind him; on the beat, into CID, learning all the time about humankind and learning too about himself.

The blue eyes were hard and cold as he contemplated this latest murder. For a few moments he allowed himself to mourn the passing of someone else's daughter, then forced such feelings aside to prepare a terse statement for the gentlemen of the Press.

Martin Enderby picked up the photo of the dead girl from his desk. She had been pretty, he thought. A blonde with a shy smile looked up at him from the black and white print. And now there was a name to match this face: Sharon Millen.

Teenager Sharon Millen's mutilated body was found today by gardeners arriving for work in St Mungo's Park.

She had been missing overnight after failing to come home from the cinema with her boyfriend, James Thomson. Police were notified of Sharon's disappearance by her parents after her father Joseph had telephoned James Thomson in the early hours. However, James had seen Sharon safely on the number 7 bus which would have taken her to within yards of her home. How she came to be in St Mungo's Park, which lies at the other end of the city, is a mystery with which the police are now dealing. They are anxious to speak to any passenger who may have been travelling on that route between 11.15 and 11.40 p.m. or to anyone who may have seen or spoken to Sharon in the vicinity of her home.

This dreadful death is now the third to have occurred in less than a fortnight. Although Chief Inspector William Lorimer assured our reporter that investigations are very much under way, there is a feeling that the police remain in the dark as far as these horrific crimes are concerned.

The question on everybody's lips of course is: will the killer strike again?

Martin read the article with a frown. Not enough about the victim.

And certainly not enough about the boyfriend. It was a pity the lad Thomson hadn't supplied a photograph of them together, but his parents had refused to let him speak to the Press. He was too upset. Only a lad of eighteen himself. Still, he couldn't be a suspect or surely Lorimer would have him in custody. Anyway, the public could easily see the pattern of these crimes now, thought Martin.

He had written a good piece on Donna Henderson, the first victim. Poor girl had been last seen leaving a city centre club on her way to a taxi rank. Only no taxi had picked her up. Then her body had been discovered in St Mungo's Park. Martin chewed over the phrase 'Murders in St Mungo's'. Or maybe 'The St Mungo's Murders'. It was suitably alliterative, anyway. Lucy Haining had met the same fate; strangulation with a bicycle chain then mutilation. Martin shuddered. He balked at the mental image of human flesh slashed away like that. God help the relatives who had had to identify the bodies.

More on the horror of three murders in ten days, he thought, starting to type some detail into his copy.

Linda Thomson knocked on her son's door quietly. The terrible sobs had subsided and she hoped that he had slept. She too had wept in her husband's arms, shocked and stricken when the police had come to bring the awful news. James had gone with them to the police station in the city centre. It had been hours before they brought him home, chalk white and frozen cold with shock. Couldn't anyone see the poor lad was in a state? His reaction clearly showed that he was innocent of any hint of crime.

Anyhow, Linda thought, anyone who knows James can tell that he'd never hurt a fly. She took the mug of tea into the darkened room and placed it on the bedside table. James was lying face down on his bed, the duvet only partly covering his legs. Sitting down on the edge of the bed, Linda stroked her son's dark hair. A long convulsive sob broke from him, but he uttered no words. He was too exhausted to speak, she thought, remembering his scream of pain earlier that day.

'Why, Mum, why?'

*   *   *

Outside the sunset glowed on the horizon, making all the foreground shapes one black silhouette. A crow sat on the rooftops turning its head this way and that, as if waiting for a mate before flying off to roost for the night. Darkness would soon gather and in the darkness unmentionable fears would rise and percolate around the city, fears which might spill over into careless talk to give a clue to these deeds of death.

Lorimer had officers scouring several haunts in the city, primed to receive any word which could lead him to the killer. The Superintendent was breathing down his neck, talking about psychological profiling. After Lucy Haining's death he had thought, 'Not yet. Not yet.' Now he was not so sure.

On a glass shelf three trophies stand. The dried blood has congealed to make a brown stain like dull varnish on the glass. Three swathes of hair adorn the shelf, blonde, red and near-black, trophies of a grisly hunter.

Outside the room where these scalps are kept, daylight has broken again. A greenish light is cast on the bare distempered walls from the uncurtained windows set high above the city. A bird flies past outside. Look and see. A concrete tower with blank eyes staring, anonymous. No one will ever find you here.

2

Chief Inspector Lorimer stood at the window of his office, hands clasped behind his back. Before him the morning had turned dull and drizzly, puddles forming in the car park below. Uniformed men scuttled across the yard to their vehicles. Doors slammed. Engines revved. Lorimer saw and heard all this without noticing it at all. His eyes and ears were in St Mungo's Park, trying to pierce through the darkness of three sinister nights.

There was nothing, nothing at all to link these victims other than the grisly manner of their death. Donna Henderson had been a hairdresser, just an ordinary enough lassie, almost eighteen. Lucy had been an art student. English family. Lived in digs near the Art School. By all accounts she had had a promising future in jewellery design, having won some award or other in this, her final year. And it had been her very final year. Then young Sharon Millen, just a wee girl really, still at school. No police records to link them, no common backgrounds. Even their appearances differed, as if the killer picked and chose for sheer variety. Lorimer understood too well that this type of killer was the most difficult to find and the most dangerous. Some crazy person with an obsession, a fetish in their sick mind, looking for victims. The scalping hadn't shown any sort of expertise, the MO claimed. But maybe he would improve his technique given time, thought Lorimer to himself. And we mustn't give him time.

He clenched his fists harder. So far there was nothing at all to show for the painstaking work by his squad. House-to-house interviews, as well as a thorough scouring of the park, had drawn a blank. The families of the victims had been questioned, their closest friends and colleagues brought in to make statements. The places they had been on the night of each murder had been turned inside out.

Donna Henderson had been murdered in West George Lane. Forensics had matched hair and blood samples. No one had seen or heard a thing and yet the murder must have taken place only minutes after she had left her companions. The killer could not possibly have known that the young hairdresser would take that particular route. The victim had been picked quite at random; yet Lorimer felt certain that a murder had been intended. Someone had lain in wait to pounce on a solitary girl in that lonely place.

The exact location of Lucy's death had taken rather longer to discover. It emerged that she had been on her way to visit a fellow student – Janet Yarwood – but had never arrived. Lucy had often dropped in on this girlfriend whose flat was a short walk away. In her statement Janet had said that she had not expected Lucy, exactly, in the sense that no prior arrangement had been made. But there had been nothing unusual about this. However, enough evidence had been found on the waste ground between the back courts of two rows of tenements to establish that Janet's flat had been Lucy's destination that night. His men had sifted through all sorts of rubbish, used needles included, and had even taken apart the beginnings of a heap destined to become a bonfire on Guy Fawkes night.

Lorimer sighed. There was nothing to link them in life, and everything to link them in death. As for poor little Sharon Millen, no trace had been found to show where her death had taken place. All they knew was that she had got on that number 7 bus and then her corpse had been found in St Mungo's Park, hidden in the bushes. Just like the others. Why? Why had he troubled to take them to the park? The initial risk in dumping Donna's body was bad enough, but the increased risk in taking two further bodies there was crazy. But I am dealing with a crazy person, Lorimer told himself. This person has apparently no motive for the killings, so why expect any logical motive for his disposal of the corpses? That young PC, Matt Boyd, had suggested a link with previous murders in the city which had been at the hands of drug-crazed youths, hallucinating and paranoid. It was Matt's answer for every crime of violence. Given the statistics, he had a fair chance of being correct some of the time.

But this was different. There was something far more calculating and vindictive about this. No fingerprints had been left and the fibres being tested by the forensic biologists were as yet without any significance. Forensic biology could uncover all sorts of clues from traces left at the scene of a crime, but it had its limitations. Often the data was only one half of an equation, meaningless until the other half could be discovered.

A consultation of HOLMES had proved fruitless. The national computer bank could show patterns of crimes all over the country. But there was none. This spate of crimes in his city had no parallel anywhere else. In one way this was a relief: it narrowed the field. Yet a repeated pattern would have offered help in establishing travel routes and other background which might have helped identify a killer.

It all came back to why. Why had he taken them to the park? Why brutalise them in such a way? Lorimer's eyes roamed around the walls of his office, seeking inspiration. There were the usual outsize maps, a statement of policing principles, various commendations and two calendars, one ringed in red to show the dates of murders committed in his Division. But it was to none of these that Lorimer turned his attention, and instead he looked to the paintings he had accumulated over the years. Some were prints, of course. A policeman's salary didn't always allow for the purchase of originals, and certainly not the famous portrait of Père Tanguy which gazed down at him. The postman looked as if he was restless with sitting and longed to be off and doing something more active. That was what had attracted Lorimer to the Van Gogh print; that feeling of a man's repressed energy. Lorimer understood that feeling only too well.

But today there was no inspiration to be had from works of art or anything else for that matter. The Fiscal had allowed them weeks to have the corpses studied by forensics, with all the painstaking details which that had entailed. And what had he to show for these weeks of investigation? For the first time in his career Chief Inspector William Lorimer was beginning to feel out of his depth. He'd cracked countless cases of mindless violence, but none had yielded up as little as this one. That none of his colleagues had experienced a case like this was little comfort.

The Press were on his back, demanding results. And so was the Super. It was time to bring in the psychologist. Lorimer frowned. He'd heard of miraculous results from these fellows, but part of him still resisted putting faith in a procedure he didn't know much about. Well, perhaps he ought to make it his business to find out now.

There was a knock at the door.

'Sir, Superintendent Phillips says he's ready to go now.'

WPC Annie Irvine waited anxiously for Lorimer to turn round and acknowledge her words. For a few moments he stood, still staring out of the window. They were all used to his moods, and put up with the long, almost rude, silences because he was such a good DCI and pretty fair-minded if his officers watched their step. At last the shoulders heaved in a resigned sigh.

'All right, Annie, I'll be there shortly.'

'Yes, sir.' She closed the door and rolled her eyes to heaven.

Superintendent Phillips, the Divisional Commander, didn't like being kept waiting and she'd be the one to catch the brunt of his short temper if Lorimer didn't hurry up. The Divcom was already in a foul mood. WPC Irvine crept past George Phillips's door. Thank goodness she wasn't the one who was going to that poor girl's memorial service.

They sat in the car until most of the mourners had passed through the gates and slowly wound their way up to the church. Rain on the windscreen made the shapes of leafless trees blurred and out of focus, like an Impressionist painting.

All the families had wanted cremations but the Fiscal had, of course, refused. The victims' bodies were still in the mortuary and would be for some time to come. Meanwhile this latest memorial service had to suffice to help the bereaved come to terms with their loss.

Lorimer wondered if wanting cremations was simply the modern trend of funerals, or did they want to obliterate in ashes the remains of these mutilated bodies? An interesting thought. Perhaps he'd put it to the psychologist and see what he made of it.

Beside him the Divcom coughed and looked irritably out of the window. Lorimer tried not to smile. George Phillips had given up smoking again and was hell to live with.

'All right, Constable,' Lorimer leaned forward and touched the driver's shoulder. The car joined the slow line of vehicles winding up to the little building at the top of the hill. Already people were queuing to enter, their black umbrellas held against the streaming rain. Lorimer stared at each one, hunting for a face to jog a memory, to spark off some clue which would set him on the long road to solving this case. Each darkened figure was a stranger. As they took their places near the back, Lorimer was distracted by a group of girls weeping desperately, holding on to each other. They must have been classmates, he thought. What a hellish murder. Lorimer felt a boiling rage inside.

As the minister asked the congregation to bow their heads in prayer, Lorimer's piercing blue stare was directed at the wooden cross on the wall. Give me a clue, he demanded, show me where that bastard is. Oh God of any pity, don't let him get away.

Later, sitting in the car, they watched as one by one the mourners left the church. James Thomson was being supported by his father. The boy looked as though he could collapse at any moment. The schoolgirls were quieter now, subdued by the service and by the necessity of encountering Sharon's parents. Bravely, the Millens had remained to receive the congregation, speechless, but shaking hands. The elderly minister stood by them supportively, speaking an occasional word of thanks. He hadn't known who we were, Lorimer thought to himself, he'd treated everyone with the same kindly courtesy. What was it about some of these church folk that they could only see good in their fellow men? Lorimer mused on this for a moment, admitting to himself that the seamy side of life had given him quite a different outlook.

What kind of outlook did the killer have? Did he know of Sharon's memorial service? Or did his involvement with her end when he left her body under those bushes, taking her blonde hair away with him? For what? Why? With Donna Henderson's murder had come a frantic round of city salons, freelancers, theatrical stylists and wig dressers. The link between the victim's profession and manner of death had seemed so obvious. Now it seemed only a cruel irony.

The last of the mourners stepped into her car and drove off. A school teacher, thought Lorimer, who was good at guessing professions from appearances.

'Nothing doing, Bill.'

George Phillips's tone was resigned. Lorimer declined to answer. Rain-soaked trees lined the road to the gateway and their car swished out into the main road leading back to town.

At the first set of red lights George Phillips turned to Lorimer.

'We'll be sending that psychologist fellow up to see you later today. Can't do any harm, and could do some good. Question is, do we let the Press in on it at this stage or not? Could make it look as though we're up to something.'

On the other hand it might be seen as clutching at straws. Lorimer stared straight ahead. He was not opposed to this development, just resentful that it had come to this in a case where he had failed to find anything significant himself.

'Fellow by the name of Solomon Brightman,' continued the Divcom. 'Funny names most of these psychologist types have. Ah well, perhaps he'll cast a little light on the case.'

Lorimer refused to acknowledge Phillips's feeble attempt at a joke. Within himself he hoped fervently that the psychologist would do just that. And it was no laughing matter.

The main building of the university was old and chilly. Stone steps and balustrades, marble-tiled floors and old creaking wooden doors gave the place a Gothic atmosphere. Lecture theatres and labs gave off from one side of a wide corridor whilst offices lay on the other. 'Doctor S. Brightman' proclaimed a small plastic plaque. Underneath, picked out in gold, was the word 'Psychology'.

On the other side of the door was a surprisingly modern office with the normal accoutrements of grey steel filing cabinets, pale pine desk and chair and several shelves of books. Solly Brightman sat behind the desk, a large ordnance survey map before him. He was a young man of thirty-two, rather foreign in appearance, due to his thick black beard, black-rimmed spectacles and handsome

Semitic features. His large brown eyes were fringed with the sort of luxuriant lashes most women would have given a month's salary for. These eyes were pondering an area on the map. A green circle showed St Mungo's Park and its immediate residential environs. Solly had ideas about these environs.

The telephone rang. He picked it up casually, without taking his eyes off the map for one moment.

'Yes, Chief Inspector. Certainly. Yes, I will. No. That's all right. I'll see you then. Goodbye.'

Solly spoke smoothly, as if the words had been rehearsed for a part he was playing, then put down the telephone. His preoccupation with the map before him made the conversation with Chief Inspector Lorimer seem quite incidental, almost irrelevant, instead of the one for which he had been waiting most of the day. Solly could see more in the map before him than simple areas of green parkland and networks of suburban streets. He saw opportunity. He saw escape routes. And he saw the emergence of a possible personality.

3

Outside the closed gates of St Mungo's Park, PC Matt Boyd stood waiting for his neighbour. He shivered beneath the police-issue raincoat. What a foul night to be on duty. Guard duty.

His shiver had expressed a disgust for the murders perpetrated within the darkened park as well as a thrill of fear that the murderer could return to the scene of the crime. His hands felt the radio in his top pocket then went to his baton concealed below the coat. Heavy footsteps told him that Henry was coming back from the chippy. Sure enough, the younger constable strode smartly around the curve of the park's railings, his breath clouding the cold night air.

'Lord, this is a miserable duty,' he spat out, turning on his heel to face the road, his back, like Matt's, to the gates behind him. He passed over the newspaper-wrapped packet.

'Ta, mate,' Matt said, unwrapping the vinegary chips and beginning to devour them greedily.

'Keep one for Rover,' laughed Henry.

Rover was the nickname for the dog-handler rather than the dog, whose name was Ajax. Handler and Alsation were patrolling the perimeter of the park constantly that night, passing Matt and Henry at the main gates about every forty-five minutes. They were due to make an appearance in less than ten minutes if their tour of the park had proved uneventful. Matt chuckled again. Rover would be lucky to see any of his chips. Still, he might give one to the dog.

The sound of the rain was a soft drilling on the pavement and a gurgle of water trickling down the drains. His footsteps were muffled by the wetness, each print illumined for an instant in the streetlight, then gone, melting into shadows. His head turned slowly from street to park, past trees and open grassland, past swishing cars and buildings shuttered against the night.

Ajax's breath came out in a faint misty cloud as he loped along, mouth slightly open showing strong white teeth. The railings took on a long curve, foliage thick and high above them as the hill banked steeply. Suddenly the dog stopped, stiff and alert. His head strained and his nose probed the air. The handler made a movement to unleash him if need be, while above them the rhododendron bushes swayed madly. Then a splintering crash revealed a white face glaring through the leaves. The handler slipped the leash and reached for his two-way radio.

In a moment there was a flurry of leaping dog and a cry as the face disappeared, falling backwards through the bushes.

Henry's radio crackled into life.

'Tango Two, this is control. Ajax has a prowler inside the park. Assistance requested. Car on its way. Over.'

'Roger, Control. Wilco.'

Henry's eyes were shining, all boredom gone. He and Matt broke into a jog along the wet pavements, ears straining for Ajax's growls. Matt paused briefly by a bin to toss away their scrunched up chip packets. A different kind of hunger was taking over.

They came around the corner to see Ajax crouching by his handler. A man leaned flat against the inside of the park railings, obviously terrified of the dog. As Matt began to climb the railings he could hear him yabbering, 'Get 'im off. Don't let 'im touch me!'

Ajax was trained to look as though he would spring at a suspect. He had full control over the man.

'Car's coming,' Henry quietly told the handler.

Matt was now standing alongside the dog, shining his torch on the man against the railings. The torchlight gave his eyes a sunken, staring look. He was a small man, probably in his sixties, thin on top with wrinkled cadaverous flesh which hung in slack, unshaven jowls. His threadbare grey coat was tied round the waist with rope. Matt felt a sinking disappointment. He was only a derelict. Still, he would be taken in for questioning. The park was out of bounds after all, and notices had been put up to that effect. Closed circuit television cameras with infrared devices were secreted in and around the park, mainly panning the area where the bodies had been found. Yet all this technology had failed to detect what one well-trained dog had found.

Matt was annoyed. For a few minutes the activity had given the impression of a breakthrough. He had been rehearsing what he would say if Chief Inspector Lorimer were to ask for a résumé of their night's duty. In his imagination he had anticipated the Chief's nod of approval and his own resulting glow.

A white escort pulled up and the tramp was hoisted clumsily over the railings and handed into the back of the car. Ajax and his handler watched them drive off round the curve of the park.

'Ah, well, back to the gate,' grumbled Matt. He set off, slightly ahead of Henry and the handler. Ajax walked obediently by their side, alert yet calm as ever, pleased by the recent excitement.

4

Solly sat in a corner of the interview room. He had not demurred when Chief Inspector Lorimer invited him to sit in as an observer.

It was highly unusual for a Chief Inspector to conduct interviews. The old man had been cautioned and a preliminary taped interview had already taken place. They could hold him for six hours and in that time it would normally be Alistair Wilson, Lorimer's smoothly urbane Detective Sergeant, who dealt with the suspect. He especially wanted Lorimer to see this fellow for himself, however, and the Detective Chief Inspector in turn wanted to see what the psychologist made of it all.

The interview room was small and square, with a window set up high; a lozenge of daylight filtered into the harsher brightness from the fluorescent tube in the ceiling. Solly sat very still, one leg crossed, attending to the conversation before him. Rather more than the man's identity had been established by the computer at the charge bar. Other computerised information told a story about this man's past. It was an unpleasant story, in which small boys had figured.

Lorimer consulted the preliminary report sheet in front of him.

'You are Valentine Carruthers. Is that correct?' Lorimer had asked. The reply had been mumbled and Lorimer had repeated his demand in a tone which made even Solly uncross his legs and sit up straighter.

'Yes. Valentine Carruthers.'

The old man's reply was spat out in defiance. It was obvious that he resented having to admit to his identity. Lorimer's response had been a surprised lift of the eyebrows. If ever a name failed to match its owner's appearance, this was one. Lorimer's eyes flicked over towards the psychologist. Was he wondering about the fellow's background? Questioning how life had let him down to the level of sleeping rough in parks?

'Right, Mr Carruthers. You were apprehended last night in St Mungo's Park.' Lorimer paused, his blue glare pinning Valentine Carruthers into helpless submission. 'You did know that the park was closed to the public?' The man nodded his response. 'And you know why, I take it?' Lorimer's unbroken gaze forced a response.

'Those murders.'

Valentine's eyes dropped unhappily down to focus somewhere below the table which separated him from Lorimer.

'Are you in the habit of spending the night in that particular park?'

Valentine considered the question. He shifted in his chair.

'Sometimes,' he said. 'It depends.'

'Could you tell me where you spent the night over the last four weeks?'

Valentine had not looked back at his interrogator whose voice, though demanding, was still reasonable in its tone. Solly wondered if the tramp was capable of remembering where he had slept every night for an entire month.

'I've been in the park most nights. One night I went down under the Kingston Bridge.'

Valentine's face was a frown of concentration.

'Could you tell me if you were in the park on Wednesday the third of November? That was four weeks ago.'

'Yes.' Valentine's answer was prompt. 'I've been in the park every night since the second girl was found.'

'And you weren't afraid?' Lorimer's question forced Valentine's eyes to meet his own. 'Didn't you worry that you might be in some danger?' The DCI leaned forward, finger jutting in the air as if danger were a tangible force.

Lorimer saw the darkness in the derelict's expression. Fear. Danger. When you live in the open like that, life becomes cheap. Emotions are whittled down to a cunning game of outwitting the elements which hamper daily survival. A killer on the loose would perhaps be irrelevant to Valentine's equation of life. He still didn't answer the question. Lorimer guessed it was probably futile but he let the words hang in the air nonetheless. Now he probed more directly into the matter which concerned him.

'I am interested to know what you saw or heard during those nights in St Mungo's Park.'

Lorimer's tone held just a hint of supplication. The old man was meant to understand that he was there to help, that his assistance might be invaluable to the police in apprehending this killer. All this was contained in a look and an inflection rather than via an obviously ingratiating approach. Lorimer tilted his head slightly before asking his next question.

'Did you, for instance, hear any cries for help, or any noises which might be taken for two people struggling?'

Valentine looked as though he would shake his head, but then the blue gaze caught him again.

'I hear all sorts of things.' His voice came out in a whine. 'Just ignore them. I leave other folk alone and they don't bother me. Most of the time.' He cast a sly glance at Lorimer. 'I'm under the trees, right, and I aim to stay there for the night.' He paused. 'Of course I hear stuff. Yobs yelling and playing their music up loud. Vans going through the park.'

'You were near the main road that runs through the park, then?' Lorimer cut in.

'Sometimes.'

Suddenly Valentine began to cough violently, the harsh rasps rising in a crescendo until it seemed as though he would retch. Lorimer winced, watching the old man double up clutching his chest. At last he straightened up, wiping away tears with the back of his hand. Lorimer let him recover for a few moments then tried again.

'Did you ever hear a cry for help?'

'No.'

'Did you hear any sound which was out of the ordinary? Something being dragged along the ground, for instance?'

Lorimer's elbows were on the table now, his face closer to the old man's. Valentine paused to consider.

'No.'

Lorimer decided to try a different tack.

'Could you see the path from where you were concealed in the bushes?'

'Oh, yes. I could see out through the leaves, but nobody could see me inside.'

The old man looked a little smug, as if he had scored a point.

'Did you see anything unusual during those nights? Anything out of the ordinary?'

Lorimer, reflecting on his choice of words, wondered what ordinary meant to a derelict. Other derelicts wandering through the night. Addicts fixing drugs. Low life passing through like a shadowy pageant. Valentine shook his head.

'What vehicles did you see passing through the park?'

'I dunno. Hard to see when it's dark. Police car sometimes. Vans.' He paused for an instant, then added quickly, 'Oh, and the old ambulance.'

'The *old* ambulance?' Lorimer sat back, curious. 'What do you mean *old*?'

'Well, you get to know sounds in the dark. The new ambulances sound different. Different engines or something. This one was old.'

Lorimer let this pass for the moment. He spread photographs in front of Valentine.

'Ever seen these women?' Lorimer leaned back in his chair, giving Carruthers space and watching his face intently. The eyes looked down on the photos of Sharon Millen, Lucy Haining and Donna Henderson. Valentine's eyes were expressionless, his bottom lip slightly open as he stared at the dead women. Finally he shook his head and looked up as Lorimer removed the photographs. He licked his lips nervously.

'That's them, isn't it?'

Lorimer ignored the question and the old derelict took his silence as affirmation.

'I think it would be best if you could find a hostel meantime, Mr Carruthers. The park is out of bounds and I really think you should be indoors for your own safety. Besides,' the blue eyes fixed him again as Lorimer leaned closer, 'we would be much happier to have an address so we can contact you again. You understand?'

Valentine nodded. He was going to be released now and he didn't look sorry. He'd almost seemed to welcome the cell and the breakfast, the constable on duty had claimed. There had been no aggro. But now he shifted restlessly in the plastic chair, eager to get shot of his temporary accommodation.

As he rose to leave the room he caught the eye of a bearded fellow in the corner. He stopped for a moment in surprise. It was obvious he had not realised the man had been there all the time. He gave a start when the bearded stranger dropped him a conspiratorial wink. Valentine scowled and scuttled out into the corridor.

'Well, what do you make of that, Dr Brightman?'

Lorimer's question was a reluctant overture to his visitor. Solly shook his head.

'I doubt if he is capable of contributing very much. He'll live in a world of his own with little sense of dates or time. He probably hears all sorts of weird things during the night. For him they won't be weird, though, just a background noise, like bullfrogs in the tropics.'

Lorimer gathered up his papers.

'Come through to my office, will you? I'd like to talk about your involvement in the case.'

Solly noticed that Lorimer didn't meet his eye. It was just as well. He might not have appreciated the huge grin that spread across the psychologist's face.

The thunder rumbles overhead. From his vantage point high above the city the watcher looks out at the sudden flashes. Squares and angles of housing blocks are suddenly lit up, looming large and bright. Darkness again.

The watcher edges nearer to the cold glass. What does he see? Lights of the city twinkling through the gloom. Dark masses of parkland, unshining. The faraway lights are frozen by another flash of lightning, turning black night into sudden shocking day. The watcher recoils from the naked light. Too bright. Too penetrating. He needs to retreat into the safe shell of his room.

*   *   *

Elsewhere in the city other watchers stood, disturbed and fascinated by the electrical storm. Solly had pulled a chair over to his window and now sat by the long, undrawn curtain, gazing at the free light show. It exhilarated him to feel an unleashed power which had nothing to do with humankind. No forethought. No motives. No manipulation. He laughed softly, like a child, when the flashes lit up the landscape. His dark eyes gleamed with delight at every crash. The storm was directly overhead now and some car alarms had begun their persistent shrill in the distance. He would sit until the crashes grew fewer and the pounding rain quietened in the streets.

Solly would have no trouble in slipping into sleep, happy with the interlude of the thunderstorm which had cleansed his mind of all the day's events and the anticipation of events to come.

Lorimer had pulled aside the green curtain after the first huge crash and flash. Light had penetrated the thin material and created a greenish glow in his room. The white lightning was naked and warm. Lorimer thought about the derelict they had brought in. He, and too many others like him, were out there now at the mercy of the elements. He had a sudden picture of soggy cardboard and heaps of rags illumined by the sheets of lightning. Poor sods, he thought, more in anger than in pity. His rage had no direction. For who was to blame for the plight of the homeless? If, like Valentine Carruthers, you had simply strayed away from the conventions of society then there was no one to blame. These things simply happened. Relationships crumbled, illusions and dreams were shattered and broken humans retreated into the safety of the outside world, sheltering as they could from the power of the elements. Like Poor Tom in *King Lear*. What was it Shakespeare had called humanity? 'A poor bare, forked animal'? Somewhere out there Valentine would be crouching like a beast below some bushes. Safe again from other wild animals.

Lorimer thought of the killer. He too was out there somewhere, untamed and powerful, like the sudden lightning. But, thought Lorimer, he could be prevented from striking again. He had to find him soon.

5

Alison Girdley walked energetically along the darkened street. The club had been good tonight, she thought, but she wanted to be home and into the shower to wash away all the hot stickiness. Her white trainers padded over the pavement. She could see the tenement building in the distance. Not far now. Just ahead, parked by the kerb, she could see a large pale vehicle. It looked like an ambulance. Curious, she thought. Why is it parked there, by waste ground? You'd expect an ambulance to be at a close mouth, associate it with stretchers, people taken away from houses.

As she drew closer to the vehicle, the driver's door opened and a white-coated figure leaned out. Alison looked up, ready to smile, expecting to be helpful. The driver waved a piece of paper in her direction.

'Excuse me.' His voice halted Alison in her tracks. 'Can you tell me where to find Jason's Lane?' Alison came right up to the door, her eyes on the paper. She'd never heard of it and was about to apologise when everything changed.

The driver leapt suddenly from his perch. Right towards her. Alison stepped back quickly. There was a glimpse of a chain held taut in both fists. A thin face with staring eyes. Instinctively Alison brought her knee up swiftly just as his hands were raised towards her face. The white-coated body sagged with a deep cry.

Now Alison was running, running as in the nightmares when you seem to be rooted to the spot pursued by a nameless terror and not gaining any ground. But the tenements were coming nearer. Her breath jerked out in sobs. Her chest was hurting.

Closer. Closer.

Don't turn around. Keep going.

The first doorway yawned near. Her whole frame was pounding

with the effort of gaining this escape. Was he behind? Don't look round.

Alison stumbled against the door in the darkened hallway and pressed the bell.

'Please. Please,' she sobbed. When the door opened she staggered in. 'Please. Police.' The two words merged in a hysterical cry.

Jess Taylor put out a hand to comfort this girl.

'What's happened?'

Thoughts of rape flashed through her mind. You saw so much about it on the telly and in the newspapers.

'What's up, love?' Mickey Taylor gently took Alison by the shoulder and propelled her into an armchair. 'Make some tea,' he whispered to his wife. Alison gulped. Her voice seemed to be constricted somewhere in her throat. The words came out jerkily.

'The man. He . . . It's him.'

'Who, love?' Mickey wondered if this girl was on drugs. She was almost incoherent.

'The one from the park.'

Mickey suddenly understood as Alison finally gave way to rasping sobs. He left her with a pat on the arm and went over to the window. A twitch of the curtain showed a bare street. No one there.

'Please,' Alison tried again. 'Please phone the police. He's down the road.'

Instead of following her instructions, Mickey went out into the night and looked down the hill. A pale vehicle was turning in the road. Its brake lights flashed on for a moment then it slowly lumbered into the night. Mickey turned back to the house.

'Was he in a van?'

Alison nodded, her tear-stained face miserable. 'It was an ambulance. I thought he wanted directions, then . . . then . . .' Her words subsided in sobs.

This was real, thought Mickey. A tremor of anger and fear shot through him. This was the horror which had been talked about by all the world and its wife these past few weeks.

He reached for the telephone.

6

Valentine Carruthers was missing. Given the nature and habits of the average city derelict this was not really surprising. But for Chief Inspector Lorimer it was a confounded nuisance.

'We've checked all the likely hostels and drop-in centres,' he fumed, glaring at each of his officers as he paced up and down the incident room. 'Each and every layer of cardboard city's been turned over. And what? No trace of him!'

Young DC Cameron opened his mouth to protest, but one look at Lorimer's face quelled him. Lorimer could have guessed the lad's thoughts easily enough. It was conceivable that being picked up by the police had given Carruthers a shake and that the old man had wandered off out of the city.

'Right. His record shows convictions for indecent assaults on minors. South of the border.' Lorimer stabbed the air with his finger as he added, 'Served his last prison sentence nine years ago and then nothing!' And in that nothing, Lorimer added to himself bitterly, his life had presumably taken a downward turn after doing time and he had ended up in Glasgow amongst the other flotsam and jetsam to be found on the shoreline of every big city. 'Okay, the old man might not have had much to add to his comment about the ambulance anyway. But I'd liked to have tied up his statement with this one from Alison Girdley.'

Lorimer brandished the file at the officers then turned on his heel.

The girl had obviously had one hell of a fright, but there was a strength in her which had made her calm enough to answer questions sensibly. Even now a photofit was being made up on the memory she had of the face in the dark. Some of her tape recorded comments were in his mind now, chasing each other around like gerbils on a wheel as he strode down the corridor.

'He opened his mouth as if . . .'

'As if?'

'As if he was yelling at me. But there was no sound.' Then later: 'I saw his teeth in the dark. They were so white.'

Gently DS Wilson had asked questions. He had led the girl back into the depths of her experience, patiently going over details once again when she faltered. His fatherly smile and reassuring voice would have helped her to know that here she was safe. Despite re-living the dark and terror she had been able to give some description.

Wilson had asked questions about his features.

'Very short hair. Cropped. Stylish, I suppose. And dark, I think. I didn't see too well. He had dark hairs on his arms. I remember that. They were bare under the white coat.'

Lorimer tried to picture the snarl, the vicious lunge with the chain. If Alison Girdley hadn't had such swift reactions . . . but then she was coming home from her karate club.

'As if he was yelling at me.'

Didn't they do that in combat sports? Wasn't there some underlying psychological instinct which made an attacking warrior yell at his opponent? Thundering cavalry charges had screamed as they approached their enemy.

Lorimer smiled slightly as he pushed open his office door. Psychological instincts indeed. Well, he knew who could make something out of that.

Solly was patiently explaining the theory of behaviourism to his first-year students.

'You see it's *learned* behaviour. It's a process of cause and event, or what you might call mental association. The rat associates lever-pressing with pellet-receiving. Press a lever: a pellet appears. If the pellets were not to appear then the rat's behaviour would change. It could no longer associate the lever-pressing with receiving a pellet.'

'But wouldn't he *remember*?' one student enquired.

'Ah, now, memory. That would come under a different topic,' began Solly. At that moment the telephone rang and five pairs of eyes watched Solly's face as he picked up the receiver.

'Ah . . . yes . . . well . . .'

The students sat mutely, ears strained to pick up any crumbs which would give them a clue to the nature of the conversation.

'No . . . that's quite all right.'

He listened for a few moments more then replaced the receiver.

'Yes, quite a different topic altogether . . .'

The students sighed in unison. Solly's single-minded approach was legendary. He was impossible to divert once he had taken an idea down a particular road.

Sometimes, Solly thought, people were afraid to look for the obvious. There was something endearing about the human mind which hared off in the direction of the tangled thicket when there were open spaces to gaze at instead.

'Yes, Chief Inspector, American Indians.' Lorimer's eyebrows had shot up in scepticism at the psychologist's suggestion. 'A warrior brave would certainly do his utmost to appear terrifying: face paint and body paint carried symbols of ancestral spirits which were believed to give the warrior power. But it's more than that. It's the disguise which can overpower the enemy. The face-painting dehumanises the warrior.'

'And the yelling?'

'Oh, the war cry. Yes. Of course they took these cries from the animals. That's why so many of their names are like Lone Wolf, Little Bear, things like that. The cries were in imitation of the animal's way of intimidating its prey.'

'I see.'

'What Miss Girdley saw was just the same, only with no sound.'

'But isn't that the whole point, to make the sound and frighten the prey?'

Solly smiled. His eyes behind the round spectacle frames were kindly.

'Ah, but he couldn't afford to be heard. He might alert someone. His yell was unheard, but effective nonetheless. The face became a wolf mask, if you like. No need for paint. Just make the grimace of a snarl. In some ways it can be said that Miss Girdley *did* hear that cry. Subliminally, of course.' Lorimer nodded, then shifted uncomfortably in his chair. 'Then, of course, it explains a lot about the murders themselves.' The psychologist paused, gazing dreamily into the middle distance. Lorimer looked irritably at his watch.

'Go on.'

Solly looked up, an expression of mild surprise on his face, then continued where he had left off.

'Warrior braves scalped their victims and kept the hair as evidence of their successes. My guess is that this killer has behaved exactly like that. His behaviour shows a pattern very like the brave.'

'Are you trying to tell me that we have an American Indian out there on the loose?'

Lorimer's tone was hovering on the derisive.

'No. Not at all. Or at least yes, but only in one respect.'

Lorimer sighed. Make up your mind, he thought silently to himself.

'Our killer displays this pattern of behaviour and therefore it follows that he has some knowledge of American Indians, some association with them, perhaps from childhood, or even through literature.'

'In other words anyone who watched *The Lone Ranger* could end up scalping young women?'

'*The Lone Ranger* rather gives your age away, Inspector,' laughed Solly. 'Miss Girdley describes a younger person.' He paused then stared into space again, talking more to himself than to Lorimer. 'A real knowledge of the ways of warrior braves might not even be essential. The aggressive behaviour displayed by the open mouth could be quite instinctive. However, I feel there is a genuine association.'

Lorimer's thoughts strayed to the other approach his investigation was taking, the coverage this case was to have on *Crimewatch UK*. He was glad that he had instructed Dr Brightman not to talk to the Press. They would have a field day with his theories. He could just imagine some of the headlines: 'Apache in the Park', 'Police Seek Redskin Warrior'.

'Our man has to have a deep-seated reason for scalping these poor young women.' Solly paused again, considering for a moment. 'This man's profile will contain the motive for what appears to be a series of senseless acts. You would look for a motive, of course?'

'Among other things.' Lorimer steeled himself against giving this odd little man a lecture on investigative procedure. He would concentrate on trying to follow his argument. 'Motive is a great indicator. Financial gain. Deep emotions. Things like that are a great help in finding a murderer.'

'But why would someone want to scalp three young women?'

'Or four. If he'd been successful.'

'Quite.'

The phone rang.

'Lorimer.'

He spoke curtly into the mouthpiece. His working day was peppered with telephone calls. It was Alistair Wilson asking for the annual staff profiles.

'I've got someone in at the moment. I'll get back to you later,' said Lorimer, wishing he could make it sooner. This psychologist dealt with intangibles. Lorimer preferred to deal with facts. He felt that Alison Girdley's attack was the first real progress he'd made towards apprehending this killer. The ambulance, the description – both were concrete. The photofit face would be shown on TV. This was something real to go on, not like Solly Brightman's nebulous psychological profile. Still, both paths could lead to the same place in the end, he thought.

'I'd check the local libraries and schools, if I were you,' Solly said suddenly. 'Look for something specific. Non-fiction. A history of American Indians, or something like it. Look to see if there's been a borrower who has repeatedly taken out such an item.'

'What if he's bought the book?' Lorimer said unkindly.

Solly shrugged and spread his hands. Lorimer felt immediately ashamed.

'Okay.'

Solly looked at his large wristwatch.

'I'm afraid I have to be going now. I have a lecture at three o'clock.' He smiled. 'Dreams.'

Chief Inspector Lorimer give him an obligatory, polite smile. Dreams, indeed!

The photofit was complete. A man's thin face glared up from the screen, small eyes, cropped hair and large ears. Lorimer remembered something about large ears, large hands, large feet . . . he could ask Alison Girdley about the hands. As an identification it was unsatisfactory, though. The features, when put together, made a fairly ordinary face. There was nothing really outstanding. Still, he'd often thought that of other photofits and marvelled at the results they had produced. This one was to be shown on *Crimewatch*. It would take all his powers of organisation to ensure that the screening was a success. Certain information was to be made known; some facts had already been printed by the tabloids but others were still under wraps. The main thing being withheld was the involvement of the psychologist. He was to remain a secret for now, thank God.

7

The air was still with that clinging dampness which is a depressing feature of the Scottish West Coast. Wet grey streets were an ocean of tarmac reflecting the grey skies. Martin Enderby emerged from the towering edifice of concrete and glass, loosening his collar and pulling down the knot of his tie. The journalist was tired after the long hours at his desk, and he paused for a moment, gazing at the dark sandstone tenements and newer yuppie flats across the street. Should he head for the car park or give in to the thirst that had been building up all afternoon? His very hesitation spelt out a weakness. With a cursory glance at the Press Bar, where he would be sure to find many of his senior colleagues, he turned in the direction of his preferred watering place, already imagining the taste of cool beer.

Inside, the bar was warm and dark. Later there would be live music from their resident folk group, but for now Martin was content to enjoy the peace and quiet and the familiar, musty smell. The reporter ordered his drink and took it to a corner table, a solid dark oak circle with an ornately carved pedestal. It was the sort of table which usually annoyed him, as there was nowhere to rest his feet, but today he was too tired to care and too intent on washing down the dust and dryness of his office. He closed his eyes for a moment. The sound of taped Scottish fiddle music and the rattle of a fruit machine were noises that scarcely impinged on his senses.

'Mind if I join you?'

With a start Martin looked up to see Diane, the slim, hungry-looking brunette whose acerbic articles in the women's page caused such letter-provoking controversy. Martin liked her. She talked a hell of a lot, but usually to some purpose and with wit.

'Sure. What'll you have?'

'Oh, it's okay, I've ordered.' She perched jauntily on the edge of the chair, crossing her legs neatly. 'How's the great white hunter, then?'

'Oh, God knows. They're putting out a story on *Crimewatch UK* so until then we have very few crumbs of information. I tell you what, though,' Martin leaned forward conspiratorially, 'I don't think even the publicity will run him to earth.'

'Why not? Wouldn't it make him wary?'

Martin took a long swig of beer then put down his glass, sucking the foam from his lips.

'Nope. My guess is that he's acting from compulsion. Nothing and no one will stop him unless he makes a real mistake, or he's caught by sheer chance.'

'You mean he hears voices in his head, that sort of thing?'

Diane's voice was teasing, and Martin wondered if she was genuinely interested. Just then, the barman stepped up, smiled at Diane and with a certain flourish placed her glass of wine on the table. She returned the smile with one of her own dazzling looks. But then she was gazing back at Martin, all attention.

'There's no reason for these killings. I mean, no motive. The killer is unknown to his victims, let's assume. His "reason" is possibly unclear even to him. Something makes him kill, something else makes him take the scalps.' He paused, glancing at his companion seriously. 'You might not be far off the mark when you say he hears voices. Think of the case of David Koresh. He claimed that God was telling him to kill anyone who opposed his cult. Quite a lot of criminals have made such claims. There's even been a TV programme about it. Seemingly perfectly sane people can hear voices.'

'Like Joan of Arc?'

Martin frowned.

'That's so long ago. I'm inclined to believe that she *did* hear God's voice anyway. No. It's the ones who behave in certain ways, as if a trigger – not necessarily a voice – had set something off.' Diane made a face. Martin could see she was becoming rather bored with voices other than her own. 'Well, then, what's new in your neck of the woods?'

'Oh, the usual. Lots of hot gossip.'

Diane gave him a wicked grin. Her column might give the impression that she was a regular tattle-tale, but she gave little away until it was committed to print. Her head turned slightly towards the bar, and she raised her eyebrows as the tape changed to an old Pretenders number.

'Thank God I'm off for some culture tonight.'

'Oh? Theatre?'

'Nope. Jayne's doing a review of Davey's exhibition. So I'm toddling off to see our ace photographer's latest offerings.'

'It's the private viewing, then?'

'Mmm,' she nodded, sipping her wine.

'He's done well, has our Davey. Commendation in the Nationals, and now this. His *own* exhibition. Not just one of many.'

'What sort of pictures are they?'

'Mostly black-and-white, I expect. None of your sensational scene-of-crime stuff. That's strictly for the paper. Mind you, they're good, too.'

Martin remembered one of his friend's pictures. It was the spot where Donna Henderson had been murdered. What had struck him most about the picture was the beautiful art nouveau lamp curled against the white sky. It seemed to throw up the real contrast of Glasgow: City of Culture and city of crime.

'Kids, I think.'

'Pardon?'

'Davey's photos. In this exhibition. I think Jayne said it was mainly studies of children. Like Oscar Marzaroli did in the Gorbals. You know.' She gave a little cat-like smile. 'Come with me, if you like.'

Martin grinned suddenly. Why not?

The gallery was part of a university building that had been thoroughly renovated in recent years. Glasgow's profile as a city of culture had spawned many similar establishments, usually small and well-lit with Renaissance music playing discreetly in the background. Here the music was drowned out by the babble of voices and laughter. The opening had attracted other photographers and artists and, Martin was pleased to note, a fair sprinkling of art critics from papers other than their own.

'Diane.'

Jayne Morganti breezed up to them, her red chiffon scarf trailing like two streamers in her wake. She was a diminutive yet striking woman of around sixty, whose black hair and animated elfin face made her seem much younger.

'And Martin.'

She kissed the air beside his chin, standing on patent-leather tiptoe to reach even that height.

'Do come and have some bubbly.'

They allowed themselves to be towed off by Jayne, giving a wave or smile to others in the Press fraternity.

'Here darlings.' Jayne handed them both long glasses of sparkling wine. 'You will just *love* Davey's piccies. I can't wait to tell the world about this little show.'

Diane laughed. Jayne's over-the-top style often included the phrase 'tell the world', her approach to art criticism having the zeal of a white-hot evangelist.

Martin strolled over to a glass table and picked up a couple of catalogues. He passed one to Diane and quietly took himself off to see Davey Baird's collection of pictures.

They were, as she had told him, mostly of children. There were faces that grinned out at him with more than childish mischief. Davey had succeeded in capturing their air of adult insouciance. Martin stopped before number nineteen. The picture showed two boys here in a back court, both street urchins in bomber jackets and garishly illustrated t-shirts. One was looking straight at the camera chin up, teeth showing in his grin. His cropped hair glistened in the sunlight. Behind him, the other had turned slightly from the camera's gaze. His smile had drooped a little and his eyes were cold and unfathomable. Martin's eyes followed the boy's to see what he saw, but it was out of the photographer's range, whatever it was, somewhere beyond the old-fashioned 'midden' where dustbins were shoved in out of the rain. Martin nodded his approval. Davey certainly had a composition that told a story with characters and setting. The plot was entirely up to the spectator, of course. There were several red dots in the corner, indicating that prints had been sold. Giving in to a moment of impulse, Martin decided that he would add one for himself.

There was only one other purchaser at the desk where a young girl sat taking orders from the catalogue. Martin had half-turned around to see where Diane was when the words, 'Number nineteen' made him swing back. Curious to see who else had fancied his print, he stared at the man in front of him. He looked like an art student with his tawny hair pulled back into a rubber band and his black leather jacket slung over one shoulder, but when Martin caught sight of his face, he wasn't so sure. The guy must be his age, at least, he thought, watching as he wrote a cheque, noting the signature's artistic flourish.

'Thanks, Chris. You can collect your copy at the end of this week. It'll take a few days to have them all framed. Everybody seems to like that one,' the girl gushed.

Martin caught her eye and smiled.

'Me too. Number nineteen, I mean,' he said, turning towards the man she'd called Chris.

The guy looked at him for a moment as if Martin was daft then his expression cleared.

'Oh. Right,' he answered. 'The print. Aye, that's another one to add to my collection. I've got quite a few of his,' he nodded back in the direction of the main gallery where the photographer was still surrounded by a clutch of admirers. The man smiled briefly at Martin then headed for the main door calling back to the girl, 'See you, Daisy.'

Martin rolled some notes out of his pocket and paid for his copy of the picture, giving the girl his name and address then strolled back to examine the rest of the exhibition. From number twenty onwards the pictures were mostly taken in sunshine, the quality of light contrasting vividly with the bleak tenement surroundings. One showed puddles gleaming in the foreground, dazzling the eye against the rows of grey houses and uneven chimney pots on the skyline. Another, taken in a rural setting, was a study of a hare on the skyline of a field, its head upwards as if gazing at the moon.

'Real talent, eh?' Diane said as she rejoined him.

'Mm. He's really hit it off this time.'

'You never know, maybe he'll do this sort of thing full-time.'

'I hope not. His shots usually tell a better story than I do.'

Martin's voice betrayed a certain jealousy.

Diane laughed and shook her head.

'Oho! Fishing for compliments, are we?'

Martin gave a lop-sided smile. He'd been short-listed for one award himself and was desperate for the sort of recognition that Davey Baird enjoyed.

'Who's giving out compliments?' a voice asked.

They swung round to see the photographer himself standing behind them.

'We were just saying how you could do this as a full-time job,' Diane told him.

Davey ran a hand over his fine blond hair and gave a hoot of laughter. 'That'll be shining bright. This is just a sideline. I still need all the work the *Gazette* can give me.' He patted Martin's shoulder adding, 'Catch up with you later. There's a guy over there I want to see.'

They watched him weave his way through the crowd, stopping now and then to shake a hand and exchange a word with someone. Martin gazed after him, imagining how it must feel to be the centre of such attention. A movement by his side made him look down.

Diane's wine was finished. She swirled the stem of her glass between her fingers thoughtfully. She's wondering if I'll fetch her another, thought Martin, who was only too aware of Diane's signals. Half of him wanted to capitulate, but his own weariness had been shrugged off by discussing the case and now he wanted to be home, doing some more research, deciding on his next line of enquiry. He had to keep the story hot for the paper, and, as he had told Diane, there was very little new information to be had. He drained his own glass and gave her a grin.

'Right, lass, I'm off!'

The exaggerated Glasgow accent was designed to make a pretence of being oblivious to Diane's come-on approach. Martin hoped he'd be allowed to succumb to it another time. As he stood up, he rumpled her dark hair just for luck.

'Oh, you . . . leave off!' she laughed, a little ruefully, he thought. Martin bent his hand twice in a mock farewell wave then slouched out of the gallery into the street.

For weeks the *Gazette* had been following the story of the St Mungo's Murders with Martin reaping the benefits. His stories had been good: just the right mixture of sensationalism and fact, not too grisly, but enough to hook his readers. These murders could really make his name as a reporter. It had taken an effort to concentrate on the outrage, the victims' friends and family and above all the menace which had to be wiped off the streets, but wasn't he using the printed word as another weapon in combating this evil hidden somewhere in the city?

As he drove to his quiet bachelor flat, Martin turned on the radio for news. There was an item about a politician and his mistress. More kiss-and-tell. It was becoming old hat. The latest royal visit overseas had created a stir. Employment figures were up. Another factory had closed down.

Martin smiled sardonically. It was the sort of juxtaposition he'd often seen at the hands of the *Gazette*'s sub-editors: the one story seeming to give the lie to the other. Martin listened long enough to hear that a cold front was moving eastwards, then switched off. The murderer had dropped out of sight since scaring Alison Girdley.

Now, Martin thought, let's make my readership speculate about the mental make-up of this serial killer. He had begun to feel enthusiastic about this angle. Talking to Diane had helped him think through a possible argument. Now there were textbooks to consult and other people's hypotheses to mull over in the search for a different sort of story.

8

Maggie Lorimer watched the windscreen wipers swish back and forth against the pattering raindrops. The car moved slowly through late afternoon traffic, necessitating constant use of brake and clutch. Maggie wasn't in any hurry, however. There would be the usual emptiness in the house, the unlit hallway, gloomy and unwelcoming. Once home she would turn up the central heating, switch on the lamps and tune into Classic FM. This last action was a necessity to Maggie, whose natural gregariousness demanded other voices around her. Even now a voice from the car radio was warning of the hazards of road works and delays from the city.

Tell me about it, thought Maggie, gazing at the rows of cars tortoising along their motorway lanes.

The voice changed and began to give the day's news in clear, precise tones.

'A body has been found . . .'

No, she thought, no, I can't stand it any more. But the voice was describing Hertfordshire and the corpse appeared to be an old man, someone who had come to grief by accident. Maggie's stomach felt weak. She had been so sure that the killer had found another victim.

Her finger flew to the button and the voice ended in mid-sentence. What if he was never found? Lorimer had spoken briefly but grimly about the difficulties in tracking down serial killers such as this one. Would he ever give up the search?

Maggie caught a glimpse of herself in the rear-view mirror. Dark curls tumbled around her pale face, greying around the hairline. Her eyes showed signs of strain and fatigue, exaggerated by the mascara she had absently rubbed into dark smudges. Lines which had once told of laughter would soon be described as crows' feet, she told herself, miserably.

Maggie sighed and pulled her gaze back to the traffic ahead. Once home she would prepare a meal for two but expect to dine alone. Despite the fact that Lorimer had always worked dreadful hours in their twelve years of marriage, Maggie had never come to terms with the disappointment of a husband who rarely appeared at dinner time. Instead of becoming accustomed to their long spells apart – for sometimes they did not see each other for days at a time – Maggie increasingly resented this lack of a pattern to their lives. Sometimes she wondered if perhaps her own day as a school teacher was so regulated by the electronic bell that she craved a similar order and structure in her home life.

The cars in front began to move faster and Maggie accelerated to match their speed. Up ahead the familiar junction appeared and she signalled left, relieved to be on the last stretch of her journey home.

The answering machine was blinking its red button as usual. Maggie kicked off her high heels, throwing her velvet coat onto a nearby chair.

'It's me. Just to remind you that it's *Crimewatch* tonight. I'll be staying over.'

There was a pause as Maggie waited for the bleep, but Lorimer's voice came again, almost as an afterthought.

'Love you.'

And I love you too, you brute, thought Maggie, tears of frustration pricking behind her eyes. How on earth could she have forgotten *Crimewatch*? Easy, her more cynical self replied, I never talk to him face to face these days, so why should I remember? At least I can videotape the programme, she told herself with a rueful laugh, then I can play my husband's face over and over again in case I forget what he looks like.

Maggie massaged the back of her neck, circling her head to rid herself of the ache that was beginning to form already. The tape bleeped a few times then continued.

'Hallo, dear, it's Mum here. Just thought I'd remind you about

44

Crimewatch. Isn't it exciting? Mrs MacDonald was asking all sorts of questions, but you know me, I just told her that I couldn't let her know anything about Bill's cases.'

No, thought Maggie, because we never tell you anything, you old gossip.

'Well, dear, must go. We'll catch up some time soon. Bye, now.'

This last phrase was spoken with a wistfulness that caught at Maggie's conscience. Damn! Here she was craving the companionship of her husband when Mum would gladly have filled the gap of lonely hours. Two more bleeps sounded before Maggie switched off the tape. She'd phone her mother after dinner to reassure her that she hadn't forgotten the TV programme. (A lie, but not one she was about to admit.) Fortified by some food she could endure hearing about what Mrs MacDonald had said at the pensioner's club – couldn't she?

9

'And now we come to a most disquieting series of murders. These murders have had wide Press coverage in recent months and you may be familiar with some of the details.'

Nick Ross's earnest, boyish face gazed towards the camera.

'I refer, of course, to the murders of three young women whose bodies have all been discovered in St Mungo's Park, Glasgow.'

Maggie Lorimer watched as the camera retreated from the presenter's face and moved to include the figure of her husband. There he was, immaculate in his dark suit and crisp white shirt (a shirt she'd ironed only yesterday), his hands clasped before him in a firm, steady manner. His whole demeanour showed that stillness which Maggie knew so well. Ross had now introduced Chief Inspector William Lorimer of Strathclyde Police and Maggie felt a stirring of pride as well as an anxiety that this live broadcast should go well. She leaned forward and pressed the record button on the video. There would be a recording taking place at Police Headquarters, she knew, but Lorimer might want to see this more privately.

And so might I, thought Maggie, so might I.

'We are grateful for the full co-operation of the families of these victims,' Ross was saying, 'in making a reconstruction of the movements of Donna Henderson, Lucy Haining and Sharon Millen. If you were in the vicinity of St Mungo's Park on the nights of Thursday October 21st, Monday, October 25th or the 3rd of November, which was a Wednesday, you may be able to help Chief Inspector Lorimer with his enquiries. Watch now and see if there is anything in these reconstructions which jogs your memory at all.'

*   *   *

Linda Thomson's eyes were focused on the TV screen in front of her. She was dimly aware of James sitting slumped in a corner, watching the screen because he had to. They all had to, thought Linda. It was macabre, but it was a part of them now, and there would never be any getting away from it.

She watched as the actress taking the part of Donna Henderson left a group of friends and plunged into the darkness of the lane. Her high-heeled shoes clicked over the cobbles. The camera showed them in close-up and for a few seconds the room was filled with the menace of the darkness and that hollow, lonesome sound of footsteps.

Ross's voice returned, reassuringly normal, talking about the forensic evidence at the actual scene of the killing.

Linda sat quite still, the cat on her knee asleep, oblivious to her turmoil. She stroked the smooth fur eagerly as if making contact with a living, breathing creature might restore normality, banish this nightmare. The cat purred in its sleep below her active fingers.

What had possessed the child to take a short cut down that sinister-looking lane? But then don't we all believe that bad things happen to other people? Linda shivered. *They* were 'other people' too, she thought. And Sharon? That still remained a mystery. Would they ever know what had happened after she had caught that bus?

The cat jumped off her knee, disturbed by a sudden grip on its fur.

Linda allowed herself a swift glance in James's direction. She remembered how she had reacted to the news about Alison Girdley's attack. Her first thought had been 'Where was James that night?' Relief to know that he had been at home with them was tempered by the dreadful guilt that she could even suspect her son of such a crime. He was so quiet, so withdrawn. Yet she knew in her heart of hearts that James was totally innocent. Didn't she?

Now the screen showed the Glasgow area on a map of Scotland. What had once been Strathclyde Region was coloured in green with a red dot indicating the city. The scene moved to a helicopter shot of the River Clyde and the bridges which ran north to south. Then the camera panned out over the city and Nick Ross used the phrase 'dear green place' as the scenes showed the city's familiar skyline then the stretches of parkland: Bellahouston, famous for its Papal visit, Queen's Park, Kelvingrove near the university and, finally, St Mungo's Park.

Solly was acutely aware of the killer. He would be crouched over his own television set, gloating. Solly felt that he was beginning to know this man now. He would have had a nasty shock when his attack on Alison Girdley failed. His ego would have been badly bruised and he would have retreated in fear and anger, like an animal snarling over lost prey.

As the helicopter circled St Mungo's Park, Solly gazed at the peripheral buildings; a church spire, old sandstone tenements and then the grey blocks of high-rise flats, bleak and impersonal like tombstones stretching to the sky. Solly had made red circles around these flats on his Glasgow street plan. Even though house-to-house enquiries had been made, he still came back to the flats. The killer was a loner. And what better place for a solitary, anonymous person than these flats which reared their pre-stressed concrete heads out of the surrounding greenery?

There were certain aspects of this man that defied profiling, but others were beginning to form a pattern to Solly. Would this programme make the killer react? The Chief Inspector certainly thought so. Solly and he had discussed the fact that the man would believe himself to be inviolable. They all had that streak of megalomania, that utter belief that their actions were those of a superior being. Often, as both Solly and Lorimer knew from their different experiences, that was the point from which their downfall began. Solly thought of the hunter in his lair. Yes. He'd pad up and down with restless uncertainty, but sooner or later he'd come out again to kill.

Lucy Haining's last known movements were being shown now, and the presenter took pains to point out that this young art student had shown so much promise. A photograph came up on the screen of Lucy receiving her award. Her young face was flushed with pleasure.

Lorimer's voice was telling the millions of viewers about the attack. The word 'mutilation' was used, no doubt producing ripples of disgust in homes all over the country. Lorimer was tight-lipped about the gory details, however. This was not an exposé to titillate or fascinate the nation. That was understood.

Now Sharon Millen's bus journey home was depicted. Nick Ross's voice became urgent.

'Did you see this girl on the night of Wednesday the 3rd of November? Were you a passenger on that bus? If so, the police urge you to come forward. Any information you may give might be helpful in apprehending this dangerous killer.'

The television screen showed the laurel bushes in St Mungo's Park where the scene-of-crime plastic flags still fluttered in the cold breeze. The Chief Inspector was explaining how the bodies had been dumped and found by unsuspecting passers-by. Hilary Fleming, holding Toby firmly on his lead, told of her discovery. She was composed now, speaking readily, buoyed up by the medication she had required since the day she and her dog had found that second corpse.

Police Constable Matt Boyd took a gulp of tea from the mug he had cupped in his hands. His eyes were fixed on the telly in the duty room. Lorimer was doing well so far, he conceded. There was no trace of anger in the man. He'd kept his emotions totally under control, giving nothing away that he didn't intend to. Matt had seen him angry and they all knew that his temper had been the product of a deep frustration over this case.

Would they ever solve it? Matt wondered, sipping tea and gazing at the familiar stretches of parkland where he'd spent so many tedious hours. There were countless murder cases where complete blanks had been drawn. If you didn't catch them quickly, the whole thing became more difficult. The scent would grow cold, thought Matt, unconsciously using an image of which Solly Brightman would have approved. But you never know. Look at the Yorkshire Ripper. Think of Fred and Rosemary West. Matt shuddered. This case had its horrors but at least there were only three dead.

'So far,' a voice said in his head.

The presenter had turned to the police officer by his side once more.

'Chief Inspector, what can you tell us about the progress which is being made in these investigations?'

The question was asked politely, deferentially, yet there was an edge to it, as if progress was not the correct word to use at all. Matt drained his mug and put it down on the floor beside his chair, smiling cynically. Progress? How would the Chief reply to that? Lorimer cleared his throat, then looking steadily at the man on his left, began his carefully prepared response.

'There are several aspects of this case which can be made public, particularly after the incident involving Alison Girdley.'

'Yes, tell us about that,' responded Ross, accepting the deflection from his original question.

'Miss Girdley was walking home from her sports club on the night of December 7th when she was hailed by the driver of a stationary ambulance.' Lorimer paused for an instant to let this information be digested. 'The driver attempted to throw a bicycle chain around Alison Girdley's neck, but she successfully avoided this attack and ran to a nearby house for help.'

Mickey Taylor took his wife's hand and gave it a squeeze. They sat side by side on the settee, watching the screen with some relish. They had been strictly warned by the police not to discuss the events of that evening when Alison had burst hysterically into their living room. Since then they had talked over everything they could find out about the crimes, avid for new developments in a case which had touched on their own unsensational lives. They had watched the TV cameras and all the paraphernalia of the television crew on their street filming Alison herself in a reconstruction of her attack. She'd been a brave lass to go through it all again, they'd agreed.

Then there had been the thrill of being interviewed in their own home. Jess had been in a tizzy about what to wear for the occasion, even contemplating the purchase of a new dress. However, she had settled for having her hair done and had worn an outfit which was smart but not flashy. The neighbours would talk about it in days to come but she wouldn't let them accuse her of showing off. No. It was too serious a matter for that.

Jess blushed as she heard her own accent from the television. How broad she sounded. And Mickey! She looked at her husband appraisingly. He wasn't as stout as that. It must be the angle of the camera, surely?

Then suddenly their moment was over. They continued to sit in silence, Mickey squeezing his wife's hand by way of congratulation, as the programme continued.

'Now. A bicycle chain. You said earlier, Chief Inspector, that this was in fact the weapon used to strangle Lucy, Donna and Sharon.'

'Yes. This is being treated as the murder weapon. Marks found on the throats of the three deceased show that this was consistent with a bicycle chain, or something very similar to it.'

'And you think that Alison Girdley was meant to be another victim?'

'We do. This was a totally unprovoked attack by the assailant. There is no doubt in our minds that this man intended to assault and to kill Alison Girdley.'

'And you believe that this was the *same* man who had killed Donna, Lucy and Sharon?'

Lorimer had been prepared for this. There had been some discussion as to whether Alison's assailant had been the killer they sought or whether this had been a copy-cat attempt at murder which had gone awry.

'We believe so, yes. The fact that this assailant was in an old ambulance is a pertinent factor. The police have reason to believe that whoever committed these crimes used an ambulance to transport the bodies to St Mungo's Park and then dispose of them in the bushes.'

The light from the television screen cast shadows on the walls as Martin Enderby scribbled furiously in his reporter's notebook. He desperately wanted to glean some new facts from this programme to add to the piece he had been writing. And he wondered what they'd say in the update.

The studio lights had become unbearably hot and Lorimer longed to take a sip from the glass of water in front of him.

'So Alison Girdley may actually have seen the man who murdered Sharon, Donna and Lucy?'

'We think so. There is a videofit picture which we have prepared on the strength of Alison's description.'

'Yes. Here it is now. Take a good look.' Ross's voice was compelling as the photofit appeared on the screen. 'If you think you know this man or have any information about the old ambulance which he was driving then please do not hesitate to telephone the incident room on this number.'

The screen flashed up the number as the presenter's clear tones repeated it twice.

'And remember, all calls will be treated in the strictest confidence.'

Now the picture reverted to the two men who regarded each other seriously behind the studio desk.

'Chief Inspector, have you any message for the public? Any advice which might lead to finding this man?'

The camera zoomed slowly in to show Lorimer's rugged face in close-up. His blue eyes seemed to pierce right through the air waves.

'This man is a highly dangerous individual. If you think you know who he is, by no means approach him but please,' he emphasised the word, 'please get in touch with us immediately. It is imperative that we catch this man.' He paused. They had decided against adding 'before there are any more killings'. It was not a wise tactic to employ scaremongering in this way. That sort of thing was left for the press to take up. Also, Lorimer felt that any admission that further attacks might take place would reflect on police work in general and on himself in particular. And yet . . .

'He is a dangerous and secretive individual. If you think you can help, then ring this number.'

Lorimer's face was replaced by the telephone numbers once more, then Nick Ross was back smiling his assurance to the viewers that such crimes were really very rare.

'We will be back with our update at 11.15 tonight. Already we have a flood of calls coming in and we hope to report on some of those later on.' Now Nick was leaning on the front of the desk, a sheaf of papers in his hand, looking quite relaxed. 'Don't have nightmares,' he smiled. 'Goodnight.'

Maggie switched off the television and sat back. She suddenly became aware of her clenched fists and the feeling of hot sweat between her breasts.

Lorimer had spoken to her about the urgency of the case, of the unpredictable nature of any savage serial killer. With one part of her mind Maggie had acknowledged all of these things, agreeing that the case was horrid and vile. But another part of her had remained detached until now. Somehow the reconstruction with trained actors had made the crimes seem more real to her. She had thought about the victims' last moments and visualised that silver chain biting into their throats.

As the scenes unfolded, Maggie had wondered about the parents. Their anguish in going through this all over again must be unbearably painful – if indeed they had been able to face the programme. Somehow Maggie thought that they would. Any link with their dead children would encourage them to watch; to see the possibility of a net being cast to entrap this sadistic killer.

And Lorimer would do it. Maggie willed him to do it. He must catch that man before . . . But her mind balked at pursuing that thought.

She looked around the room. It was not a masculine room in any way. The sofas were pale apricot and green, matching the leaf green of the curtains. Colours that were impractical for family life. But then there would never be a family now. She had chosen the colour schemes and planned the interiors, despairing of ever dragging her husband around a furniture shop. Lorimer seemed content to leave such decisions to her, although he was terribly fussy when it came to hanging any of his precious pictures. They at least were his; these

Glasgow Boys prints, that Rosaleen Orr with its rich colours and hidden depths that took pride of place. Maggie loved her house, and yearned for it to be *their* home, but more and more it seemed that her husband was merely a passing stranger, a bedtime companion.

Maggie pulled herself back to the memory of Lorimer's performance on *Crimewatch*. She felt her shoulders relax as she thought of Lorimer and his single-minded pursuit of the killer. This was what he was good at. This was what was important. What she wanted from her husband seemed selfish, almost trivial now, by comparison. Perhaps she should resign herself to this way of life instead of trying to fight against it.

Maggie closed her eyes wearily. The tension in her chest had created a real pain. She wanted to weep, but couldn't.

10

So that was it, then. The overhead lights dimmed and the studio sounded hollow as lines of cable were trailed across the floor. The cameras retreated silently, mounted by technicians crouching like monstrous insects, huge headphones clamped over their ears. Lorimer's shoulders were stiff with tension. He filled his lungs deeply, making himself relax.

Nick Ross was saying something to his production assistant so there was a moment's respite, a gathering together of energies before they headed back into the courtesy suite.

'Well done, Chief Inspector.' The blond head turned in Lorimer's direction, the calm, intelligent face creased in a beam of satisfaction. 'Now, let's get you out of this shambles.'

He indicated the army of technicians and youngsters with clipboards who had descended on the area, and ushered Lorimer out into the corridor. As they made their way to the room where drinks would be waiting, Ross chatted inconsequentially about family, holidays in Scotland; all designed, Lorimer knew, to ease his tension. He had used that gentle ploy himself and appreciated it from another professional. There would be no more said about murder until Lorimer had visibly unwound. And then?

Telephone lines were already jangling. Amongst the genuine calls were cranks and time-wasters, Ross had told him, but sometimes, just sometimes, a call would come through like a seam of gold appearing in a darkened mine.

The update to the main programme would be made by Ross himself, letting viewers know if there were any immediate results to be had from their various appeals. Lorimer would remain behind the scenes listening as information came filtering through.

Lorimer found himself in a small, windowless room which had

the heavy smell of new carpeting. Some of those who worked on the programme were talking loudly and lighting up cigarettes. The producer handed Lorimer a square-cut glass containing malt whisky. It was a presumption, Lorimer thought, that was actually justified. Not only did he indulge in his national drink, he was in real need of one at that moment.

'Water?'

A small brown jug was proffered.

'Just a splash.'

There was no more he could do now but wait. It was irksome to have matters whisked away from him like this, and Lorimer realised that he felt exactly the same about Solomon Brightman. There were always training courses that stressed the need for teamwork and co-operation in police work. To fly solo was not only foolish and egotistical but dangerous. It showed a craving for power. Lorimer knew that his need to be in control fought battles with the common sense which delegated authority. But common sense usually won. Indeed, it had been his ability to work in a team that had impressed his superiors all the way up through the ranks.

The whisky slipped over his throat and burned a yellow warmth inside. By going to the psychologist, by involving this television programme, he was not admitting any inability on his own part, or that of his department. It was necessary to cast a wider net than he alone could wield in order to catch this killer, and Solomon had told him that it was highly likely the man they were after would watch the programme.

'He won't know beforehand that there will be any reference to his killings, but he will *expect* some sort of recognition. The obsession with self will make him glory in his deeds and want to see them displayed,' the psychologist had said.

Lorimer knew a lot about killers and their utter conviction that they were invulnerable. They all believed that they could never be caught. Some of them had appeared shrunken and bewildered when the law had finally put a stop to their evil progress. Others continued to display an arrogant bravado until the day a judge sentenced them to a suitable term of imprisonment. What about this man? A vision of his photofit face came to Lorimer's mind.

Unsmiling, clean shaven, with close-cropped hair, he could be a soldier, a policeman even, or any ordinary respectable citizen. It was frightening how normal-looking appearances hid such evil within. With a shudder Lorimer remembered the benign, smiling face of Thomas Hamilton, the warped murderer of that class of infants and their teacher in Dunblane.

'Chief Inspector?'

A small woman with dyed red hair and round black spectacles stood in front of him.

'A telephone call for you.'

Still cradling his glass, Lorimer followed the woman out into the corridor. They walked along until she stopped by the door of a well-lit office.

'You can take it in there. That's a separate line.'

Lorimer nodded and the woman closed the door softly behind her.

'Hello. Chief Inspector Lorimer speaking.'

'It's Solomon.'

Lorimer's heart sank. Somehow he had hoped for a respite from cowboys and indians.

'I want you to do something for me.' Lorimer waited, curious despite himself. 'Can you ask the presenter not to mention the case in his update?'

'*Not* to mention?' Lorimer's voice was incredulous.

'Yes.' There was the usual pause that Lorimer had come to expect between Solomon's statement and elucidation. 'He'll be expecting to hear more about himself. I want you to provoke his vanity by keeping him guessing. If he hears nothing it will seem to him that his case is not important any more, despite the earlier programme.'

'But if there *is* real information coming through . . .' Lorimer hesitated. He felt, like Solomon, the delicate control that this television show was exercising over their unknown killer.

'You don't want him to go to ground?'

'I don't want any more dead bodies either!' Lorimer snapped back.

There was another pause in which Solomon's sigh was just audible.

'If no one appears to have telephoned, it's just possible that he will dial that number himself.'

Yes, thought Lorimer, from a call box. The bastard isn't a fool.

'Chief Inspector,' Solomon's voice sounded almost wistful, 'I really would like to hear his voice.' He paused again and when Lorimer did not reply he continued, this time adopting the manner of a teacher speaking to a stubborn child. 'There are certain aspects of this case I'd like to discuss with you. May I see you about four o'clock tomorrow?'

Lorimer was suddenly torn between annoyance at the man's presumption and a desire to laugh at the absurdity of taking orders from him.

'Chief Inspector?'

'All right. I'll see what I can do. Tomorrow at four then.'

As he put down the phone he could just imagine Solomon's wide smile.

Nick Ross was not smiling when Lorimer suggested that the update should make no mention of the St Mungo's murders.

'But we have all these calls giving possible names!'

'And we both know that it's going to take days to corroborate them. By that time he could be anywhere.' Lorimer's mouth hardened. 'Our psychologist working on the case believes we may provoke our man into making a call himself, if there is no mention of him during the update.'

Nick Ross's eyebrows rose. A psychologist had not been mentioned by this Chief Inspector from north of the border. That *would* have given extra spice to the programme. A frown of irritation passed over the presenter's face, the only sign Lorimer had of his displeasure. Somehow it made him feel guilty, as if he had no right to conceal any aspect of this case.

Solomon was right. At twenty past midnight the switchboard registered the call.

11

S olomon was late. One of his third-year students, an earnest
Scandinavian who towered over him, had sought his approval
about the research techniques needed for his dissertation. Calmly,
Solly had reassured the young man, pointing out the best ways to
obtain the data he required. As a result it was twenty-five past four
before he emerged from the building into University Avenue and
looked up and down for a taxi.

Beneath his placid appearance he was experiencing some excitement. Chief Inspector Lorimer would be waiting, probably with
justified impatience, for this meeting. Solly knew that his credibility
was on the ascendant since the murderer's phone call. Now he had
to capitalise on that.

At last a taxi appeared over the brow of the hill, its FOR HIRE
sign blazing orange. Solly gave his destination and settled back
to think.

'I'm sorry, Chief Inspector, Dr Brightman appears to have left. Can
I take a message?'

Lorimer resisted the temptation to be rude. The secretary at the
Department of Psychology was undeserving of the brunt of his
temper. He'd save it for Dr Brightman.

'No, thank you. I expect he's on his way.'

Lorimer put down the receiver. Since yesterday everything
seemed to have changed. It was like looking through field glasses
and adjusting the focus. Certain areas now came sharply into view,
others remained hazily in the background. One thing was certain,
and that was the way that the killer had played into their hands.
Well, to be fair, into the hands of Solomon Brightman. Lorimer
had spent quite a lot of the night reconsidering the psychologist's

ability to make an impact on this case. Even now a copy of Canter's treatise lay in his desk drawer. He had been impressed in spite of himself, even from the little he had begun to read.

A rat-a-tat was knocked on his door and Solly's bearded face peeped round. His habitual smile was sheepish.

'Chief Inspector.'

'Dr Brightman.'

'I'm sorry for the delay.'

'Well, now you're here, let's get down to business.'

Solly sat by the window and unbuckled his battered, soft-hide briefcase. He glanced up and gave a shy smile, as if he were about to offer an explanation for his lateness.

'You have the recording?' he said instead.

'Of course. Do you want to hear it now or would you rather discuss . . . whatever it is you're so anxious to tell me?'

Lorimer did not try to disguise the sarcasm in his voice. Immediately he was annoyed with himself and wondered how to counter the resentment that this mild-mannered young man provoked in him. Their working relationship had to improve, he thought, or rather his own attitude to it.

'I'll come straight to the point.' Solly crossed his legs and leaned forward slightly. 'Why was there no rape?'

Lorimer stared at the psychologist for a moment before answering.

'But there isn't always a sexual motive in serial killings.'

The dark head of the psychologist nodded up and down and the huge eyes peered owlishly from behind the tortoiseshell spectacles. He took a cursory glance at the notes he had extracted from his briefcase.

'I'm concerned that there is no evidence of any sexual motive. Unless this man is simply a fetishist – and I don't believe he is – there should have been signs of sexual activity. The crimes point to the sort of killer who would achieve a sexual gratification from strangling his victims.' He paused, as if to let this sink in. 'Both strangulation and the taking of trophies normally coincide with sexual activity.'

'You mean rape?'

'Not always. As you know yourself, some of these serial killers are impotent and use their victims' fear to heighten their own sexual urges. The absence of semen or any other bodily fluids is surprising.'

'Perhaps he was clever enough to know about DNA finger-printing?' Lorimer suggested wryly.

'I think he's even cleverer than that, Chief Inspector.'

The psychologist uncrossed his legs, stood up and turned to look out of the window. When he spoke again, it was almost to himself.

'I think he is very clever indeed. In fact, I believe he's leading us up the garden path.'

Lorimer waited, hands clasped under his chin, staring at the enigmatic figure before him. He had the sudden feeling that something momentous was taking place. It was a sensation that left him outside, like an observer. For once, he was surprised to note, such a feeling did not trouble him.

'Chief Inspector.' Solly had turned round and Lorimer saw the bearded face, solemn and sad, as if some profound insight had wiped away that customary smile. 'I don't think we're looking for a serial killer. Oh, I know he's killed three young women' – Solly held up his hand to forestall Lorimer's protest – 'I know he went for Alison Girdley. But it just doesn't fit.'

'What doesn't fit?'

Solly sat down again with a sigh.

'He kills three girls with a bicycle chain. He scalps them and retains their hair. Then he takes them to a park where they will be found by a member of the public. Why?'

'If I knew why, I'd have had a better chance of apprehending him by now,' Lorimer replied testily.

Solly nodded sadly again.

'He wanted to kill. There is no apparent sexual motivation. There is no sign of any preliminary torture or menace. We have Alison Girdley's statement showing that he lured her near enough to lash out and kill. That's all he wanted. To kill.'

'Or to obtain scalps?'

'If he is a genuine fetishist he would be likely to have a history of mental illness. Your trawl of the hospital records would have uncovered something. Probably.'

'Wait till you hear what he says on the tape,' Lorimer replied, pulling open his desk drawer.

He removed a cassette from a jiffy bag then slotted it into the tape recorder on his desk. Solly stared intently as the play button was pushed. There was a moment's silence, then a nervous throat-clearing before a Scottish voice proclaimed: 'I killed those girls.' There was a pause that would have done justice to Solly's own deliberate manner. 'Can you guess what colour I'm going to have next?' Another pause was followed by a snigger then the sound of a telephone being put down.

Lorimer watched the man opposite as he listened intently. Solly's gaze never wavered.

'Again,' he said.

Lorimer rewound the tape and they listened to the words falling into the space between them.

'So.' Lorimer fixed his blue gaze on Solly. 'Do you still rule out the theory that we have a killer who is fixated with scalping young girls?'

Solly did not reply immediately, but sat frowning in concentration, biting his lower lip.

'I agree that the victims were selected at random,' he began, then added, 'Mostly.'

'Mostly?'

'Yes. I believe one of these girls was known to him. I believe that he has very cleverly tried to make us think that we are dealing with some maniac who compulsively kills and scalps young women for some sort of perverted pleasure.' Solly shook his head, then continued, 'I don't believe that. I think he is putting up some sort of smokescreen. He has killed two young women at random to cover up the premeditated murder of a third.'

Lorimer's eyes hardened, but not because he disbelieved the psychologist. He had encountered some violent criminals in his career, but never anyone capable of such cold-blooded intent.

'You mean Donna Henderson was deliberately stalked and killed, then the others were used to make it look like a spate of serial killings?'

'Yes. Perhaps. He puts a deliberate signature on these deaths; the chain, the scalping, the removal of the bodies to the park. He wants us to think that there is a serial killer on the loose. But it's all too deliberate. Too neat.' Solly's voice drifted off in thought.

'You really don't think this is a serial killer, despite the attempt on Alison Girdley's life?'

'No. He's clever. He's well read.' Solly's grin returned. 'He may even have been a student of psychology.'

Lorimer returned the smile.

'God help us.'

The two men looked at each other for a long moment. Solly continued to smile and then nodded, acknowledging the new sense of co-operation between them.

'Well,' Lorimer's tone became brisk again, 'We'll have to go back over the Donna Henderson case with a fine-tooth comb. If what you believe is true, there are going to be some disgruntled police officers raking over the same facts and figures.' Lorimer took a deep breath. 'How would you profile him?'

'The tape helps, of course, but I would say he is white, single, in his early thirties. He *may* suffer from some sort of personality disorder.'

'Schizophrenia?'

'Possibly. He may well be as outraged as the next man when he reads about the murders, if he does have such an illness. But it's early days to speculate on his mental health. He's probably a professional who works and lives on his own. He's not taking the scalps home to mother. Usually, multiple killers have backgrounds of deprivation in their childhood: a lack of moral guidance. So he may have been orphaned or illegitimate.'

'I'm still concerned about that ambulance. How does it figure in your profile?'

'Yes. That's interesting. I wonder if he uses it for transporting equipment of some kind. A pity the Girdley girl didn't see inside.'

'She won't think so!'

'There is one thing that bothers me.' Solly looked up, the smile nervous now. 'You won't like this, Chief Inspector, in view of what I've said, but . . . This man may not have started out as a compulsive killer. His intention might simply have been to cover his tracks.'

Solly's pause was loaded with significance and he spoke softly, 'But he may have become a compulsive killer.'

Lorimer could hardly believe his ears.

'You're right. I don't like this. First you say that he's not then you say that he might be. Dr Brightman, you seem to have a habit of contradicting yourself.'

Solly shrugged his shoulders and raised his hands, palms upward, in an exaggerated gesture.

'I said once that he was a hunter. It's as if he has acquired a taste for blood.'

'You think he'll kill again, then?'

'Oh, yes. I don't think that voice on the tape realises just what he has said. He intended it to mock us, and to make us continue to believe that he would go on killing. What he may not realise is that he has begun to enjoy it.'

Despite the stuffiness of his office, Lorimer shuddered. For a few minutes he had felt a sense of relief with Solomon Brightman's theory. If the killer was a cold-blooded murderer with one of the more recognisable 'ordinary' motives, then the killing might have stopped. But now? There was a chilling truth in what the psychologist said. Lorimer had never experienced a case like this, but he had read about killers who had killed for profit, jealousy, revenge or whatever, then found a perverse delight in blood-letting. Often it was paranoia that set in. But sometimes killing just became easier, the killer drawing a sense of power with each death.

'Chief Inspector.' Solly stood up, putting his papers back into the briefcase. 'May I have a copy of the tape, please?'

Lorimer drew out a second tape from the jiffy bag and handed it over.

'Thank you.' Solly sat down again to fasten the briefcase. 'Oh, were there any other phone calls of any significance after the programme?'

'Possibly. We're working on them, but it will take time to sort out the nonsense from the genuine calls. And even they might be well-intentioned but misleading.'

'Yes.' Solly stood up again. 'Well, Thank you, Chief Inspector. I hope this has been helpful.'

Lorimer stood up and walked over to open the door. He paused for a moment, considering. His fingers gripped the door handle.

'Dr Brightman . . .'

'Yes?'

'Thank you.'

The grin returned with its full force and the psychologist put out his hand.

'Oh, I think it's my pleasure.'

12

M aggie heaved the canvas bag off her shoulder and let it drop with a thud to the floor. Secondary five's ink exercises and the juniors' tests were a chore she would put off until later.

The hall was dark and quiet. Maggie stretched out her arms to ease the ache then let herself slump. Her body felt very small when end-of-the-day weariness set in. With a sigh she stepped out of the flimsy shoes and shuffled through to the bedroom to find her sheepskin slippers, the first of several little comforts which meant home to Maggie. She would pad slowly back through the hall to the kitchen, turn on the fluorescent light and press the button that brought her Classic FM.

These two brightnesses gave her enough stamina to make some decent coffee. Good coffee was important to Maggie. Snuggled into the kitchen chair, she would clasp her stiff fingers around the mug, letting the fragrance tickle her nostrils before she took that first sip. Sometimes, especially during holidays, she was aware that her body craved a break for coffee at just this time in the afternoon. Would she persist in this pattern of behaviour even when she was an old lady in retirement in some dim and distant future?

For a woman who resented long periods of solitude, this was one time when it was good to be alone.

For twenty minutes or so Maggie let herself drift, hearing the music as a background comfort, sipping the coffee until the cafetiere was almost empty. Only then would it be time to return to a sense of reality, sift through the day's mail and check the answering machine.

Lorimer hadn't called. Still, that was hardly surprising. He would have been at the studio until God knows when, then he'd had the early shuttle to catch back to Glasgow. Maggie knew he would be met at the airport and whisked off to Headquarters where he would remain until . . . Until he decides to come home, she thought gloomily.

Today had been particularly difficult at work. Many of the staff had seen *Crimewatch* and were naturally curious to sound her out. Behind the coffee cups she could see eyes glancing her way, appraising her. As always, she played down Lorimer's involvement, but after being the programme's most horrific focus it was impossible to avoid discussion of the case. Someone said they knew someone who knew the father (or was it the uncle?) of the third victim, Sharon Millen, and then a subtle form of verbal sparring broke out, several voices raised in assertion of who had the nearest link to those directly involved. Maggie felt lost in the myriad of tenuous connections.

They had begun to discuss the possibility of another murder taking place.

'What does your husband think?'

Maggie, who had lost the thread of the previous conversation, had been startled by the directness of the question. The Head of Modern Languages had fixed her with a steely glare.

'I don't know. I hardly ever see him.'

The words were out before Maggie could stop them. The woman's raised eyebrows and patronising smile were what Maggie had tried for years to avoid. Sure, everyone discussed their home life to an extent, but Maggie had learned to be circumspect about her husband's work and remained non-committal about her marriage. Now there was an embarrassed silence in which she felt like a fugitive caught in a sudden arc light.

Sandie, her friend in Secretarial Studies, nudged her and laughed, 'Ah, well, what it is to have a famous hubby! Jack won't be on the box unless we win the lottery!'

There were a few laughs, which broke the tension, and Maggie shot her friend a look of gratitude. She was spared any further quizzing as the bell signalled the end of morning interval. As she smoothed the biscuit crumbs from her suede skirt, she determined to make herself scarce at lunchtime. There would be no more digging into the case if she could avoid it. Nor into what had started to titillate her curious colleagues – the state of her marriage.

The coffee cup was empty yet there was still some warmth between the porcelain and her fingers. She would sit quite still until the very last strains of the Moonlight Sonata had played across her senses.

With the presenter's voice came that sense of waking up, coming back to the present and reality. Maggie stood up stiffly, ready to begin again. She would tackle the tests first then prepare some food. That way the fifth-years' jotters could command her entire attention during the evening.

It was almost ten o'clock and Maggie's neck was sore from sitting too long in the one position. Her tray of dirty dishes lay to the side of the settee, away from the growing pile of marked exercise books.

The front door closed and she could hear Lorimer turning his key in the lock.

As he came into the living room Maggie's dark head rose from her work and turned towards him. The standard lamp behind her threw the angles of her face into sharp relief, but her expression softened as she saw him.

'Had a good day?' His smile was rueful, sweeping over the jotters spilled around her feet.

'The usual,' Maggie sighed, then stretched out her hands in welcome. Lorimer put his coat over a chair and caught her hand, kissing her upturned mouth.

'Glad you're home,' she murmured.

'Like a cup of tea?'

'Oh, I'll get it.'

'No. Stay where you are. You look bushed.'

Lorimer disappeared and Maggie could hear cupboard doors opening and closing. She closed her eyes, unable to concentrate any longer on the jotter on her lap.

'There you are.'

Maggie looked up at her husband and took the tea. He seemed quite relaxed for a man who had been on live television less than twenty-four hours ago.

'Well?' she asked.

'Well, what?'

'Oh, you know. How did it go?'

Lorimer moved to sit beside her and Maggie slid the rest of the jotters over the edge of the settee. Their mugs of tea sat side by side on the low table as Lorimer slung his arm around his wife's shoulders, drawing her against him.

'It wasn't what I expected. I suppose it never is. Everything was much smaller. The studio, the rooms. And there were so many people. God, no wonder it costs so much to make television programmes. The wages bill must be astronomic.'

'What about Nick Ross? What's he like?'

'Exactly as he seems. A nice, sharp bloke. Very aware. Very professional.' Lorimer paused, glancing briefly at Maggie's profile. 'Did you see the programme?'

'Of course.' Her tone was full of injured protestation, covering up the guilt that she felt. No one would ever know that she'd almost forgotten her husband's appearance on TV.

'And?'

'You were great.'

Lorimer grinned and Maggie knew he'd wanted to hear these words from his wife, biased or not.

'Did you get lots of telephone calls?'

'Yes, we did.'

Lorimer shifted away from her and took a long drink of tea. Maggie waited. She wouldn't push. If he wanted to talk about it he would.

'We think there have been several sightings of the vehicle – the ambulance – but that's not certain yet.' He paused again, and Maggie reckoned he was debating whether she should know about the developments that had already taken place. She knew it was a rule that he only told his wife what he'd already said to the media.

'Why was there no mention of the murders in the update? Were there no responses by then?'

'I asked them to leave the case out,' Lorimer frowned. 'It was a strategy to see if we would get a call from the killer.'

'And did you?'

'Yes.'

Lorimer was looking away from her now, and Maggie could see the tension in her husband's neck. She longed to ask 'Will you find him?' but dreaded that her question might sound like a criticism.

'Well,' she said briskly, 'It can only move things forward. You looked really good on television. Everyone said so.'

'Everyone?'

Maggie giggled. 'Well, Mum. And Mrs MacDonald.' Her thoughts flicked to her colleagues in the staff room, then shut them out again. 'The reconstructions looked quite scary. Were they accurate?'

'Oh, yes. They'd done their homework, all right.' Lorimer's arm came round her shoulders again and then he was holding her tightly. 'Maggie?'

'Mmm?'

'Let's go to bed.'

They rose from the settee, still holding on to one another, then Lorimer reached out and switched off the lamp. The room plunged into semi-darkness, making vague shapes of the discarded objects on the floor.

13

The yellow flames are seeping out beneath the tyres, catching on the dried heather and old winter grass. One flame shoots up over the radiator grille and, as if at a signal, others leap up to join it, hissing against the wet bodywork. The vehicle rocks slightly. Perhaps the force of this combustion has made it shudder.

The watcher by the trees listens to the roar as the fuel tank ignites. A splash of colour floods the ambulance, shrivelling the paintwork. Sparks fly up into the night sky and he is reminded of that magical feeling on bonfire night. The crackling grows louder, but not loud enough to muffle the thuds within the vehicle. He listens. Soon there is only the roar and crackle of flame to be heard. He watches. The fire has done its worst and now the pale shape of the van has gone, leaving behind a blackened outline.

He laughs softly. No one will find you now. Cinders and ashes will leave no secrets behind.

When the report came through, Lorimer was almost expecting it.

'Totally burned out?'

'It's a complete wreck, sir,' the officer remarked, 'but there's no doubt it's the one we're after.'

Since *Crimewatch UK* there had been some useful information about the ambulance; enough to identify it as the one seen by Alison Girdley. Lorimer had a hunch that it would be trashed. He and Solly had no false ideas about their quarry: he was no fool. Given the interest in the programme, he was bound to get rid of the incriminating vehicle.

'That's not all we found, sir.'

The voice on the line cut into Lorimer's thoughts.

'Oh?'

There was a moment's hesitation which Lorimer recognised as the forerunner of bad news.

'No, sir. There is . . . there was a body inside the van.'

Had he? Would he have? Lorimer felt cheated for a moment. A cowardly suicide may have robbed him of bringing this criminal to justice. A wave of shame swept over him. He should be glad the bastard was dead and gone. No more young women would be picked off in such a gruesome manner.

Lorimer listened to the officer's voice giving details of the locus. It was a good forty minutes' drive from the city.

He put the phone down. Well, that was that. Another case over, and no thanks to him. Circumstances had overtaken him and the end had come so abruptly. The only satisfaction, he thought wryly, was that he was not the only one who would feel cheated. Solly Brightman's theories could never be proved now. But whatever elation he may have expected did not manifest itself. Instead, Lorimer felt flat and tired, as if he had succumbed to a bad cold. Would they ever identify the killer now? It was possible, but unlikely. There would be the usual scientific formalities, of course, but a charred corpse hardly made for the best of identifications.

Suddenly Lorimer felt an unreasonable surge of anger. How dare he cheat his way out of capture like this! That didn't fit at all. Lorimer shivered. He was beginning to follow unfamiliar patterns of thinking.

Lorimer felt the familiar buzz which occurred whenever he set foot on the locus of a murder. It was certainly not suicide. The first indications were that the body had been bound and left to die in the ensuing blaze. Very likely this was a fourth murder to add to the tally. But would they be able to identify the victim? And why had he been in the ambulance?

The Fiscal was already there watching the pathologist's examination as Lorimer stepped over the plastic cordon. He smiled briefly, acknowledging Lorimer's presence, then looked back at the young woman who knelt by the charred body on the ground. Lorimer scanned the scene with growing eagerness. The ambulance was a blackened shell now, with the rear doors twisted off at an angle. The dried winter grass was scorched for yards around, an acrid smell still lingering in the air. Uniformed policemen, their acid yellow jackets bright against the muted foliage, searched painstakingly around the area, eyes trained for anything which might raise a question in the long search for an answer.

Overhead a skylark poured out its notes, piercing the damp, grey air, oblivious to the little drama far below.

The moorland was mostly scrubby heather and curled dead bracken the colour of a pheasant's wing, except where an occasional hazel or rowan struggled for survival. Following the line of the road, a row of poplars reared their empty heads like scraggy, upended broomsticks. It was a bleak yet commanding landscape, thought Lorimer, his eyes finally coming back to the locus.

The Procurator Fiscal stood, hands thrust into his Burberry pockets, watching the proceedings with interest. Lorimer had a lot of time for Iain MacKenzie. He might be only in his early thirties, but he had already gained a reputation for being a tough customer who did not suffer fools gladly. The pathologist rose to her feet and stripped off a pair of thin surgical gloves. An earlier drizzle had soaked her blonde hair, plastering tendrils of fringe to a tanned forehead.

Lorimer grinned at her.

'Haven't seen you for a while, Rosie.'

'Oh, I've been away in Rwanda.' She wrinkled her nose. 'What a rotten job to come back to!' she exclaimed, looking up at the drizzly clouds.

Lorimer chuckled. Rosie Fergusson loved her work, but wasn't crazy about the great Scottish outdoors.

'Working for Her Majesty, I presume?' Lorimer asked.

The Sunday supplements had run various articles about the aftermath of the Rwandan massacres. Rosie's name had been mentioned more than once.

'Yeah. You know how it is,' the pathologist rolled her eyes, making light of her position as advisor to the Government in matters of forensic science.

'Not really. Care to enlighten me?'

Rosie twisted round and looked at him shrewdly. For a moment she seemed to consider then shook her head. 'You don't want to know. Believe me.'

Remembering the photographs of mass graves that had illustrated the articles, Lorimer found it hard to imagine this pretty young woman sifting through the debris of such appalling human tragedy. Rosie rarely betrayed any emotion about her job. Instead, she usually adopted a flippant attitude that was one of the tools of survival in her profession.

'Let's have a look before you bag him up.'

Lorimer stepped closer to the body, which was under a plastic tent protecting it from the elements.

'The van was found first thing this morning,' Iain MacKenzie told him. 'A postman spotted it on his way to Strathmirrin. Sensible fellow didn't touch a thing but got the local police sergeant out of his bed straight away.'

Lorimer gazed down at the charred body of the victim. His arms had been tied behind his back and the ankles were twisted together, suggesting that they too had been bound.

'He wouldn't usually look like this,' said Rosie, following Lorimer's gaze. 'If his limbs had been free, the whole body would have been curled into a pugilistic attitude.'

Lorimer nodded. He had seen burned corpses before and remembered the aggressive fists bunched against the onset of death.

'Time of death?'

Rosie shrugged. 'Hard to say. Within the last twelve hours certainly. Probably some time after midnight.'

Lorimer tried to picture the scene. A conflagration bursting out in the middle of nowhere against a darkened sky. Who might have seen it? They were not too far off the beaten track. Anyone passing along could have seen a light from the blazing ambulance on the low-lying moorland. These days, however, most folk wanted to keep their noses out of any trouble, especially on a cold February night.

'Fire started with petrol, I suppose?'

'Yes, petrol all right. He must have had it in the ambulance, driven here and then . . .' The Fiscal shrugged. 'What we don't know is if there was an accomplice. How did he get away? There are no tyre marks on the ground to indicate a second vehicle, but if somebody had arranged to pick him up?'

He left the question dangling tantalisingly for Lorimer, whose task it would be to figure out this piece of the puzzle. Somehow Lorimer could not envisage a second person there. Suddenly he wished that he had asked Solly to come along.

Iain MacKenzie strolled across to where the burned-out ambulance stood. Lorimer matched his stride, careful to walk by the plastic flags and leave the grassy area undisturbed for the officers still about their business. The young Fiscal stared at the wreckage.

'Our man has tried to get rid of the evidence,' he began, nodding towards the blackened hole inside the old ambulance. 'Thinks he's covered his tracks' – he paused, glancing over his shoulder – 'and disposed of our chum over there.'

'Well, we'll just have to see what forensics can find, if anything,' replied Lorimer.

He tried to keep a growing excitement out of his voice but saw that he had failed when Iain MacKenzie's eyes gleamed in a conspiratorial smile. The Fiscal would be glad to see that his Chief Inspector had the bit between his teeth again. There had been little enough to go on in this case.

'Going after Alison Girdley was his first mistake. Let's hope this one is his last.'

Lorimer nodded in agreement, his mind already racing ahead to the immediate procedure of the day: the Fiscal would have given instructions to the pathologists and the police forensic team. The two men turned in time to see the body being bagged ready for its journey to the city mortuary. Iain MacKenzie looked at his watch.

'Rosie will be doing the PM in a couple of hours. I need to be in the office for a bit. See you there about midday?'

'Fine. Who's on with Rosie?'

'She didn't say.'

The blonde pathologist would have had an early start after the Fiscal's telephone call. Before leaving, however, another call was necessary to alert her partner. The double doctor system on this side of the border was a legal condition ensuring the highest possible veracity in criminal pathology work. One of them would lead the post-mortem examination, the other act as observer and note-taker.

'God, I hate this weather!' Rosie Fergusson gave a shudder as the two men returned to her side. 'Give me Africa any day.'

Lorimer looked in fascination at the burnt corpse lying on the steel table. It was a difficult leap for the imagination to make. Only yesterday this had been a living, breathing human being.

Lorimer never forgot the feeling he had experienced the first time he had witnessed a murder PM. It had been strange how unreal a dead body looked. The bloodless skin gave the corpse the appearance of a dummy, not a real person at all. Seeing that first victim had crystallised all Lorimer's thoughts about murder. The very lifelessness of the corpse had spelt out clearly to him how terribly evil it was to commit such a deed. To take away forever that vital spark which changed a meaningless husk into a man. Lorimer wasn't an adherent of any particular religion but he did believe in the sanctity of life. What took place during a murder was the robbery of that treasured animus within a person. To Lorimer it was the ultimate violation, and while the police as a body were often reckoned to be hardened to such feelings, it was sometimes that very respect for life that made some men and women join in the first place.

Rosie was cutting into the thoracic area now, watched by Dan, her colleague on today's rota. She scooped out the dark red lungs with expertise born of much practice. Lorimer and the Fiscal were on the other side of the viewing screen but could communicate easily with the pathologists through the intercom. The body lay just under the window, its organs glistening in display. The pathologist's hair was tied back as she investigated the intricacies of the body on the table. The blue t-shirt and trousers topped by an emerald plastic apron gave her the air of a fishwife, especially when she moved around the table to reveal the yellow wellies which were a compulsory part of the pathologist's garb. Dan and she conversed quietly, occasionally being interrupted by questions from the intercom.

'Was he dead before the fire?' Lorimer wanted to know.

'No. This chap was alive and probably conscious when the fire began. There are sufficient soot deposits in the air passages to show this.'

'What exactly do you look for?' Iain MacKenzie's voice was full of professional interest.

'If there is carbon monoxide present in the victim's blood along with soot in the air passages, and if these passages are acutely engorged, then we can be certain that the victim was alive at the time of the fire.'

'How old do you reckon?' asked Lorimer.

'Well, he's not a young man. The teeth are fairly decayed and some are missing. I'll know more when I have a look at the coronary arteries. He had TB, you know,' she went on conversationally. 'You can see these cheesy-looking areas in the lungs.'

Something was stirring in the Chief Inspector's mind as he stared at the body. Rosie paused to let the two men look, then continued, 'There are marks on the neck and jaw which look like skin cancers.' Lorimer waited expectantly. Rosie was great at this sort of thing. 'I think he's been a derelict, poor soul. And,' she went on, looking at Lorimer significantly, 'there was enough of his clothing to confirm that.'

In every murder case the pathologist examined the body fully clothed from the body bag, tagging any items for further forensic testing and as exhibits for the process of the law.

'There were remnants of clothing under his back that remained intact. The coat he'd been wearing was tied round his waist with rope. Actually we have loads of fibres to be sent up for testing, believe you me.'

Lorimer shook his head, wondering that there was anything left at all. Rosie looked up and smiled.

'Why don't you two hop off and have a coffee in the kitchen? Dan and I will be a wee while yet.'

Lorimer took one long look at the brown and blistered corpse. He was reminded of wooden sculptures he had seen portraying victims of the holocaust. Each gaping maw had proclaimed the final agony of death.

Iain nodded towards the kitchen. The rectangular room was

painted in Dior grey like the rest of this building. All windows were hazy with obscure glazing, giving a permanent sense of being cut off from the world. The only colours came from the large planters of artificial flowers. Here the seasons ran riot, sunflowers mingling with daffodils and anemones in unlikely shades of vermilion and turquoise. Lorimer had thought to himself more than once how appropriate these artificial flowers were in a place reserved permanently for the dead.

There were more tasteful arrangements placed in the viewing room where victims might be identified by their families. Today the formalities of identification had been made by officers at the scene, since there was no way of telling who the victim was. Next of kin might wait months before knowing that a family member was lost to them. It happened all the time.

Rosie and Dan were still absorbed in their work with the body on the tray. The vital organs had been replaced, neatly bagged within the torso. Fluid samples had been taken, and already there were containers labelled to be tested in the lab.

'We'll be able to examine samples of tissue,' Rosie said, her voice coming clearly through the intercom. 'There were sufficient intact, you know.'

Lorimer raised his eyebrows but made no comment. To him the remains on the table were just that; remains. To a trained pathologist, however, there were innumerable clues to show who this sorry creature had been. Rosie was chatting away cheerfully. She might have been discussing the weather.

'There may be an infiltration of polymorphonuclear leucocytes into the tissues and into the blister fluid. That would be quite consistent with burns that are sustained by a vital organism. Also there are reddened areas that show the burns were sustained in life.' She stood back to indicate areas of flesh that showed these patches of red. 'Do you know, we may even be able to send fingerprints to your lot. You might do a quick ID, if he's got a record.'

There was such bad blistering that a positive identification was unlikely from simply looking at the face or body, but in his mind

Lorimer tried to match another face to the corpse below him. If his hunch was correct, then he would soon know from the fingerprint records what had become of Valentine Carruthers.

14

Martin Enderby couldn't believe his luck. Usually it took a combination of wheedling and cunning to extract decent information from the police. Now they had offered him his story on a plate. The burned-out ambulance was definitely the one mentioned on *Crimewatch UK* but there was even more to it than that. A body had been recovered from the wreckage, identified as a derelict who had 'been helping the police with their enquiries' regarding the St Mungo's murders. Chief Inspector Lorimer had forestalled any bombardment of questions from the Press by issuing a statement.

'We are treating this death as suspicious,' he had said. 'However we do not have any reason to believe that the victim was involved with the murders of the three young women found in St Mungo's Park.'

Martin had grinned at that. Okay, the guy hadn't been the killer, but he was involved in some way, otherwise how could he have ended up dead in that ambulance? Lorimer had clammed up at that point, though, almost as if he wanted the gentlemen of the Press to dig deeper for him. And maybe we will, thought Martin. It shouldn't take too much digging to find out about the derelict. His name was still being withheld until any relatives could be traced.

Martin looked up as a shadow fell across the computer screen on his desk.

'Davey, my man, just who I need right now!'

He swivelled round on his chair to face the photographer. Davey Baird looked down at him quizzically.

'How d'you fancy a wee drive out to Strathmirrin? Take some piccies of a bonfire site?'

The photographer's thin mouth curled in a sardonic grin.

'A bit early in the year for Guy Fawkes, isn't it?'

'Guy is just about right. Some poor guy copped it out there. Burned to death in that ambulance they were looking for. You know – the one on *Crimewatch*.'

'Tell me more.'

Davey settled himself onto an adjacent chair, straddling the seat and resting his arms over the back. He listened intently as Martin outlined the events at Strathmirrin.

'I've already interviewed the postman over the phone, but I'd like to get down there this afternoon while the light's still reasonable.'

'Sure. Now okay?'

'Great.'

'Right, I'll just grab my gear and see you in the car park.'

The afternoon had settled into a typical February day where light on the horizon was like a sweep of mother of pearl against the grey, oyster-coloured clouds. In the fields new lambs waggled their tails in ecstasy, butting their long-suffering mothers. The colours were still the shades of winter: dried yellow grasses and darker patches of heather and bracken. Martin's cassette intoned a Smiths tape. The old ones were still the best, he always asserted. Davey pressed the window button to let in a stream of cool air and the music spilled out, making the lambs gallop away from the roadside.

'Whereabouts are we headed, exactly?'

'Through the village of Strathmirrin, over the hill and down onto the moor. We'll have a bit of a walk from the road. Still, it's not that far, I'm told.'

Martin grinned at his companion. Normally it was a case of taking whatever photographer you were given but he'd been lucky in having more than his fair share of the ace freelance. They had pooled their resources together on several assignments involving this case. Davey had taken great pictures in the park and at the known sites of the murders. Of course, the wrecked vehicle would have been towed away by the police by now, but Davey would still manage to record something memorable about the site.

They passed through the little village of Strathmirrin in minutes. The cottages and old coaching inn which boasted such colourful hanging baskets in high summer looked strangely abandoned in this late winter light. Martin slowed down as they breasted the hill, looking for the site of the fire. It wasn't difficult to spot. A little way off the road a police landrover was parked, a small van beside it. Davey glanced over, raising his eyebrows.

'We're not the first, then?'

Martin parked on the grass verge then helped Davey unload his gear. Below them a copse of fir trees screened the sweep of moorland from the road. A sheep track meandered downwards through the heather and round a curving hillock that concealed the site of the fire from the road above. It was a difficult, but not impossible, route for a heavy vehicle to negotiate. The police landrover was not too close to the locus, thought Martin. Perhaps that was deliberate, though.

As they scrunched through the wet heather they could see several figures by the site, some in uniform. A camera tripod was balanced carefully in the tussocky grasses.

'Damn!'

Davey shrugged. 'It's all one. You'll do a better story.'

Martin laughed ruefully. 'And you'll take better pictures.'

'Of course!'

As they drew nearer Martin could see that three of the figures were police officers. He did not recognise the other two men. The photographer by the tripod was aware of Martin's approach and waved a warrant card in his direction as if to prevent any distraction. So. A police photographer. Martin felt relief. They were the first from the Press, then.

The second man in civilian clothes was a strange-looking fellow. He was standing staring at the burnt grass as if it had been the site of an alien landing rather than a spot ravished by mere human violence. His arms were folded across his chest and the breeze ruffled his thick black beard. Although Martin's professional curiosity normally prompted him to speak to any interesting stranger who came into his orbit, there was something about this character's bearing which he didn't like to disturb. It would have been like violating the private moment of someone at prayer, he thought.

Davey was circling the burnt grass, his gear weighing him down to a slow walk. At last he stopped by a spot where the sun fell behind him. Martin watched as he fished a band from his pocket and tied his long hair back in a ponytail. No stray hairs were allowed to float across his lenses. Satisfied that his colleague was now at work, Martin sidled over to the figure by the police tripod.

'Martin Enderby, the *Gazette*,' he said, offering his hand.

'Thought it would be your boys,' answered the photographer curtly, returning to his work.

Martin waited patiently until the man had clicked off sufficient frames for his purpose. 'A friend of yours?' he asked, indicating the dark figure still standing on the fringes of the site.

'Only just met him today,' the officer replied. 'Colleague of DCI Lorimer's.'

Martin nodded, hoping for more, but the photographer was already packing up his gear. 'Ready, Dr Brightman?' he called.

The still figure moved out of its trance. Martin was amazed at the transformation on the man's face as he grinned boyishly at the photographer.

'Oh, yes, I do think so. I really do think I am ready.'

Then he rubbed his hands in a gleeful gesture and waved cheerily as they passed Martin on their way to the unmarked van.

Well, thought Martin to himself, he's an odd one. Dr Brightman? Could he be new to the Forensics Department? Perhaps he would give Glasgow University a little call later on.

Davey was several yards from the site by a group of windswept saplings. He looked down on the area, snapping quickly then moving slightly to catch a different angle. Martin waited impatiently. The photos would be terrific but Davey sometimes became detached from their purpose and looked only for a picture's compositional value. At last he appeared satisfied and returned to Martin's side.

'Find anything out from those two?' he asked

Martin shrugged. 'Not really. Someone new to Forensics, I think. Anyhow, I shouldn't expect there would be much left to test after a fire like that.' He indicated the expanse of bald and blackened earth. 'Seems to have done a thorough job.'

Davey didn't answer, his eyes on the van now moving off in the direction of Strathmirrin. Martin followed his gaze. Whatever the prize-wining photographer was seeing, he couldn't make it out. Ideas for a winter landscape, perhaps?

'Right, let's get back and put this lot together,' he said at last, looking at his watch. Other folk might have time to stand and stare but he had a deadline to meet.

15

Donna Henderson's life lay in fragments within a plain buff folder. Despite the ubiquitous computer, hard copy was still the first point of reference for officers, and the lever arch files were stacked high in Lorimer's Division. He sat with the folder open in front of him, examining statements several months old. Parents, friends, colleagues and neighbours had all contributed to the picture of who Donna had been. An ordinary lassie, Lorimer had decided at the time; one whose ambitions lay no further than the next good night out with her pals and maybe a holiday abroad, if she could save up her tips.

The young hairdresser had left school at sixteen to train in a local salon. She had apparently been happy enough to sweep up the floors, make tea and learn to shampoo clients' hair. Then the take-over had come. A larger group of salons had bought out the shop and Donna had been given the chance to travel into one of their Glasgow branches. She had been thrilled at the prospect, a friend had said. Despite the cost of travelling into the city every day, Donna had loved her work there and was keen to learn. The senior stylist had been tactful about her progress. Enthusiasm had not been lacking, but she was not a fast learner. Nevertheless her cheery manner had been an asset to the city salon and she was both punctual and conscientious. Ironically it was that very conscientiousness that had been her downfall, Lorimer thought. A more rebellious spirit might have stayed out later with her pals and risked parental wrath; at least she would have travelled in company rather than seeking that solitary taxi home.

A taxi she had never reached.

Lorimer flicked through other statements. No boyfriends of any note. A few dates at the pictures in the company of lads she had known at school. Except one. Darren Hughes had met Donna at the Garage, a well-known city night spot, and had seen her twice thereafter. She wasn't really his type, he'd said. Too chatty. He'd thought they'd shared the same taste in music, but apparently Donna had favoured a band that Darren considered passé and he'd lost interest quite quickly. Donna hadn't appeared too bothered by the brief fling. A bit of necking in the back row of the cinema was about as far as the relationship had progressed. He might interview Darren again, but there was no obvious motive for murder.

Why the hair? Again and again Lorimer had tried to make sense of this aspect of the girls' murders. 'Can you guess what colour I'm going to have next?' that voice had asked. There would be a few attempts at a voice match, Darren Hughes amongst them, but Lorimer had the strong impression that the voice on the telephone belonged to someone who had not yet sat across the table from him in the interview room.

Solly Brightman considered the murder to be deliberate and well planned. That was as may be. The psychologist was coming up with more answers now that he had been to Strathmirrin to see the locus of Valentine Carruthers's murder. There was more to it than they could possibly guess, he had told Lorimer, driving the Chief Inspector into a barely concealed rage of frustration. He knew *that* already. Donna might have seen something incriminating, Solly had suggested. She could have been a threat to this man without even knowing it.

Now other questions must be asked of the people within this dossier. People who would show a greater reluctance to face the nightmare all over again and whose memories might be less reliable. The shock and aftermath of murder sometimes wiped out whole areas of memory for those close to the victim and they would cling to older memories of a younger, safer Donna. Lorimer had toyed with the idea of a client being involved. The trouble was that the city salon enjoyed a lot of passing trade and so not all their clients would be listed in the appointment book. It was like looking for a needle in a haystack. But someone would have to make the effort to sift through that appointment book and to question the other employees at the salon yet again. Lorimer rolled his eyes to heaven. The Super had brought Solly Brightman into the investigation, but he would not necessarily provide the extra manpower to enable Solly's theories to be tested. It's always the same, Lorimer had fumed to his wife. The lack of manpower was the bugbear of every Division in the country. In a case like this, the bottom line was a longer day for the more senior detectives. Unpaid overtime, just part of the job. No wonder Maggie was cheesed off most of the time.

He closed Donna's file and picked up the one marked 'Carruthers V'. The full post-mortem report would take three weeks to prepare. Rosie had given him a start, though, by answering at least one question: who? His mind flashed back to the old derelict he had interviewed. He recalled the hacking cough, his cunning eyes and the wheedling tone of voice. Yet, despite his past he had felt sorry for the man, down and out as he was with no protection from the elements. And, he thought grimly, no protection from whoever had ended his unfortunate life.

But what was the connection between a young hairdresser and an old tramp? Had Donna been involved with charity work which might have brought her into contact with Valentine Carruthers? He doubted it, but it might be worth contacting Glasgow City Mission and checking out that line of enquiry. They might throw some light, too, on Valentine's nocturnal movements.

Someone, somewhere, badly wanted rid of a young girl and an old man. The other two victims were camouflage, so the psychologist would have him believe. There is something wrong here, thought Lorimer, but until he could put his finger on it he would not dismiss Dr Brightman's line of thought. Solly certainly would not wear the suggestion a young DC had made that Valentine had simply strayed into the abandoned ambulance and been the victim of hideous circumstances.

The old ambulance, he had noted, had run through the park. For the hundredth time Lorimer cursed himself for failing to follow up the old man's comment. Perhaps he had been trying to hint at something he knew? Solomon believed now that Valentine Carruthers had known a great deal. The disposal of the old man by fire had taken some forethought and planning. So a thorough investigation into the tramp's background was essential. Who were his cronies? What might they know of the old man's involvement in the park?

'Get yourself down to Kingston Bridge,' Lorimer had instructed his youngest DC. 'See if he took our advice and found a hostel. Ask around. Get to know his haunts.'

Lorimer hoped that gossip from amongst the street people would be forthcoming. It would certainly be welcome.

'He thinks it's finished,' Solly had remarked at their last meeting. 'He will believe that he has burned every shred of evidence to link him to the murders, including his association with Valentine.'

'But is it finished?' Lorimer had asked and Solly had shaken his head slowly.

'Not at all. The paranoia he has displayed will only escalate, and his behaviour become equally unstable as a result.'

'He could kill again?'

Solly stared the Chief Inspector straight in the eye.

'Perhaps he already has.'

The ambulance had been sighted all over the United Kingdom, apparently. The process of elimination was tedious, given that every call to the *Crimewatch* programme had to be treated as potentially helpful. Now, however, there were several possible leads. One in particular interested DS Alistair Wilson, and it was this one that he needed to discuss with Lorimer.

'Chap over on the South Side. An Asian bloke who deals in second-hand cars and scrap metal. A bit on the shady side, if you'll forgive the pun, but no form as such.'

Lorimer was scanning the report rapidly.

'Says the vehicle went missing last October.'

'Yes, sir. Can't think why he didn't bother to report it.'

DS Wilson's voice was heavy with sarcasm. They both had a fair idea why the garage owner had not felt it necessary to involve the police in his business. Dodgy vehicles which should have ended up in the scrapyard were all too often sold on for a better profit to unscrupulous characters willing to risk driving about minus a tax disc and MOT certificate.

'What made him report it now?'

'Says he saw *Crimewatch* and felt it was his duty as a respectable citizen. He was all too anxious to know if someone had spotted it in his premises, is my guess.'

'He's probably hurt the VAT man over the years, but he's not going to be had up for murder. Sangha. Ravit Sangha,' read Lorimer. 'He and his brother run the business, you say, and the brother does the scrap metal side of things.'

'Sangha says that he has no record of who brought the vehicle to him,' continued Wilson, 'but he remembers it had been previously used by some type of rock band. He'd paid cash, of course.'

Lorimer read through Sangha's statement once more while Wilson waited expectantly. It was up to his DCI to take the next initiative. In bringing the statement to his boss, he was already hinting that more could be done without actually asking for extra manpower.

'What do you think?'

'I could always go and see him again, lean a bit harder,' Wilson smiled.

Sometimes his pleasant gentlemanly manner in dealing with the public was a blind for the hard steel beneath.

'Do that. A second visit might shake him up sufficiently to jolt his memory. I want to know who owned that vehicle and where it went after it left Sangha's yard. There's a surprising amount of forensic evidence sitting in the file doing nothing. If we know the previous owner we can eliminate at least some of it.'

Ravit Sangha's garage was situated on the corner of a busy dual carriageway and the main road leading to a sprawling housing estate on the South Side of Glasgow. The blue hoarding proclaiming USED CARS in white painted capitals overlooked a shabby yard with grimy whitewashed walls. There were cars lined up somewhat haphazardly, only a few displaying a price sticker on the front windscreen. Dark stains on the forecourt told of old oil spillages and there were empty plastic drums heaped into a far corner. The office was a jerry-built affair resembling the huts in school playgrounds: the sort that linger on far beyond their shelf life as 'temporary accommodation'. Ravit Sangha may well have expected to progress to something bigger and better over the years, but the whole place had an air of defeat as if the receivers were not far off.

And now trouble had come in the shape of one old used ambulance. Why had he bothered to telephone? DS Wilson had asked himself. Sangha had been highly agitated at that first interview, protesting his good citizenship far too much for the Detective Sergeant's liking. Lorimer was right. There had to be something more. Like where had the vehicle really come from and whether it had really 'gone missing' from Sangha's yard. Answers to these questions would direct this inquiry forward for a change. Trawling through Donna Henderson's case was becoming a wearisome exercise.

Less than an hour later the two CID men were on their way back to Divisional Headquarters. DC Cameron risked a glance at his sergeant as they weaved through the afternoon traffic. Grim satisfaction was registered on that usually expressionless face. Cameron smiled and found himself wishing that he could be a fly on the wall when their visit was reported to Chief Inspector Lorimer.

Lorimer's raised eyebrows were just the reward DS Wilson expected as he narrated the events on Glasgow's South Side.

'You were spot on about the VAT,' Wilson confirmed. 'When I began to hint about the serious consequences of defrauding Her Majesty's Inspectors the poor buggar became almost pale.'

A hint of a smile flickered over Wilson's mouth.

'So what was the real reason for contacting us when he had a can of worms like that to hide?'

Lorimer clasped his hands tightly together. He could sense an undercurrent of excitement in Wilson's manner and knew the DS had something to tell.

'A phone call. Some bright citizen had seen the ambulance in the yard and decided to put the frighteners on our friend Sangha.'

Lorimer inclined his head thoughtfully. Wilson picked up the cue.

'Reading between the lines it's probably no more than some idiot mouthing off the usual racial nonsense,' he went on. 'Still, it's been enough to bring Sangha running to us before we came to him.'

'What about the brother?' Lorimer rapped out.

'Ah, yes. Well, he sat there looking at us as if we'd crawled out from under a stone. Didn't say a word at first but he backed up brother Ravit's story once the thought of years of missing VAT loosened his tongue.'

'I can imagine. And then it all came out?'

Wilson nodded. 'It all came out. They'd paid cash for the ambulance from some rock band or other calling themselves The Flesh Eaters. No vehicle registration document, let alone MOT or insurance.'

'Still, with a name like that they shouldn't be hard to find,' remarked Lorimer.

'Also we have a description of two of them,' Wilson added.

'Fine. So we know where the ambulance came from. Any idea what happened once the Sanghas took possession of it?'

Lorimer's light tone belied the expression on his face. He was staring at Alistair Wilson. He knew his sergeant's ways so well.

Wilson paused to watch the effect of his words on Lorimer's face.

'Ravit Sangha sold that ambulance to Lucy Haining.'

16

'But we don't need him any more. We can drop the whole investigation of Donna Henderson's murder, look at Lucy Haining's case and concentrate on the leads from *Crimewatch*. What do we need Brightman for?'

George Phillips sighed irritably. 'I'm reluctant to sever the relationship between the university and ourselves, Bill.' The Divcom gave a dry cough. 'I really do think we should allow Dr Brightman continued access to the case.'

Lorimer glared at his superior, not caring to conceal his annoyance.

'Let him sniff around meantime. I'm sure he'll have his uses,' Phillips concluded, shuffling some papers on his desk to indicate that this conversation was terminated.

Lorimer fumed to himself all the way along the corridor. George Phillips had been deliberately vague and his own remonstrations had cut no ice whatsoever. He suspected that there were wheels within wheels that he knew nothing of concerning the Divcom's desire to use a psychological profiler. Maybe he would read something about it in the Chief Constable's next annual report, he thought angrily, as he slammed shut the door of his own room, shaking Père Tanguy's picture.

Lorimer looked up at Van Gogh's postman. The sitter clearly wanted to be up and off about his business instead of staring at the artist for hours on end. Lorimer took a deep breath. Perhaps that was a bit like Solomon and himself, the one looking at shapes within a framework of his own creation, the other out and about in the world, trying to make sense of the disparate facts that he could find. He ran a hand through his hair.

Solomon Brightman would keep his afternoon appointment after all, despite Lorimer's attempts to cancel it indefinitely.

'No, I do not accept that I was wrong. I simply told you that the murderer had killed a targeted victim known to himself, and used the others as camouflage.'

Solomon Brightman spoke in his usual unhurried manner, refusing to show any anger to match that of Chief Inspector Lorimer.

'We've spent far too many man-hours going over the Donna Henderson murder again, and now ordinary detection methods have given us quite a different lead.'

Solomon raised his hands and shrugged in that fatalistic gesture that annoyed Lorimer so much.

'The *Crimewatch* programme can hardly be considered ordinary,' he said reasonably.

Lorimer gritted his teeth. He was stuck with Dr Brightman now and so any further argument would only be counter-productive. Solomon may have been having similar thoughts for he suddenly changed tack.

'I'd like to look at the place where Lucy Haining was actually killed,' he said.

'All right. I'll arrange for a uniformed officer to pick you up.'

Solomon shook his head. 'I'd rather just wander around unobtrusively, you know.'

Lorimer resisted a smile, thinking a less unobtrusive-looking character would be hard to find. He then swivelled round from his desk and pointed at the maps pinned to the wall behind him. They were enlargements of specific areas in the city.

'Here. This is Sauchiehall Street and these are the streets leading up to the Glasgow School of Art. Over the hill just there' – his finger stopped at a point on the map – 'you'll find the waste ground.'

Carefully Solomon made a sketch of the area, writing the names of the intersecting streets and copying the cross which signified the place where the young art student had met her death. Up until now Solomon had concentrated his attention on St Mungo's Park and its immediate environs. The city locations had suggested no more

than places of dark opportunity. Doubtless young Sharon Millen
had been killed in just such an area.

Deep down Lorimer knew that they had both been guilty of one
simple assumption; that the first killing had been the one to be
carefully planned and that the others were simply random slaughters
intended to obfuscate the whole picture. Now they were faced with
the possibility that the killer had been cold-blooded enough to begin
covering his tracks with Donna Henderson's murder.

'A practice run?' Solomon had suggested earlier.

He had not been surprised to read the disgust on Lorimer's face.
Whoever this killer was, his profile was adding up to show a man
of Machiavellian cleverness and ruthless disregard for human life.

Martin Enderby put the phone down thoughtfully. So. Not Forensic
Pathology after all. Dr Brightman was not only a trained psychologist, but he was researching a book about criminal profiling.
Here was a tasty bone for a hungry newshound indeed. And
the book would be a good enough reason to set up an interview.
Then . . . Martin grinned to himself. Then he'd see what else he
could find out about the St Mungo's Murders. He picked up the
phone once more.

'I'm sorry, Dr Brightman has just left.'

'Oh, just my luck!' Martin groaned, affecting the tone of an
anxious student trying to locate his tutor.

'Is it urgent?' The secretary's voice became concerned.

'Well, sort of. Do you know whereabouts he might have gone?'

'He was heading for the Art School, I believe. He should be there
within half an hour.'

'Thanks. I'll maybe catch up with him there.'

Martin replaced the phone and grabbed his jacket from the
back of the chair. The Art School! Was there some new lead
concerning Lucy Haining that he should make it his business to
find out about? Martin's long legs took the stairs two at a time.
Whatever Dr Brightman might stand and stare at this time, he
wanted to see it too.

101

17

Sauchiehall Street certainly expressed the dichotomy of Scotland's largest city, thought Solomon, as he turned into the main thoroughfare and headed west. Buses rumbled along Hope Street between ranks of pedestrians impatient for the lights to change. More than once, Solomon had held his breath as some old dear rushed out, defying the traffic. They seemed to lead a charmed life in this city, for he'd never seen an accident yet. Once in the pedestrian precinct, Solly slowed down, taking a professional interest in the mass of humanity coming and going. Snatches of conversation floated past him, accents betraying both the cultured and the couthy.

'C'm ere, youse!'

A young mother wheeling a buggy yelled at her two older offspring who were weaving in and out of the human traffic. Giggling, they dashed over to their mother's side and Solomon watched, amused, as they made faces behind her back. Pensioners sat on benches, some merely staring at the world going by, but others intent on feeding the feral pigeons. Behind him the *Big Issue* sellers were plying their wares outside Marks & Spencer's and the shopping mall. In doorways buskers expressed their social outrage in plaintive song to the world at large, but to nobody in particular.

Solomon glanced up at Mackintosh's elegant Willow Tea Rooms, an early twentieth-century gem, though the School of Art was the real jewel in the celebrated architect's crown. Here and there, tucked into quieter side streets, were the galleries where contemporary artists now made their names. Solomon had wandered around some of them occasionally, his eye favouring the brighter abstracts which commanded attention. But today he would not be distracted from attending to a much more sombre view.

Leaving the main street, the psychologist began the steep climb which would take him up to the Art School and beyond, to Garnethill. A young traffic warden was taking note of a white Toyota whose owner had left it overlong at the meter. She kept her head down as Solomon passed, grinning to himself. He had never learned to drive and affected to despise governments which allowed too much road traffic and contributed to hazards like pollution and road rage. Death from a traffic accident provoked a certain resigned sadness, of course, but the deaths of Lucy Haining and the other young women were an outrage that society must refuse to accept.

Solomon crossed over to where the School of Art towered above him. It seemed stark and bleak today, casting its shadows towards the area where one of its students had ended her bright prospects. As Solomon glanced at his makeshift map, he did not notice a tall figure standing above him on the steps to the main entrance.

At first his eye was caught, not by the main building at all, but by a vehicle parked on the opposite kerb. The blue Art School minibus bore an uncanny resemblance in size and shape to an ambulance.

Solomon crossed the street to take in the vista of this celebrated School, itself a work of art. High over the entrance swung a bow of black metal serving as a token arch. Its keystone was a plain black box, rudely interrupting the flowing line like some purely functional appendage. Yet on closer inspection it became a sinister rectangular mass glaring at the world with one all-seeing indigo eye. Below the black-banded windows, unkind spikes and knotted buttresses of thin metal led the eye downwards to the railings with their abstract motifs.

The curving stairs made a pleasing invitation to proceed up towards the entrance, but the grubby white doors set with purple and blue eyes did not beckon. Rather it seemed a challenge to enter this holy of holies. Solomon smiled to himself, catching sight of a blonde student who now lounged against the railings. Clad all in blue denim, she was flicking cigarette ash onto the hallowed steps, seemingly oblivious to the mystique around her. Perhaps familiarity with the School as a workplace bred contempt? Solomon looked around him. To one side the newly cleaned Victorian tenements of Dalhousie Street fell away steeply. On the other side a conglomeration of concrete and glass pressed close, its ugliness in sneering contrast to the refinement of the School of Art.

He would return to wander the interior and tread the floors where Lucy Haining had daily trod. But not yet. Pausing to look both left and right, Solomon eventually decided to retrace his steps and continue up Dalhousie Street towards that cross on his map.

As the sun shone down on the streets it was hard to see this place as one where evil had stalked. There was such an air of normality, the public going about their business. Three schoolboys in green uniform passed him by, laughing and chattering; an Asian woman swathed in cloths of gold and brown glided along, her plastic shopping bags rustling by her side.

Solomon slowed down as he came to the square of waste ground. This was where murder had taken place. Nobody had seen anything suspicious on that cold winter night and, looking at the adjacent buildings, Solomon could see the advantages of choosing this as a place to conceal an act of murder. The tenement building on one side was covered in scaffolding for what seemed a long-term project. Each and every window was boarded up. Blind eyes overlooked the patch of ground. Today, men in white overalls were clambering over the tubular scaffolding. The psychologist could hear them whistling as though the air around them had never been contaminated by evil.

He walked around reading what he saw like some familiar language. The proximity to the School of Art had added a dimension of creativity to this long-neglected area. On top of the lamp-posts squatted fat black metal pigeons looking as though they were quite capable of muting down the length of each tall, thin pole. In some ways, Solomon thought, this was typical of much of Glasgow's urban regeneration where smart new developments in red brick with landscaped corners cocked a snook at their older, worn out neighbours. On the far side of the waste ground, tenements huddled together, some with neo-classical features still clinging to the stonework; a few still hopelessly grimy with more than a century's dirt.

Continuing to walk round the perimeter of the site, he came at last to where the killer must have taken Lucy. A narrow lane bounded the area on one side, flanked by a high brick wall. Uneven cobbles, which were more like bricks stuck haphazardly into the ground, caused him to stumble. Above the wall, branches of barbed wire swung menacingly on metal brackets. The psychologist shuddered. Even in broad daylight it felt unsafe to walk here. Suddenly he stopped and stared. Built directly into the wall was a strange house on two storeys, resembling the back portion of a warehouse. And then, just as he stood there, a young woman emerged from the front door, closed and locked it behind her, and marched purposefully down the lane. Solomon looked at the house again. There were two doors, one at street level and the other like the entrance to a store, set on the first floor. Each was painted a bright, defiant red. There were windows on this side. He presumed the police had questioned the residents to no avail and, with a resigned sigh, turned to the waste ground itself. The ashes of bonfire night were now only a black patch in the winter grass. A few scrawny ash trees would create a screen from the road in high summer, but as yet they were leafless.

Lucy had used this lane as a short cut to her friend's flat. The killer knew that, Solomon told himself. He walked back up the lane then turned and strolled alongside an imaginary Lucy, engaging her in . . . what? Conversation? Argument? He stopped before reaching the red-doored house and tried to imagine the situation. Had her killer taken Lucy by the shoulder in an embrace that was meant to look protective but that was actually steering her towards her death? What had made the girl stop on her journey? The scalping had taken place in a corner of the ground where the shadows from the wall and trees were darkest. Yet the place would never have been discovered had Janet Yarwood not intimated that Lucy might have been on her way to see her: she often came that way. Painstaking police work, thought Solomon, ungrudging in his admiration for Lorimer's team. The lane would have done just as well. In fact, it would have been a duplicate of Donna Henderson's murder, and that, surely, had been his intention? Had something gone wrong, then? Had Lucy struggled, run towards the waste ground in an attempt to break through the line of trees but been caught by the killer's deadly chain?

Solomon was aware of the silence. From where he stood, the city's roar of traffic was muffled by the thick wall and there was not a soul in sight. The killer must have stood here, his victim at his feet, ready to transport this latest corpse by ambulance to St Mungo's Park. The lane had a no parking sign at its entrance, Solomon had noted. Mon–Fri 8.45–5.15 p.m. Any vehicle outwith these hours would be legally parked and hardly noticed. Had he stopped in the ambulance and beckoned Lucy, the way he had with Alison Girdley? But Lucy knew this ambulance; she had been the one charged with its purchase in the first place. So. She knew her killer, maybe even liked him, and would wait patiently while he drew alongside her and called out her name. Or was he parked there already? One way or the other Solomon felt that there had been an implicit trust on the part of the girl. The killer had beguiled her somehow or else she was unaware of her danger. Why? To answer that, he must find out much, much more about Lucy Haining and every person she had known in her student life. It was not only a murderer he was looking to profile.

The lane took Solomon back out to the street that ran downhill to the city centre. Here Garnethill overlooked the city from all points. To the west, the white spires of Trinity speared the sky. Beyond lay the university and Solomon's own small patch of belonging. Down to the north the buildings faded into misty greys, the street lights beginning to cast a weak glow. South lay the river. As Solomon walked back along Scott Street, the Art School appeared like a safe canyon against the wilderness outside. Huddled into the steep incline was the side door to the Centre for Contemporary Arts. Even as he glanced that way a couple emerged from the building. The CCA was open late every evening, he knew; sometimes it hosted a club night but mostly it was simply a hang-out for students, art students in particular. Solomon wondered if the centre had been investigated in the course of Lorimer's lengthy inquiries. He made a mental note to ask – tactfully.

Straight ahead the river Clyde lay hidden, caught between the amalgam of buildings sprawled on either bank. Traffic criss-crossed the intersecting streets like a never-ending game in an amusement arcade. Push in a coin, see the buses ride the grid. Buses, taxis, post office vans, cars, ambulances . . . Their dim roar was like an animal breathing in its sleep, unseen and languorous in daylight but lurking by every watering hole come sundown.

The ambulance would have slipped into the main stream of night-time traffic then crossed through the gates of St Mungo's Park. On impulse Solomon hurried down the last few yards to Sauchiehall Street and hailed an approaching black taxi.

It was that half-light of evening that motorists so dislike when the taxi drew up at the park gates, the evergreen bushes looking burnt orange in the glare of headlights. The park was no longer manned, though infrared detectors and closed circuit television cameras remained discreetly in place. But the gate was firmly shut. Solomon looked back at the retreating taxi that had swung an effortless u-turn and was now heading towards the city. The journey had taken sixteen minutes. What had been going through the killer's mind during that journey? He had already made the dry run with poor little Donna Henderson, so he knew what to do here. But how could he be sure that a police presence would not disturb his activities? Even more so with Sharon Millen, he thought. Unless . . . Could the killer have had information about police movements? Or had he simply strolled around to check whether it was safe to repeat his original performance? Any cold-blooded murderer would seek to cover his tracks, but someone in the police force would have insider knowledge that could work to his advantage.

The photofit of the killer showed a trim, clean-cut individual. They had even made a joke about him looking like a copper. Yet so many men of this age group had that cropped hairstyle; defiant punk or a convenient attempt to disguise a receding hairline.

Solomon leaned against the park railings, forcing himself to consider this possibility. A sudden vision of Lorimer's steely blue glare flashed across his mind. The Chief Inspector would not take kindly to this idea at all. Oh, no, indeed.

18

It was almost too easy once he'd stopped to think about it. Martin had missed the black-bearded psychologist, who had not been at the School of Art after all, it seemed. The journalist had hung around watching the students come and go for a good half hour. He'd watched the entrance like a hawk, waiting to see whether Brightman would emerge, but the only figure he had recognised was Chris, the art student who'd bought that print at Davey's exhibition. Martin had smiled as he passed him by on the street but the guy had just looked right through him as if he wasn't there and walked on. Only minutes later a janitor from the School's design workshop had strolled up and asked a few bland questions. The man's meaningful look had almost encouraged Martin to whip out his Press card but, preferring anonymity, Martin had feigned the air of a tourist overawed by the sight of Charles Rennie Mackintosh's great work. The janitor's look had remained sceptical, though, so Martin had taken himself off, cursing the time wasted. Later, however, the way to weasel information out of the psychologist had come to him in a flash of brilliance.

Martin chuckled to himself as he slotted the cassette tape into his machine. Diane's sexy voice made the hairs on his neck tingle and there was a growing warmth in his groin. A small involuntary sigh of pleasure escaped him as the thought of her flickered across his mind.

The preliminary courtesies of the interview were coming to a close and Diane's firmness of tone signalled the beginning of more interesting dialogue.

'Tell me, Dr Brightman, what sort of response does psychological profiling receive from the police?'

'In general, you mean?'

'Well, I know it's used a lot in the United States, but is it well thought of here in Britain?'

There was a pause in the conversation and Martin could imagine Diane, legs crossed, smiling in encouragement at Dr Brightman, researcher into what made murderers tick.

'Yes and no,' came the reply. Martin expected Diane to pounce on that prevarication but she kept a measured silence. 'There have been cases in England where the techniques of criminal profiling have been used to great effect. The results are often surprising to the investigating officers when regular methods have drawn a blank.'

'Do you feel that regular methods, as you call them, are out-dated, then?'

'Oh, no.' His rejoinder was swift this time. 'I have great respect for the methods used by the police. In many ways we follow similar lines of thought. We do not only ask why something like a murder took place but we try to stand in the murderer's shoes. Like Father Brown.'

'Pardon me?'

'G.K. Chesterton.' Martin and Solomon replied together, and Martin grinned. He must remember to tease Diane about that one. But Solomon was enlarging for her benefit. 'The Father Brown stories. He was, in his way, the classic profiler. He put himself in the murderer's shoes, so to speak: tried to think as he would. Clever, really. A priest, you know. The confessional and all that.' The psychologist's voice drifted away as if his thoughts had taken wing elsewhere.

'So the police are beginning to use psychological profiling here in Scotland?'

Diane was clever, thought Martin. Brightman had not actually mentioned Scotland yet.

'Ah, yes. It is not only confined to their counterparts south of the border. Oh my, no.'

'And the Scottish police value your services?'

There was another silence. Hello, thought Martin, anybody there?

'I did not say that the Scottish police used my methods,' the psychologist began slowly.

'But they do?'

'Yes.'

The admission seemed reluctantly drawn from him.

'Will you use any of the cases in Scotland in your book, Dr Brightman?'

Clever girl, thought Martin, take him round the houses.

'Ah, that depends.'

'On what?'

'Well. I think a certain case might generate much interest to readers. But then again I could not use it until there is a satisfactory outcome.'

'You mean until a particular murderer is caught?'

'That might not always be the same as a satisfactory outcome.'

'But surely that's what you are aiming for?'

'Usually, yes.'

'Tell me, Dr Brightman, this particular case – has it anything to do with the St Mungo's murders?'

Diane's voice was a mixture of innocence and guile. Martin recognised the 'you can tell *me* all about it' quality she so often employed. And exploited. Another silence followed. Martin was trying to picture the bearded psychologist, hand on chin, perhaps, considering. He wondered how much of Diane's tactics he could see through. All of them, probably. He was a psychologist after all. Perhaps his answers were like police statements to the Press, carefully calculated to serve their own ends.

'The St Mungo's murders should never have happened,' Solomon said at last. 'There is so much still to understand . . .' There was another pause. Go on, urged Martin, listening to the tape whirring in the silence of the room. 'I do hope to see a satisfactory end to it all. Sometimes I feel quite close to him, then it's as if I never knew him at all.'

Martin held his breath. Was the psychologist thinking aloud, forgetting Diane's presence?

'And Lucy Haining?' Diane's question fell like a drop of water into a still pool.

'They knew each other, of course. To know one may be the key to knowing the other . . .' Martin imagined Diane scarcely daring to

111

breathe, fearful of disturbing Brightman's train of thought. But then the psychologist cleared his throat. 'The book won't be published for some time, of course. There are several cases to be examined as well as techniques to be explained.'

Was the change of tack deliberate? wondered Martin. Had he sensed that he was venturing into the heart of his case whence he would not let this young woman journalist follow?

'Now I'd love to hear about the techniques of criminal profiling,' she exclaimed, as if that was her sole reason for interviewing Dr Solomon Brightman in his West End home. There was a short laugh from the psychologist before he continued.

'Ah, the secret formula! I'm afraid you will be disappointed in me. The techniques are really no more nor less than studying the behaviour of individuals. It's what psychologists do all the time.'

His voice sounded kindly.

'But I thought . . .'

'You thought we clever people had devised a bag of tools to unlock the brain of a killer? It's just the tools of our trade put to a particular use.' There was a pause during which Martin tried hard to picture Diane's perplexity. Or was she merely stifling a yawn in the silence? Somehow he didn't think so. He felt she must be drawn to Brightman, just as he himself was now drawn, fascinated by what would come next.

'Did you enjoy your years at school, Miss McArthur?'

'Well, yes, I suppose so.' Diane sounded puzzled by this seeming digression.

'Were you interested in history, geography and statistics?'

'Well, yes . . .'

'These are the subjects we use in our investigations. With the police,' he added as an afterthought. This time Diane seemed lost for words. Brightman continued. 'The history is the history of the criminal, his background and so forth. The way he executes his crime and the patterns of crimes – if they are numerous – tell us about him. For instance, the difference between an organised and disorganised murder reveals a certain divide in behaviour that lets us begin to figure out a criminal.'

'And geography?' Diane broke in.

'Well, the locus of a crime is often revealing. Many criminals commit their crimes near to their own homes. At least to begin with. The pattern of crimes then helps to show us where home might be. We would look very carefully at maps, access to transport then, perhaps, clusters of crimes. Statistics are used all the time, you know. The computer cuts down a lot of cross-checking of data. But it needs to be done.'

Martin switched off the tape and swore softly. Brightman had led Diane into a morass of generalities. He had been in control all along, taking Diane deeper and deeper into the trees; deliberately blinding her to the wood. Martin gritted his teeth in frustration. He had hoped that there would be some nuggets of information about Lucy Haining, but so far there was only one tantalising suggestion that she had known her killer. Martin rewound the tape, clicking off and on until he came to the part he wanted to hear again.

'They knew each other, of course. To know one may be the key to knowing the other . . .'

Martin wrote this down in his spiral-bound notebook. He would have to listen to the rest of Diane's interview, but he doubted it would yield up any more than these two sentences. Just how much did this fellow really know?

Later Martin regarded his reflection in the bathroom mirror as he shaved. The firm jawline was raised at an angle as he automatically changed direction with the blade, keeping his neck skin taut. Diane had done well to continue with Dr Solomon Brightman for another twenty minutes while he had expounded theories but had given nothing else away.

'To know one may be the key . . .'

Martin had made a rapid decision. He had to find out much more about Lucy Haining than he had initially dug up all those weeks ago. And he knew the very person who might help him in his search.

Flinging down the damp towel, Martin began to whistle to himself.

19

L orimer didn't like it at all.

'Do you realise exactly what you are inferring? That one of my men . . .' He broke off, glaring at Solomon, the words sticking in his throat, then turned wearily and shook his head. 'I just don't buy that. Granted, he's clever. Devious. He plans. The *organised* mind you talk so much about. But that's it.'

Lorimer looked over his shoulder to where the psychologist still stood, the ends of a woollen scarf wound about his gloved hands. For a moment the other man's face was impossible to read and Lorimer wondered if he would simply walk out of his office and never come back. But then the door swung open and George Phillips strode heavily in.

'Ah, Bill . . . Oh, Dr Brightman, how are you?'

Lorimer caught the imperceptible shake of Solomon's head as George Phillips launched himself towards the desk, thrusting a sheaf of papers at his DCI.

'That's the latest from Europe. At least their figures make us look like a slightly more moral neighbour.' Three strides took him across the room then he turned, his massive frame filling the doorway. 'Or do they just catch more of 'em?'

His smile was sardonic as he left. The room was suddenly silent and Lorimer was uncomfortably aware of Solly standing there, waiting patiently.

'Oh, sit down.' Lorimer gestured to the only easy chair by the window and slumped into his own swivel chair behind the desk. 'See these,' he waved the documents in the air. 'Statistics. Someone over in Brussels is probably paid a fortune to produce these. And what do they tell us? That there are more cases of paedophilia on the other side of the Channel.'

Solomon raised his thick eyebrows, but said nothing.

'It's nonsense. We probably have as many perverts as they do. We just haven't brought as many of them to justice. That's the trouble with statistics. Do your job well and the figures seem to soar. The more effective we are, the more the Press report cases and the poor old British public think that paedophilia is running riot.' He swept his hand upwards, indicating the row of ledger files. 'See that? Robberies with violence, child abuse, murder . . . maybe a serial killer . . . and you have the temerity to suggest that one of my team is bent?'

Lorimer stopped, realising that he was beginning to lose control. Solomon cleared his throat.

'Lucy Haining spent over three years in Glasgow. I would like to find out how these years were spent, whom she befriended. Little things over and above what you already know.' He raised a hand. 'I'm not suggesting that your background information was unsatisfactory. But you must see that things have changed?'

'Yes.' Lorimer looked down at the papers on his desk, avoiding Solomon's eye.

'She was one of a series before,' Solomon insisted gently, 'and now she may be the reason for all the murders.'

'What do you want?'

'A free hand. I need to ask questions, be able to talk to her friends, her teachers, anyone who knew her in and out of the Art School.' Solomon leaned forward. 'I need a picture. If I can understand Lucy Haining's world, then the profile of this killer may become much clearer. He knew her and she undoubtedly had dealings with him. She bought the ambulance. Who else knew about that?'

'We have had officers asking just that question,' Lorimer replied.

'And?'

The DCI shrugged. 'Nothing so far. Nobody else at the Art School knew about it or saw it. However, we've made some progress regarding the previous owners.' When Solomon didn't reply Lorimer continued, 'A rock band. Couldn't track them down immediately. They sold the vehicle to help fund a lengthy trip to the States. They're on their way back now. In fact' – he looked at his watch – 'if I'm quick,

I'll be meeting them at Glasgow Airport within the next half-hour.'

'Lucy Haining,' Solomon began again.

'Do what you want. If you find anything, and I mean anything concrete at all, I want to know. Even,' he sighed heavily, 'if I don't like it.'

Glasgow International Airport was, like airports the world over, a watershed between the mundane and the exotic. Lorimer barely glanced at the acres of car parking, car rental premises and dormitory hotels spread out before the airport buildings. The motorway had arched upwards, sweeping them above the airport and for a few seconds he ignored the familiar spires of Paisley on his left, scanning the tarmac to catch sight of the massive aircraft below. Then the police car dipped down on to the approach road and Lorimer drew his gaze away.

After a word with the uniformed duty officer, Lorimer and his driver made their way to the end of the long glass corridor where travellers departed and arrived hour after hour. The detective joined the small clutch of people waiting for their friends and relatives. A toddler in a red ski suit and bobble hat ran to and from his mother, delight on his face each time he trespassed a foot or two into the forbidden entry zone. Lorimer's eyes skimmed the group but there was no face familiar to him, just citizens going about their lawful business, it would seem. For a few minutes he would be as anonymous as they were. No, not simply anonymous, but part of them; one of those ordinary folk waiting for those who had flown in from far away places. Travellers always seemed to bring a bit of stardust back with them along with the straw hats and terrible souvenirs. Those, like himself, who were on this side of arrivals instantly felt the difference.

Several businessmen, briefcases in hand, strode briskly past the group. These were men to whom flying was like catching a bus. No stardust clung to their sharp city suits and Burberry raincoats. Suddenly the bobble-hatted child gave a squeal and hurled himself at a tall young man in cords and a lumber jacket. In the noisy embraces that followed more and more passengers filtered through, diminishing the waiting group.

117

Lorimer looked at his watch again then his eyes bore down the corridor. He had photographs of the members of the rock band and he anticipated no difficulty in identifying The Flesh Eaters.

There they were.

An inappropriate name for these young men, thought Lorimer, eyeing them up. They all looked as though a square meal would do them the world of good. Each band member carried the ubiquitous duty free bag, splashes of yellow and red against their sombre clothing. As they drew closer, Lorimer observed their unhealthy pallor, which might have been the result of jet lag. Fleetingly he wondered if any traces of illegal substances had been found in the wrecked ambulance.

The band members walked two by two, the front pair deep in conversation. The nearest lad was small in stature, his bullet-shaped head grey with stubble. Lorimer noted his cleanly shaven chin with some surprise, however. A plain gold hoop winked from his left ear. The navy duffel coat was so worn that it looked like something recycled from the sixties, and probably was. The lad was gesturing to his much taller companion who nodded down to him. Lorimer was aware of the others, but the animated small fellow drew his attention.

'DCI Lorimer.'

His voice carried discreetly far enough to alert the four band members. Other passers-by barely gave them a glance.

'Your agent may have let you know to expect us?' Lorimer's voice was polite and slightly apologetic. They stopped immediately and the small fellow put down his duty free bag carefully.

'No. He didn't.'

The rejoinder was spoken in a reproving tone, but what interested the detective was the decidedly middle-class accent. The eyes that glanced at the ID card cupped in the officer's hand were bright and intelligent.

'What's all this about?' he continued.

Behind him the others exchanged bewildered looks, more puzzled than guilty, thought Lorimer, instantly dismissing thoughts of dope in their hand baggage.

'I'll explain as we go to collect your luggage,' Lorimer smiled encouragingly, then gestured towards the BAGGAGE RECLAIM sign. The small band member ran a hand over his cropped head then picked up his carrier bag decisively.

'Lead on, Macduff!'

There was a snigger behind him which he acknowledged with a grin.

'Tosh MacLaine.' The lad stuck out his hand, to Lorimer's surprise. The brief handshake immediately put things on a more business-like footing and Lorimer took an appraising look at the band. Of the four, MacLaine was probably the oldest. He certainly had an air of self-assurance. The wee ones were often the cockiest, Lorimer reminded himself.

The detective's explanations were brief. He explained that their former vehicle had been involved in a fire under suspicious circumstances: that the police would be grateful if the band members could assist them in their inquiries. Lorimer explained about eliminating old traces.

'But if it had been in a fire . . .' MacLaine said.

'It's amazing what's left behind.' Lorimer smiled his best enigmatic smile.

They had arrived at the baggage hall and the conversation was interrupted by the need to locate the carousel carrying their luggage.

'Hinny, you and Fleck grab a couple of trolleys. I'll stay with the Inspector here.'

MacLaine took out a packet of Marlboro cigarettes and offered one to Lorimer.

'No thanks. And it's Chief Inspector, by the way.'

'Right. *Chief Inspector.*' MacLaine lit up and closed his eyes as he inhaled deeply. 'What now?'

'We have cars waiting to take you all to Headquarters. We need to ask you some questions, then, if you are agreeable, we would like you to give the police doctor some samples, like hair, to match what we already have in the labs.' There was not even the flicker of a smile on Lorimer's face as he took in the young man's skinhead cut. 'The sooner we can do this the better.'

MacLaine looked thoughtful for a moment then shrugged.

'S'all right by me. The boys are pretty bushed. Won't take too long, will it?'

'No. We'll have a car to drop you all off home later and you can make some phone calls to let your family know, if you like.'

MacLaine shrugged again. 'Hinny'll want to phone his bird.' He broke off. 'Uh huh, looks like we're in business.'

He dropped his half-smoked cigarette, grinding it under the sole of his sneaker, then headed towards the carousel where the others were lifting off the baggage. Lorimer remained where he was, giving MacLaine the opportunity to pass on the arrangements to his band. The detective's own practised manner had disarmed them and they seemed grudgingly co-operative. Or were they so tired that there was no reason to protest? Lorimer regarded them shrewdly. There was no questioning by these lads, yet, of why they'd been picked up from the airport. It had been Lorimer's own idea to have them all in together like this. Once they'd dispersed there might be difficulty in locating them again. Rock bands were always on the move. Lorimer was glad to have some positive action anyway. There'd been such a huge amount of work on this case for such little return.

As they piled into the two waiting police cars, Lorimer looked back at the airport building. The automatic doors would open and close all day and night as travellers came and went. Suddenly it came into his mind that Donna Henderson had been saving up for a holiday abroad.

Lorimer turned his face away from Glasgow International Airport and nodded to his driver.

20

'The rock band? Tell me about them.'

Maggie Lorimer put down her red marking pen and gazed attentively at her husband.

'Well, they looked a right scruffy bunch but there was more to them than met the eye. Two of them were graduates. Psychology.' He said the word with such distaste that Maggie burst out laughing. 'Anyway, they were all co-operative enough lads. Forensics have some samples to match up now, we hope.'

'But what about their tour? I mean, are they going to be a success story?'

'Couldn't tell you. They have an agent in London, if that means anything, and they've made an album, but you'd need to be up to date in your *New Musical Express* to know if they're rated at all.' Lorimer grinned. 'Ask your kids at school.'

'Oh aye, sure. As if teachers are supposed to have any opinion about rock bands. Our Head of History probably thinks Iron Maiden was a young Margaret Thatcher,' she giggled.

Lorimer looked over at his wife. She had more in common with her pupils than they might ever guess, he thought. Maggie Lorimer had never been much on the side of the Establishment, a real little banner carrier in her student days, according to her friends. It was ironic that she'd become a policeman's wife.

'What else happened today?'

'Oh, the usual,' Lorimer began in his non-committal way. Then he sat up suddenly. 'Actually there is something. Hang on a sec.' He disappeared into the study then came back waving an invitation. 'Something for you.'

'For me? What is it?' Maggie put out her hand for the card.

'A party. George Phillips's sixtieth.'

'Well,' Maggie said, scanning the invitation, 'the Moat House! Very posh. I'll . . .'

'. . . need something to wear?' Lorimer mimicked her.

'Oh, you!' She lobbed a scatter cushion which he caught expertly. 'You won't be working?' she asked, an edge to her voice.

'Not if I can help it. All work and no play makes Bill a dull boy.'

'Good. Good.'

Maggie Lorimer nodded to herself, a wide smile on her face as she turned back to the pile of marking. Lorimer picked up the invitation and tucked it behind the clock on the mantelpiece.

'Solomon Brightman will be there.'

'Oh, the great Dr Brightman?' Maggie looked up again. 'Will I like him, do you think?'

Lorimer shrugged. 'I'll be interested to see what you make of him.'

'Hm.' She grinned impishly at her husband. 'I wonder what he makes of Chief Inspector Lorimer?'

Lorimer raised his eyebrows in mock horror but privately his wife's words struck home. Just what did the psychologist make of him? Had he been less than co-operative, perhaps? Did Solomon Brightman see him as a mere pen-pusher, a manager delegating authority to officers like Wilson who did so much of the legwork? That was what a DCI's job was all about. The management of murders.

With a touch of impatience Lorimer brushed aside this piece of introspection and turned his attention to the document he had left by his chair. The ongoing detection into a paedophile ring had taken some priority over the St Mungo's murders for the Divcom. European feelings were running high over certain of their nastier cases and there were possible links to incidents on his own Division that made interesting reading. He had a meeting with other senior officers from all around the region. Information had been trickling in for a good while now. From what Lorimer could see, there was a fair bet that children were being abused in the backs of cars, rather than in specific locations like homes or the usual seedy rented rooms. It made the case all the more difficult to pin down and meant a pulling together of many of the Divisions.

Lorimer poured himself a whisky, his mind already on the patterns of crime he might find in these documents.

Solomon Brightman poured boiling water into a generous measure of Ribena, his eyes gleaming in anticipation as the steam rose above the earthenware mug. It was one of those damp misty nights when winter refuses to concede to any notion of spring and Solomon felt that the cold had seeped into his bones. Still, it had been a useful evening and he still had the portfolio to examine. As he sipped the hot blackcurrant, he pondered on his next move.

Lorimer's face came vividly to mind, the deep furrows between those glacier blue eyes, the downturned mouth showing signs of stress. What had prompted him to become a detective? Solomon wondered. The life was one of constant pressure, he knew. Budgets were notoriously tight but the flow of crime took no account of police resources. The man was driven, though. It wasn't just a matter of fulfilling his own ambition or even of pleasing his superiors. Lorimer wasn't that type. He really cared, mused Solomon. The murders of those young girls were like a personal affront. Maybe because he had no family of his own? I care, too, Solomon thought to himself, but I know how to stand back from it. Lorimer becomes involved in these people's lives. The psychologist took another sip of Ribena, imagining the Chief Inspector on stress management courses. He probably ignored every word the lecturer spoke, engrossed in whatever case he was involved in at the time. Solomon smiled at his suppositions. Lorimer would be an interesting man to profile but he really must concentrate on the matter in hand. Lucy Haining's personality might well begin to emerge from the contents of her portfolio.

Solomon had been surprised to find that the dead girl's work was still at the Art School.

'But I thought that her parents . . .'

'Well, they didn't want any of Lucy's things,' the Principal's secretary had explained, a note of apology in her voice.

'Didn't they come up to Glasgow, then?'

'No.' She had paused for a moment before continuing. 'It was her friend who packed everything up for her. So sad. All these boxes and materials. Such a waste.'

'Which friend?' Solly had enquired.

'Oh, Janet Yarwood. She was Lucy's tutor, of course. She wants to put on some sort of retrospective exhibition. Maybe when the final-year students exhibit in the summer term.'

Solomon recalled the conversation, his mind already turning over Lucy Haining's possessions. Possessions that her parents didn't want. Then the secretary had mentioned the portfolio. It was still in the office. Yes, of course he could borrow it. If he just left a contact number?

Solomon drained the last of the sweet blackcurrant and put the mug aside. The large portfolio was resting against the wall as if waiting for him to uncover its secrets. Solomon unzipped the cover and drew out a large stack of drawings, their tissue coverings rustling. Designs for Lucy's final-year jewellery project were revealed on the first sheets. There was an obvious African influence here, thought Solomon. Some sketches contained pencil notes written in Lucy's spidery hand giving details of materials she would have used in the final creation of these unusual pieces.

Solomon turned the pages slowly, careful to smooth the tissue back onto the pastel drawings. Here was real talent, he thought, as page after page revealed elaborate designs. Some were on a theme of silver and gold, with rare touches of colour, enamels and lapis. Others used painted wood and inks, their shapes rounded and bulging like parts of human anatomy. Suddenly the designs were replaced by a series of life drawings. Portions of bodies were sketched in some detail. Solomon could see the influence in Lucy's jewellery now. There seemed to be a preoccupation with buttocks, breasts and shoulders. A few life drawings followed, mainly of young boys. These were good enough to sell to a gallery, thought Solomon. The young artist had had a talent that was not confined to her chosen medium.

He gazed thoughtfully at the boys; sitting, recumbent, slouching against a wall. There were details of heads, some on darker paper, white highlights giving the young eyes a sad and luminous quality. There was even a sketch of an old man, bent with age but still grinning up from the page. Solomon put it down to lift the next sketch from the diminishing pile when something about the old man's face made him take it up again. A shiver suddenly shot down his spine as he recognised the grinning face. For the image captured in Lucy's drawing was one he had seen in police custody.

It was Valentine Carruthers.

21

Lorimer stared at the face that lay on his desk. The image of a burnt corpse kept interfering with Lucy's drawing. But now he knew so much more about this old man whose name alone had aroused his curiosity.

His team had not been idle following Valentine's disappearance and their discoveries had multiplied considerably after his death. Other Glasgow derelicts had provided information about old Carruthers's recent way of life. Pieced together with his police record, newspaper cuttings and a particularly detailed report from a rehabilitation clinic in Leeds, the present file made sad, but interesting reading. Solomon's discovery had prompted further investigation at Glasgow School of Art, adding several more facts to the sum of knowledge about the old man. Much of his past life had been recounted during therapy sessions in the rehabilitation clinic. Lorimer sent out a mental thank-you to the psychotherapist who had kept her files in such meticulous order.

Valentine Carruthers's life story had ended in agony and flames but it had started in a world of relative luxury, Lorimer read. The Carruthers family boasted several generations of sons who had made their fortunes at sea. One had even risen to the rank of Commander. Valentine had broken with that tradition, however. His father, apparently a rather taciturn man, had married a young Frenchwoman. According to the psychotherapist, Valentine's mother had never wearied of telling him how his parents had met. Valerie Bouverat, dark, pretty and petite, had captured the attention of the young Lieutenant Carruthers one night at a party in the Officers' Mess.

Lorimer read on, imagining the conversations between the therapist and Carruthers. Confidential discussions, of course, up until now.

His parents' marriage had not been a great success but nor had it been an unqualified failure. Mrs Carruthers had apparently found her husband's long stretches at sea hard to bear. With his spells ashore becoming increasingly tedious, the Frenchwoman had lavished her pent-up affection on her little son, who had grown up to be a rather pampered child, shy of the father whom he rarely saw and tongue-tied in the presence of adults.

Mrs Carruthers had fought a long battle to keep her little boy at home when her husband would have packed him off to school at an early age, Carruthers had claimed, and it was not until his mother became ill that the twelve-year-old Valentine was sent away. What followed was a familiar story, according to the therapist. *Public school buggery is a well-known fact of life, and there are those adults in society who constantly claim that the sordid practices of their boyhood did them absolutely no harm. Valentine Carruthers was not one to voice such an opinion.* Lorimer read the therapist's handwritten notes, then continued piecing the whole picture together. Young Carruthers had left school and drifted into the civil service, eschewing the family tradition of taking to the high seas. Then his mother's death had given him the excuse to cut all ties with home and make his own way in the city of London.

Lorimer pictured the old man years before, pouring out his life story to this therapist. How much of it was true, he wondered, and how much the self-pity of a man trying to make sense of his wasted life?

Nothing much seemed to be known about his twenties but Lorimer guessed that his later preference for young male company must have begun at least by then.

His first conviction had come on his thirty-first birthday. He lost his job, spent two years in prison and came back to society to find that his life had changed forever. There had been nothing like the modern provision for rehabilitation of child abusers then and Valentine re-offended regularly, coming to the attention of the police several times in the twenty-five years that followed. He was well into his fifties by the time any attempt was made to turn him away from paedophilia. His crimes were detailed in the Press, his neighbours hounded him from their communities and eventually the man travelled further and further north. Until he reached Glasgow.

Valentine's descent into dereliction was not so very surprising, Lorimer thought. Rejected by a fearful society, unable to control his desire for the company of small boys, he had slept rough and taken what pleasures he could whenever he had dared. Nonetheless the Chief Inspector's natural revulsion was tinged with pity.

They had met in a park, according to the statement by Lucy's tutor. Meeting Lucy must have opened up new horizons for the old man, thought Lorimer. He imagined how she had sketched the tramp impassively, as she might have sketched a robin's nest or an old mossy log. He would have made an interesting subject, that was all. Then Lucy had offered to pay him to sit in her children's drawing class. The old man would have accepted this without hesitation.

It must have been hard to sit still surrounded by these earnest young faces, Lorimer thought, his mouth tight with distaste. They had become accustomed to their wizened subject, however, and saw no harm in accepting his polo mints and sherbet lemons. Questions recently asked of the youngsters in Lucy's drawing class had so far suggested that none of them had been interfered with by the old man. In fact they had felt sorry for him rather than afraid.

Then the murders had begun. Lucy was strangled and Valentine pulled from the bushes in St Mungo's Park. His disappearance and horrific death had raised all sorts of questions but one thing was certain. The killer must have known them both. And if he had been known to both Lucy and the old man, then who else in the world of the Art School had encountered him?

22

Martin slid a handful of coins into the *Big Issue* seller's mittened hand then strode through the archway to Royal Exchange Square. Canopies over the smart shops and restaurants fluttered in the wind as he made his way round to the front entrance of GOMA. At one time the building had housed the Stirling Library, a reference library which had become a refuge for vagabond students and city derelicts alike. Right outside, the equestrian statue of the Duke of Wellington was the butt of playful citizens who regularly crowned His Grace with an orange and white traffic cone. Now the area was pedestrianised and the neo-classical building was Glasgow's home for the Gallery of Modern Art, its acronym part of the city's vernacular. The exhibits had attracted much attention, and had polarised opinion at first, but now it was accepted as just one more facet of the city's complex personality.

Jayne Morganti was waiting for Martin in the top-floor restaurant. She had chosen a table by the window and sat gazing over the city rooftops, one arm flung out across the back of her chair. Martin paused for a moment and grinned at the picture she made. She was striking a similar pose to Adrian Wisniewski's mural figures whose elongated limbs created graceful arcs above the diners. Deliberate or subliminal? he wondered to himself, taking the stairs two at a time to the upper floor.

'Darling!' Jayne mouthed two large kisses in the direction of Martin's cheeks as he bent his large frame over her. 'Thank God it's not busy! I can't stand it when there's a crowd of school children squishing these revolting little sachets of sauce over their chips!'

'Ha! So much for taking art into the classroom, then.'

'Oh, they're welcome to come in and look around, darling, I just wish this place could be a bit more civilised at times.'

Martin glanced around at the brightly coloured walls and ceiling and thought there was something rather abandoned about the sprawl of figures whose youthful faces were turned aside as if hearing something in another distant landscape.

'Maybe they should put up a sign: GROWN UPS ONLY.'

'If only.'

As Jayne raised her eyes to heaven, a tall mini-skirted waitress appeared and took their orders for drinks. Martin settled his long legs under the table.

'Well now,' began Jayne briskly, 'to what do I owe this lovely lunch invitation? I take it you want to pick my brains about something, mm?' As she tilted her head to one side, her long silver earrings caught a sudden shaft of sunlight.

'They're nice.' Martin's finger circled his ear meaningfully.

'Oh, them.' A red fingernail caressed the silver. 'My assegais.'

'Your what?'

'Assegais. You know. Tribal spears. That's what they're based on anyhow. Actually,' she broke off to look Martin straight in the eye, 'I wore them especially for you.'

'Oh! Not trying to make a conquest of me, by any chance?'

'Behave yourself. I'm not into toyboys any more, and anyway, you're far too tall to suit me. No. I wore them because they were one of Lucy's designs.'

Martin's jaw dropped.

'Lucy Haining? But how did you know . . . ?'

'. . . that you wanted to talk to me about her? Oh, a little bird told me. You know what newspaper grapevines are.'

Her dark eyes sparkled mischievously and Martin found himself impressed as always by the older woman's vibrant sexuality. Maybe it was her Italian blood that gave Jayne Morganti such raw energy.

'I'm right, then?' she chuckled throatily but before Martin could reply the waitress returned with their drinks and took their lunch order.

'Cheers! To your sleuthing.' Jayne laughed merrily as their glasses clinked.

'To my sleuthing. But how did you know, you horrible woman?'

'Your little friend, Diane. She's quite smitten, poor child.'

'Oh.'

For a moment Martin wondered just how much the two women had discussed.

'It's all right. All your secrets are safe with me, darling.'

Jayne's husky contralto voice was deliberately teasing. She took a sip of wine then flicked the earring once again.

'About Lucy,' Martin began, 'just what do you know about her?'

'Well, you know I presented the award last year and so, yes, I met Lucy at the Art School. What can I tell you? She was interesting. One of those very pale creatures with dyed red hair and lots of dark eye make-up. Very Gothic without being spiky. I tell you what did come across. She was terribly ambitious. Knew exactly what she wanted to do and wouldn't let anyone stop her.'

'Someone did,' Martin remarked quietly.

'Yes.' The light went out in Jayne's eyes and suddenly Martin was aware of the wrinkled hands clasping her glass and the crepe-like skin on her throat not completely hidden by the devoré scarf. 'Tell me, Martin, why do you want to know so much about Lucy? I mean, apart from more copy for these wretched murders.'

Martin hesitated.

'I guess I fancy myself as Clark Kent.' He spoke lightly, trying to recapture his bantering tone, then added in a drawl, 'Which makes you my Lois Lane, of course.'

'Oh, no. That won't do at all. Diane would be most put out to hear you say that!'

'Well, let's just say I need to know as much about Lucy as you can tell me.'

Jayne looked away from him, staring over the city skyline as she spoke.

'I remember thinking what extraordinary talent she had. Jewellery design is painstaking. The ideas can be large – immense, like landscapes – but the execution demands such attention to detail. Her whole approach was like that. She could see an overall picture then work laboriously on the details. I admired her. She'd a hard time of it, like a lot of art students. Materials are so damned expensive. I'm

sure some of these kids would sell their bodies for their art. Lucy
made extra money taking these children's life-drawing classes. She
was on a full grant. No parental contribution. In all senses. There
was no backing from home at all. I gather mummy and daddy
disapproved.'

'Of what?'

Jayne sighed and turned her gaze back to Martin. 'Lucy herself,
I think. Certainly of her being an art student. They didn't come up
for the award ceremony. She said she wasn't bothered but I think
it hurt. Anyway, she had her little display in Princes Square and I
bought these lovely things. She wasn't making much from actually
selling her jewellery. She'd cover her costs, I suppose. Wouldn't use
plastic when she could buy real gemstones.'

'What do you know about her tutors?'

'Ah. Now there's an interesting lead for you to follow, darling.
She seemed very cosy with one particular lecturer.'

'Lecturer or lecher?' Martin joked.

Jayne raised one skilfully pencilled eyebrow.

'A lady lecher, actually, darling, but you never know, do you?'

'Name?'

'Janet Yarwood. Lucy's advisor of studies. *Actually*, Lucy used to
drop in to Ms Yarwood's flat regularly. That's who you should take
out to lunch next, my dear. I'm sure she can tell you everything
about Lucy you'd want to know. And lots you don't,' she added
wickedly.

Martin raised his glass.

'Thanks, Jayne, but let's not tell the world all about this. At least
for now.'

Jayne smiled again and inclined her head knowingly.

23

It was unusually mild for the first day of March. Spring crocuses had responded to the sudden sunshine and Lorimer could see them beyond Police Headquarters, dappling the public gardens with colour. The midday sunlight had split his desk into halves of shade and dazzling brightness. Lorimer shifted the forensic report into the shade. It made interesting reading. What would the killer make of a list like this, Lorimer thought, running his eye down the names of fibres which had survived that terrible conflagration. Some of the names were unfamiliar, cloaked in scientific jargon, but the forensic biologist had appended his own translations. There were now blue ticks against several items in the list that had tallied with fibres provided by the Flesh Eaters. Lorimer's eye paused on one item circled in purple: Kanekelon – Japanese hair fibre (manufactured).

What on earth did this mean? he wondered, reaching for the telephone.

A few minutes later he replaced the handset and sat motionless, fingertips together, staring unseeing at the drift of spring flowers outside. Forensics had not matched this particular fibre with any of those given by the boys in the band. Surprising, really, mused Lorimer, when the fibre had come from a wig. Performers might have been expected to dress up a bit. But no, the hair had come, like so many of the intact fibres, from beneath the corpse, whose dead weight had been instrumental in preserving these traces from the flames. Kanekelon was a fibre only manufactured in Japan and used in the most expensive of modern hairpieces and wigs. So. Was he to infer that the killer had used a disguise?

Lorimer frowned. Alison Girdley had given a reasonable description of a dark-haired man with close-cropped hair. It just didn't make sense. There was something tickling the edges of his mind, an irritating tic that wouldn't go away. From experience he knew that plodding routine work brought more results than flashes of brilliant insight. Nevertheless he kept going over the murder cases, visualising the girls' last walks in their city, trying to see who had leapt out at them with that deadly chain. Lorimer closed his eyes, letting the heat from the window soak into his face, enjoying the sleepy peacefulness for a moment. Then with a sigh he stood up to twist the rod, closing the vertical blinds, and work once more in the shade. He looked back over the list and the purple-circled word.

Suddenly Lorimer recalled the locus of the burnt-out ambulance and his conversation with the Procurator Fiscal. Had there been an accomplice on that occasion effecting a get-away from that bleak spot? And had it been a woman, perhaps? Lorimer tried this possibility on for size and felt a frisson of excitement with the thought that it might just fit. During briefing sessions the team had thrown about the suggestion of an accomplice but this had been rejected on several counts. Added to that, Solomon Brightman had been most insistent that the killer worked alone. But what if he had used someone on only this occasion?

Lorimer replaced the report on his desk. Like most of the traces, this hair fibre would have to lie dormant until – or if – a suspect could be found.

Lorimer looked back at the calendar. Circled in black with felt-tip pen, like a bad omen, was the date of George Phillips's party. The DCI was ambivalent about his superior's retirement. There was a fair chance that he'd be in line for the job of Superintendent himself, and he didn't know if that's what he really wanted. When he had time to think about it, which wasn't often, Lorimer knew he'd hate to be passed over for the job. And there was Maggie. She had always made a big thing of his promotions. All the same, it would take him further away from hands-on detective work and deeper into the world of management. His present job had plenty of that already, and Lorimer sometimes felt as if he were pulling against the forces that bound him to this office. The other circles on the calendar stared out at him. Red for murder. Red circles around these dates when three young women and an old derelict had met their untimely end. There was no way he'd even be considered for George Phillips's job if they remained unsolved.

Solomon remembered his first trip to Glasgow when he had remarked with some surprise on how green it all was. His expectations had been limited to a city of brick and stone but now he was as proud of his adopted city as many of its life-long citizens. He had quickly realised that although Glasgow's accolade as European City of Culture had been thought risible by some envious cynics, that same city could well have won an award for being the greenest, having more parkland within its boundaries than any other in Europe.

St Mungo's Park was only one of many large expanses where the public could stroll, walk dogs, listen to bands on a summer evening or bed down for the night, like Valentine and his fellow dossers. Solomon himself enjoyed the daily walk from Glasgow University, along Kelvin Way and across Kelvingrove Park on his journey home. The outrage of murdered girls being dumped in one of the city's dear green places went deeper than simple horror at the killings. The concealment of these corpses in a public park had offended Glaswegians as strongly as if they had been left in their own back gardens.

Several times the psychologist had deliberately walked through St Mungo's Park, squirrels rustling below the laurels and rhododendrons. A vehicular road ran through from west to east and Solomon had paced along the route that the ambulance must have taken, trying in his mind to locate its destination.

High-rise flats bent their shadows over the main road opposite the park gates. They were a legacy from the sixties; pre-stressed grey concrete towers, like streets up-ended. Other tower blocks had been obliterated by the demolition squads a mere three decades after they themselves had replaced streets of Victorian tenements.

The residents in St Mungo's Heights had been questioned during a door-to-door exercise by Lorimer's team but their responses had been fruitless. Despite this, Solomon had found himself standing on the path by one particular clump of laurels, no longer cordoned off by police tape, staring at the high flats as if they held a secret. Their geography was right. With Lorimer, he had discussed the possibility that their killer could have been making for the flats after disposing of the bodies. Lorimer had been convinced enough by his argument that killers tend to live near the area where they leave their victims. There was plenty of statistical evidence to back this up. It was only later in the careers of multiple killers that they travelled further afield. Solomon felt certain that somewhere not too far away was home to the person who had taken the lives of those three girls.

One of Lorimer's unanswered questions still plagued the psychologist, however.

'Where did he park the ambulance?'

Nobody in St Mungo's Heights admitted to any sight of the old vehicle and a thorough search of lock-ups had yielded nothing. Its whereabouts had remained a mystery until they had stood beside its blackened wreck miles away from the park and the city.

It was not to St Mungo's Park that Dr Brightman directed his taxi cab that spring morning. Reading Week had given him the luxury of several hours to play truant from his office and he headed south of the river to the elegant suburbs of Pollokshields. The trees were still bare but colourful patches of polyanthus brightened the well-tended gardens and the daffodils were just beginning to nod yellow heads from the verges, coaxed by the unexpected warmth of the sun.

Solomon stood at the gates of Bellahouston Park where the pathway forked upwards. A sign indicated the dry ski centre to his left and another showed the way to the House for an Art Lover. Reflecting that the City Fathers catered for all tastes, Solomon made his way along the tree-lined path that curved up and around to reveal the house that Charles Rennie Mackintosh had never built. It was a century since the celebrated architect had submitted his designs for that German competition. His submission had come too late for him to win the major award but he had been given a special prize nonetheless. Now the house was built, thanks to the efforts of a few determined men and women, and stood serenely looking towards the hills of the west.

Solomon gazed up at the clouds scudding across the blue spring sky and had the sudden impression that the chimneys and pillared gables were soaring through space. His gaze drifted back to the house and wandered along the front, searching for the entrance.

Janet Yarwood was waiting for him just inside the café door. She looked much older than he had expected. Her clothes sagged awkwardly on a thin frame and the psychologist was absurdly reminded of a moulting bird with its neck feathers missing. She came towards him, unsmiling, and thrust out a skinny arm.

'Dr Brightman.'

'Yes, hello. Miss Yarwood?'

'Ms.'

She gestured that he should follow her and led the way out of the reception area and through a white door.

Solomon stared about him as he was ushered up to the Post-graduate Centre that was part of the School of Art but located away from the city centre and housed on the upper floor of this building. He noted the familiar Mackintosh features all around him. What would the celebrated architect, who had died in such poverty, have made of all this? Watching Janet Yarwood's thin ankles disappearing up the stairs ahead brought Solomon back to the matter in hand. At last he was shown into a brightly lit office. Sweeping his glance over the partitioned desks and pinboards that were cluttered with notes and cartoon drawings, he realised it was used by several of the students, not just Ms Yarwood.

'Please sit down.'

The woman dragged a chrome and blue swivel chair from under a desk and Solomon sat. She pulled another from the empty desk opposite and perched on it, nervously rubbing her fingers as if they itched. Solomon smiled politely, wondering if he wanted to put her at her ease or not. Her agitation at his visit was understandable yet there was more than normal tension here.

'It isn't easy for you to be asked questions again, is it?'

His voice was gentle and reassuring but the restless fingers were scratching her face now and the small bird's eyes never left his gaze.

'What do you want to know?' The words were rapped out harshly.

Solomon wanted to say *Tell me about Lucy* but he held back the question that seemed to shout aloud into the room.

'Perhaps we could have some tea?' he suggested gently.

Janet Yarwood's mouth fell open in surprise, then, without a word, she slipped off the chair and fetched the kettle that Solly had spotted amongst the discarded mugs beside a filing cabinet. She continued to stare at him with undisguised hostility as he smiled serenely in her direction. At last her head turned away as she prepared the tea, banging the mugs loudly on the metal surface. The psychologist studied the grey hair cropped severely above a scrawny neck. He knew from Lorimer that she was a mature student in her late twenties, but a stranger would have assumed her to be at least forty, he thought. Her blue jeans, which were several sizes too large, were secured by a thick leather belt, and the baggy t-shirt served only to emphasise her lack of chest and stick-like arms.

'There.'

The mug was put in front of him so violently that the tea slopped onto the varnished desk. Janet Yarwood stared at the pool of liquid helplessly. It was as if the act of bringing the tea had finally used up her reserves of energy and she could do no more. Solomon mopped up the spill with a hanky then took a sip of the sugarless tea.

'She was very special, wasn't she?'

The gentle voice and the question were too much for the woman and she began to sob; harsh, racking sobs that made her thin shoulders heave. Solomon watched as she clutched the edge of the chair. He had seen grief like this before in mothers who had lost a child. He waited until the sobs subsided, until Janet Yarwood gave a shuddering sigh and wiped her eyes with the back of her hand. He sipped the tea again and this time it was a command rather than a question.

'Tell me about Lucy.'

The night sky was broken with fast-flying clouds and the silhouettes of starkly bare trees whipping this way and that. Against the sodium glow from the city, their curving branches were like dancers' arms, swaying in some frenzied Highland fling. Solomon rarely closed

140

his curtains in the bay-windowed living room, preferring to look down over the park at the city lights twinkling in the distance. That evening, however, contemplation of the skyline had given way to the mess of notes scattered around his feet. Lucy Haining, Janet Yarwood, the killer seen by Alison Girdley . . . pieces of an indeterminate jigsaw puzzle were nevertheless beginning to take on some shape and form.

Janet's revelations were now committed to paper: both what she had told the psychologist and what she had so patently failed to say. As Solomon was bent over his word processor the door buzzer sounded.

'Yes?'

'William Lorimer.'

'Oh, right, just come up.'

Solomon activated the button releasing the main door of the close then went across to the window, looking down to the street below. There was nobody there. Evidently Lorimer was already on his way up the three flights of stone stairs. Solomon padded barefoot through to his front door, his dressing gown flapping against his legs. He unlocked the door, letting it swing open, then turned back to the kitchen, ready to play host to his unexpected visitor. He had filled the kettle jug and switched it on when he heard the footsteps in the landing.

'I'm here,' he called out, opening a wall cupboard and rummaging for some chocolate biscuits that he kept for such occasions.

Afterwards, talking to Lorimer, Solomon could not recall exactly what had happened. He had had the impression of a shadow rising on the wall to his left and, as he turned to greet his visitor, the shadow had engulfed him.

His neighbour across the landing, seeing the open door later that evening, had called out then come in anxiously, finding poor Dr Brightman sprawled on his kitchen floor. Ambulance and police car had arrived in rapid succession and, in the dark hours long before dawn, Lorimer had been alerted to the incident.

'It's Solly. He's been attacked,' he told Maggie briefly, already reaching for his clothes.

*   *   *

For several hours Lorimer sat looking grimly at the pale face of his fellow-investigator. A blow to the head had caused concussion but the medical staff assured him that there was no serious damage. The constable who had taken a statement from Solly's neighbour had called in to brief the Chief Inspector on the incident. The psychologist's home had been ransacked but until he regained consciousness no one could tell if anything of value had been taken. Certainly the usual hardware prey to the average burglar was still in place.

At last the thick dark eyelashes fluttered and Solly stared at the figure seated beside him.

'What happened?'

His voice came out in a whisper, the glazed look in his brown eyes showing that he was still some distance away from reality.

'Some bugger whacked you over the head.'

Solly stared blankly, the words apparently not registering, then he turned his head slightly and groaned as the pain thudded through his skull.

'But it was you!'

Lorimer smiled indulgently, shaking his head. The poor fellow was still confused.

'I'll fetch the nurse.'

Lorimer rose to go but Solomon tried to raise his head from the banks of pillows.

'No. Wait.' His voice, though weak, held a note of urgency. 'You came to my flat tonight – you spoke on the intercom.'

Lorimer stiffened. This was not the rambling of concussion. The psychologist's eyes were fixed on him now, waiting for an answer. Lorimer sat down again.

'I've been at home, my friend. A rare occurrence, my long-suffering wife would tell you.' He paused. 'Whoever came to visit you tonight, it wasn't me.'

'But he said . . .' Solomon trailed off, trying to clear the fog in his brain. 'He said William Lorimer.'

'Then it certainly wasn't me. I only use my Sunday name in court.'

A light dawned in Solly's eyes and Lorimer noted the sudden tension in his face muscles.

'Then who?'

'I hate to think,' replied Lorimer. 'But once you're fit to go home you can go through your things and see if there's anything missing.'

'Did he make much mess?'

'Afraid so. Oh, nothing disgusting, thank God. Just pulled stuff out of drawers and dumped it. Seems he was looking for something.' Lorimer looked at the white-faced figure under the covers and his eyes narrowed in speculation. 'What can you remember about your own movements during the evening?'

'I had supper, soaked in a hot bath, then sat down to type up my notes.'

'Did you have handwritten notes, then?'

'Some. The rest are in here, I'm afraid.' His grin was weak as he indicated his sore head.

'Did you have any phone calls, or any other visitors?'

'No.' He paused. 'Sorry. Yes, there was one call but it rang off when I answered.' He looked up at Lorimer as they both drew the same conclusion. 'Not a wrong number?'

Lorimer shook his head. 'I doubt it. How long after that call did it take for the doorbell to ring?'

Solly shut his eyes as if the effort of thinking hurt his head.

'Sorry. I don't have a clue.'

'Okay. We'll just assume for the present that you had a visit from an intruder. It may have nothing at all to do with the case. On the other hand,' his blue eyes blazed with a light that made Solomon shiver, 'it could be that we're closer than we know to some guy who prefers female scalps.'

'If it was . . . Why didn't he kill me?'

'Perhaps he thinks he has.'

Solly settled back on his pillows, exhausted.

'I think I really will fetch that nurse now,' Lorimer said softly and slipped quietly from the darkened room.

Alone with his whirling thoughts, Solly tried to remember. But all he could see was a giant shadow on the wall: a shadow with no substance.

* * *

143

Twenty-four hours later Lorimer, accompanied by his wife and Solomon, drew up outside the psychologist's flat. Maggie had insisted on coming with him to the hospital.

'He's on his own, poor soul, and someone has to give him a hand.'

She had warmed to the younger man from the first, her woman's sympathy bridging the gap of any possible strangeness. Solomon, a lifetime of Jewish mothering behind him, accepted Maggie taking charge without demur.

They had driven in silence, apart from asking the necessary directions to Solomon's house in Park Circus, out of respect for his still throbbing head. Lorimer looked up at the graceful Victorian buildings then at the vista beyond and gave a low whistle.

'Some view you've got here!'

Even from street level the panorama of the city was exceptional. Solly managed a weak grin.

'Even better from upstairs.'

'Top floor?'

'Yes. Sorry.'

'Don't apologise,' Maggie broke in, 'I need the exercise. Been sitting all day.'

Eventually they stood at Solly's front door. Maggie and Lorimer exchanged glances as they noticed how the psychologist's hand shook as he turned the key. Lorimer hadn't exaggerated about the mess. A snowstorm of papers littered the living room carpet; desk drawers lay upturned on the floor. Even the bookshelves had been emptied, their contents now a jumbled heap.

Maggie's face fell at the shambles but 'Tea?' she asked aloud, with a brightness in her voice that Lorimer was sure she did not feel. Solly responded with a grateful smile.

'Camomile, perhaps?'

'Just ordinary tea for me,' Lorimer butted in.

'You'll find everything in the kitchen.'

'Right-o.'

Left to themselves, the two men surveyed the room, wondering where to begin.

'Is there any reason for this other than the Lucy Haining case?'

Lorimer clasped his hands and leaned forward, trying to read Solomon's expression. The younger man sat staring impassively at the swirl of papers on the carpet. Lorimer waited. He had realised during his visits to the hospital just how little he knew about the young Jewish psychologist. His home and family background had been of no interest whatsoever until Maggie, with her woman's instinct, had asked all the pertinent questions. He hadn't even known if the fellow was married or not, for heaven's sake. Now a dozen thoughts whirled around the policeman's head.

Solomon sat back in the sagging armchair and sighed a small sigh.

'I'm afraid not,' he said at last. 'I rather wish there were.'

'No jealous lovers or belligerent students with a grudge?'

Lorimer's tone was deliberately light and the young man smiled as he shook his head.

'The students like me, it seems and, alas, there are no beautiful women in my life to be fought over.'

'Well, there should be! I can't imagine why they're not queuing up at your door!'

Maggie set down a tray on the desk.

'Thank you for these kind words, Mrs Lorimer.'

Solomon's tone was self-deprecating though he smiled his sweet, boyish smile and Lorimer saw for the first time what his wife had seen immediately. Solomon Brightman was indeed a striking man, his pale face, dark beard and bushy hair at once exotic and intriguing.

Lorimer took the mug of tea from his wife and sipped before continuing with his questions.

'Can you think of anything you had in here last night that someone might have wanted?'

'Someone who knew we were working together. And someone who wanted me to think they were you,' added Solomon, thoughtfully.

'Right.'

'I visited Lucy Haining's tutor at the Postgraduate Centre,' Solomon began slowly, his hands warming around the ceramic mug. 'She gave me certain information that I was going to pass

145

on to you today. Or was it yesterday? I'm afraid I'm rather losing track of time.'

He paused. Maggie was trying to catch her husband's eye but failed, her gaze wandering back instead to the young man whose brown eyes still seemed fixed on a pattern on the carpet.

'Janet Yarwood is not quite what she seems. Her statement described her as a fellow student of the victim but she's a postgrad Art student, in fact. Specialises in life drawing and portraiture. She was' – he paused once more then continued as if deliberately choosing his words – 'a friend of Lucy's. One of her tutors in her final year. It seems that Lucy had been helped to set up a children's life-drawing class by this woman in order to make a bit of extra cash. Ms Yarwood apparently took a special interest in her.'

'But I thought that Lucy Haining was a jewellery design student?' Lorimer objected.

Solly nodded. 'You're right, and I thought that was a bit odd too. Janet Yarwood had asked specially to be Lucy's tutor and help her with obtaining materials and things for her bangles and what not.'

Maggie smiled discreetly at Solomon's description of the dead girl's designer jewellery. She doubted if he had ever taken any interest in anything so worldly as the stones, settings and metals for female adornment. She glanced down at her own sapphire and diamond engagement ring, letting the gems flash against the lamplight.

'I would say,' Solomon frowned as he paused, 'that Ms Yarwood's interest in Lucy Haining was not altogether healthy.'

He glanced swiftly at Lorimer and Maggie.

'Go on.'

'She doted on that girl. Oh, I don't know for sure what her sexual orientation may be but, allowing for that, her relationship with Lucy verged on the obsessive. In fact,' his voice trailed off as he expressed his thoughts aloud, 'I wonder if young Lucy had some kind of a hold on this woman.'

'Could *she* have killed Lucy?' asked Maggie, then bit her lip as Lorimer flashed her a look of annoyance.

'I think this woman is capable of anti-social behaviour. Murder?'

Solomon shook his head and sipped absently at the camomile tea. 'She cherished Lucy. But I don't believe she killed her.' Solomon's voice was sad and soft, as if remembering something Janet Yarwood had told him. 'No. We're looking for a man. The man Alison Girdley saw. The question that vexes me now is, was he – or is he – known to Janet Yarwood?'

'And?'

Lorimer leaned forward to place his mug on the coffee table. Solomon pointed at the mess of papers on the floor.

'I've made notes about most of the men known to Ms Yarwood and Lucy. Or at least the ones she's telling me about. That's what I was doing when you . . . or rather when my attacker arrived,' Solly smiled weakly.

'Right. Let's get a move on.' Lorimer knelt down swiftly, gathering up the papers and shuffling them into a neat pile. 'You start with this lot.' He handed them up to Solly then turned his attention to the tumbled drawers and their contents strewn further into the room.

Despite his aching head, the young psychologist leafed patiently through the sheaf of documents, sorting them into piles.

It was some time later that the three finished searching through all the papers, Solomon having checked and double-checked for missing information.

'I can't find that list of names. Male acquaintances of Janet's. Doesn't matter, though. It should be on the computer,' he said at last. 'Unless . . .'

He rose painfully to his feet and stepped across to his desk, switching on the word processor. Lorimer stood behind him, eyes fixed to the screen as Solly scrolled up the notes he had so recently typed in. It made interesting reading to the DCI. Solly's scientific observations were peppered with comments which showed a deep understanding of the human condition. Reading the comments, Lorimer suddenly felt an overwhelming sense of pity for the woman who had lost her young friend.

'Let's see that list. It should be . . . oh, dear.' He turned to Lorimer. 'Deleted, I'm afraid. However, all is not lost.' He pressed a tiny button on the side of the machine and when nothing happened he turned to Lorimer with an apologetic smile. 'My back-up disk. He's taken it.'

'Hell's teeth!'

Solomon swung round and gave his familiar shrug.

'Now we know why I was mugged, at any rate. Someone knew what Janet Yarwood was telling me. Or she went on to let them know what she'd said.' He frowned and looked up at Lorimer. 'It must be someone who knows we are working together.' He paused to let the implication of his words sink in. 'She may well know who our killer is, without realising it. But,' he added seriously, 'he must also know that she could give us a lead.'

'If it is him,' Lorimer began then added impatiently, '– and we don't know that yet – then he's closing the net around himself. We narrow things down to those around the Art School who were close to both these women.'

Lorimer stood up suddenly, a frozen look on his face.

'Do you have the Yarwood woman's home phone number?'

'Yes. Why?'

'Phone her.'

Solomon searched back through the piles of notes then pulled out a handwritten sheet. Maggie watched the two men intently as the number was dialled. Time seemed to stand still as the phone rang on and on.

'Maybe she's out,' she suggested hopefully, looking at her husband's grave expression. But even she was shivering with apprehension as Lorimer reached for his mobile to call Headquarters.

24

J anet Yarwood had lived alone in a block of new flats five minutes'
walk from Glasgow School of Art. Now the entrance to the street
was jammed with police vehicles and already some residents were
finding it difficult to gain access to their own flats. Uniformed
police officers were firm but polite with curious passers-by who
had been drawn towards the street cordoned off from the adjoining
main road.

Inside, DCI Lorimer and Dr Solomon Brightman waited for the
arrival of the pathologist. Lorimer's phone call had triggered off a
chain of events leading up to the forced entry into Janet Yarwood's
flat. Her body, still clothed in the t-shirt and jeans which she had
worn at her meeting with Solly, lay on the hall carpet. Blood had
leached out in a huge stain, mainly from the gory mess of her scalp,
and the white walls were spattered in dark red like some obscene
action painting.

'Guess what colour I'm going to have next?'

The voice on the tape echoed in Lorimer's mind as he looked
at the remains of the artist. Had he anticipated this killing even as
he'd spoken? Somewhere, if he really did keep them, a grey scalp
was now added to his collection.

Solly, still weak from his own ordeal, had covered his mouth and
turned away from the horror on the floor. He had written about
murder, thought about it, theorised, but he hadn't expected it to
be like this in reality, Lorimer thought wryly. There was a smell,
almost a taste to it, as if the brutal act had left traces of death swirling
unseen in the air around the mutilated corpse. Lorimer found him
in the artist's sitting room, arms clasped around his body, rocking
back and forth as if trying to relieve a pain deep within. He put a
hand on his shoulder but said nothing. His sudden fear about Janet

Yarwood had been horribly realised. Swift enquiries had shown that after Solly's visit to the House for an Art Lover, the woman had failed to turn up next day as usual. Lorimer had spoken to one of the postgraduates, a Christopher Inglis. He'd been a bit puzzled that Janet hadn't turned up, he'd said, but it hadn't worried him. Inglis thought someone had phoned her home to see if she was sick. But if she was ill in bed maybe she just didn't want to answer the phone? After all, it was only a day since they'd seen her.

'Hi, Bill.' Rosie Fergusson's voice broke into his thoughts as the blonde pathologist appeared in the doorway. 'Just fill me in on this one, will you?'

She made a pointing gesture at Solomon, mouthing 'Who's that?' but Lorimer steered her by the elbow away from the lounge and back into the hallway.

'I'll make the introductions later,' he whispered, then began to run through the details about the body on the floor that had been Janet Yarwood, aspiring portrait painter.

'Twenty-nine. Single. Lived alone. Bed hadn't been slept in. Last seen by her colleagues the day before yesterday. Chap upstairs heard her radio on that night, so we might assume she was home. Over to you.'

Already the pathologist had pulled on gloves and was kneeling by the corpse. A few minutes later Lorimer had the answer he was looking for.

'Yes. She's been dead about forty-eight hours or so.'

'But you can't be sure until you've done more tests,' Lorimer mimicked the young woman's voice and she grinned suddenly, recognising the banter that often occurred on these occasions, lightening the grimmer reality of their respective jobs.

'Well, one thing we can be sure of, and that's the nature of the killing.'

'And?'

'She was stabbed several times. Look. See here and here.'

Rosie pointed with a pencil to areas on the corpse which were heavily bloodstained.

'But her neck?'

Lorimer crouched over, indicating the wounds he had seen three times before in recent months. Rosie shook her head.

'I can't be certain yet but the scatters of blood look like she was alive when she was stabbed. Let's see.' She flipped back the dead woman's eyelids. 'No sign of any haemorrhaging.' The mouth was examined gently. 'There you are. Strangulation was post-mortem. That tell you anything?'

Lorimer nodded, his face grim. It was all adding up to give credence to Solomon's profile. The too-deliberate signature of strangulation and mutilation. The killer had had a reason for doing away with Janet Yarwood, just as he must have had for the murder of Lucy Haining. Yet he was cocking a snook at them with the bicycle chain and the taking of another scalp. Had the old ambulance not been a burned-out wreck, doubtless the body would have ended up in St Mungo's Park, he thought bitterly.

Leaving the pathologist to her task, Lorimer made for the victim's bedroom. It was small and tidy, the bed made and a pair of felt slippers neatly placed beside the bedside cabinet. The sight of the slippers gave Lorimer his usual qualm. A living, breathing human had been taken away and that horror outside left in her place. His lips tightened in determination as he continued his search of the room. A jewellery box lay on the dressing table with various ceramic pots and tiny vases placed strategically around. He looked at the walls and again his glance fell on the bedside tabletop. There were no photographs. Perhaps a portrait painter had no need of them?

Lorimer turned to the dressing-table drawers and began to rummage. Underclothes, jerseys, socks ... nothing much here, he thought. The bedside cabinet was more revealing. Notebooks and papers had been shoved higgledy-piggledy in the two sections of the cupboard. His hands searched delicately through the contents. Bank statements, insurance policies, all the usual paraphernalia of adulthood. There were several letters which Lorimer scanned. He made a note of two names and addresses for next of kin then, realising that he would have to process many of the documents for further information, he took the pile out with him into the hallway. Leaning against the lounge door, one eye on Solomon's back, he tapped out a number on his mobile.

'Lorimer. Get me DS Wilson.'

There was a pause during which Lorimer glanced down the hallway. The pathologist, the scene-of-crime officer whose name was Fred, and the forensic biologist were working away methodically in the midst of all that carnage. This was just a beginning for them. Tomorrow they'd be back to find further samples.

'Alistair? I want you to run a check on Lucy Haining's bank accounts. Find out all you can as far back as, oh, let's say the last year. OK? Right. I'll be over shortly.'

He put the mobile back into his overcoat pocket then returned to the lounge where Solomon was still sitting.

'Solly.' The dark head turned in Lorimer's direction. 'There's someone I'd like you to meet.'

Solly rose to his feet as Rosie walked in briskly behind the DCI, stripping off the surgical gloves with a loud snap.

'Ah, the famous Dr Brightman!' Rosie exclaimed, extending her hand. 'How do you do?'

Lorimer watched, amused to see Solomon's first reaction to the petite blonde. Expert on human behaviour he might be but Lorimer enjoyed observing how swiftly the young psychologist had found his most charming smile. An eyeful of Rosie was a fairly good antidote to the horrors that Solly had seen elsewhere in the flat.

'I've heard about you before,' Rosie said mischievously.

Solomon stared blankly at the woman for a moment then his face cleared in understanding.

'Of course. Glasgow University.'

She smiled, nodding. 'I don't spend all my time in the City Mortuary, though it feels like it sometimes. Lorimer tells me you're profiling this guy.' She indicated the area outside the room, as if the killer's presence still contaminated the locus.

'Yes. You know about my, um, accident?'

'You were mugged in your own flat, right?'

'Maybe I was closer to our suspect than I'd have wished.'

'So it might have been you laid out on my slab!' Rosie teased.

Solly blushed suddenly at the thought of this attractive young woman examining his naked body. Noticing his discomfiture, Lorimer clapped Rosie on the shoulder.

'They're an insensitive lot, Dr Brightman. She's just winding you up.'

Just then a grey-bearded man put his head around the door.

'Ah, Chief Inspector.'

'Back to work,' commented the pathologist, recognising the scene-of-crime photographer. 'Right then,' she tapped Solly's arm gently, 'I'd best get on out there. See you later, maybe.'

'I can have one of the boys take you home,' Lorimer suggested, seeing Solly slump back into the soft folds of the settee, but the psychologist shook his head.

'I'm all right now. I'd like to stay while you look around the flat.'

'Up to you. There may also be a few things to do in the office before I see my bed tonight.'

Lorimer checked that the scene-of-crime boys were still in the flat then began to look around the room. Janet Yarwood had been one of the many solitary people in this city. She had told the psychologist several things about Lucy Haining that Lorimer remembered from the report. Now, thought Lorimer, just as Rosie could read for signs of death, it was time that Janet Yarwood's home told him something about her life.

First-floor flat, lounge window overlooking the street below. A door directly opposite led to the hall and the other rooms, and there was a small kitchen off the lounge. The only wall without window or doorway was dominated by a huge batik hanging in bright pink, black and white. At first the design seemed abstract but on closer inspection Lorimer saw that it was in fact a representation of a zebra and foal against an African sunset. Remembering the influence on Lucy Haining's jewellery designs, Lorimer made a mental note to look for other African artefacts. Most of the furnishings were old and shabby, in contrast to the newness of the building itself. Instead of a carpet, there were several durries laid side by side, leaving a broad strip of unvarnished floorboard under the window. Here a collection of artist's materials were gathered: boxes containing tubes of paint, larger tubes of primary-coloured acrylics, brushes of various sizes sticking out of pottery jars and stacks of unframed canvases, face to the wall. Curious about their subjects, Lorimer flipped them over. They were all studies of children. Had any of the models come from Lucy's life classes? he wondered. But perhaps they were simply early studies for commissioned portraits. At one end of the room, under the garish batik, was an old square table. Someone had stripped and varnished it at one time and the warm oak glowed in the lamplight. A large blue pottery bowl was filled with exotic fruits. Had she meant to eat them, he thought, or were they a subject for still life? Two squashy chairs and the settee were draped in plain undyed linen, contrasting with the striped multicoloured rugs.

His eyes wandered over the walls, noting the artist's taste in paintings. There was an abstract of Moorish buildings in solid colours that picked out the bright rugs, several tiny embroideries collected within one frame and, he was heartened to recognise, an original Anda Paterson. The blues and mauves showed ancient women and their donkey coming from market. Lorimer looked at the picture, oblivious for a few minutes to the rest of the room. At last he jerked his eyes away and moved on to the kitchen wall where, he was surprised to see, there was simply a blank. A swift appraisal of the whole room caused him to frown. It was unbalanced somehow, this empty space. He moved closer, then drew in his breath sharply as he saw the holes. Tiny particles of pink plaster lay in the cavities from where, unless he was much mistaken, picture hooks had been wrenched.

Lorimer stepped into the hall where the scene-of-crime photographer was busy. A sudden camera flash illumined the wrecked body on the floor and Lorimer pursed his lips together in a gesture of angry disgust. What a bloody awful waste.

'Fred. In here, please.'

The photographer followed him into the lounge and Lorimer pointed to the wall.

'There. It looks like someone may have taken some pictures off the wall.'

'Mm. Theft, you think?'

The man's grey eyebrows rose in speculation. Lorimer shrugged briefly. He was quite sure that any art thief worth his salt would not have left Anda Paterson's gem behind. Whatever the nature of the missing pictures, they had been taken for a reason other than theft. The photographer fitted on a different lens then snapped a few close-up shots of the tell-tale holes.

'Thanks.'

'Sure. Anything else, just let me know.'

Lorimer stepped back to appraise the room once more then decided it was time to investigate the kitchen.

There were plants everywhere. The original fittings of the kitchen were light grey but the colour had virtually disappeared beneath the foliage. Huge untidy spider plants hung over the tops of cupboards and there were pots of streptocarpus ranged on the window sill. Every available work surface held tins or trays full of cuttings and an enormous spiky yucca dominated one corner. Many of the plants were in flower already, and Lorimer guessed that the kitchen window faced south. There was even a delicate orchid, its pale pink blooms wilting slightly. Lorimer picked up a plastic container and sprayed a mist of water over the plant. He recalled the plain face of the young woman whose remains would shortly be zipped into a body bag and carted off to the mortuary. It was not surprising that she had surrounded herself with such things of beauty. Her own adornment had not been important, if Solomon's theory was correct. There had been nobody else to please. Except Lucy, a little voice reminded him.

Lorimer stretched his shoulders back, realising for the first time that night just how tired he was. Out in the hall the body had been hidden away in a black bag and already there were men being instructed by the pathologist to take it away. Rosie shook out her blonde hair as Janet Yarwood left her flat for ever, then turned and smiled as she caught sight of Lorimer.

'Does your friend need a lift home?'

Solly was on his feet now, swaying from weariness. 'Thanks,' he said before Lorimer could reply. 'I'd appreciate it. Not taking you out of your way, I hope?'

'That depends where you live.'

'Oh. Not far from the university.'

'In that case, Dr Brightman, it's no bother at all.'

'Right. I'll leave you to Rosie's tender care then,' Lorimer said, sketching a salute and watching the pair of them leave. Hopefully he'd not be far behind.

Had there been a hint of something in Lorimer's tone? Solly wondered. Was that a twinkle in the pathologist's eyes?

As he followed the woman out into the night, past the fluttering cordons and the duty policemen still guarding the locus, Solomon breathed in the cold air in great gulps. Rosie held open the passenger door for him and he sank into the leather seat. They remained silent on the journey, Rosie covertly examining the man whose dark lashes were now closed over eyes that had seen too much. Her fingers reached out for a moment as if she had a sudden urge to stroke the tumble of thick curls back from his forehead, then she drew back and smiled to herself. Let him sleep for the moment.

In fact Solomon was still very much awake, his head spinning not with thoughts of his undeniably attractive driver, but with recent memories of a much plainer creature altogether.

25

The two men walked down Gibson Street avoiding puddles in the cracked pavement. Lorimer had turned his coat collar against the downpour and walked head down, hands thrust into his pockets. Solomon, oblivious to the rain soaking his black curls, was talking excitedly, arms waving in wide gestures. A group of students waited for the lights to change. Lorimer raked them with his policeman's eyes, only half-listening to the psychologist. Huddled and giggling beneath a black umbrella with its spokes awry, they seemed like children compared to the way he remembered himself in his student days. That was definitely a sign of age.

Gibson Street was, for Lorimer, the epitome of student life. Sure, it had changed in the last couple of decades but most of the buildings were still intact, except for a jarring gap where a row of elegant yet decrepit tenements had stood. Now it was a muddy area where the students parked their cars and vans. Lorimer couldn't help glancing over on the other side of the road to see if the sign was still there. The Manor had been the all-time hippy hang-out, a squat for visiting bands and home to the more interesting children of a psychedelic age. Rumour had it that Pink Floyd had once stayed over. Lorimer looked in vain. The sign above the door lintel appeared to have gone.

This was Solly's patch now.

The newer, upmarket restaurants and bijou interior designers told of a greater general affluence amongst the residents. In his day, his and Maggie's, there had been the thrill of the exotic as Eastern cuisine first began to take its hold on the city. The old Shish Mahal had been their favourite. God, he thought, you could have had a mutton vindaloo for shillings back then. The Asian grocery stores had proliferated, too. There weren't so many about now, though.

The Chief Inspector had deliberately met the psychologist after his classes and was now accompanying him on his way back home. He had established the younger man's routine from casual questioning the previous day and now he wondered if Solly was aware of his role as guardian angel. He had come straight from the City Mortuary to Glasgow University and had just given Solly the latest information obtained from the art student's bank accounts.

'But this is tremendous, it explains everything!'

Solly was practically dancing around the puddles.

'Everything?'

'Of course. Lucy Haining was receiving regular sums of money that tally with Janet Yarwood's withdrawals. The dates coincide.'

'And the other regular payments? Where did they come from?'

He wanted to hear Solly's answer. Would it fit in with his own ideas? Solly stopped and beamed, oblivious to the rain trickling down his beard.

'Blackmail. It fits. Lucy Haining was blackmailing somebody.'

'Janet Yarwood?'

The psychologist shrugged. 'Possibly. Though the woman would have given her money only too willingly.' He stopped suddenly and looked straight at Lorimer. 'For love. There was no need for threats.'

They walked on.

'So, you think Lucy Haining was killed by someone else. Whoever had been paying her large sums of money for three months before her death.'

'Exactly. Someone paid Lucy to keep her mouth shut.'

'And eventually shut it for good.'

Solly nodded eagerly. 'It was carefully planned. This man had decided that Lucy was either too big a threat to him, or else the payments had to stop.' He grinned at the policeman. 'You like it?'

Caught by his child-like enthusiasm, and despite the fact that he'd already worked through the same ideas, Lorimer found himself grinning back.

'I love it. Not only that but we can begin looking around for an artist who fits the bill. An artist who'd rather remain anonymous.'

Lorimer looked shrewdly at Solomon. The psychologist pulled at his wet beard as they walked on. Then he circled the air with his hand as he spoke.

'Janet Yarwood was a postgraduate student but she would have a small income from her post as a tutor, wouldn't she? Enough to pay her mortgage?'

'That wasn't her only income. We've found that there had been a fairly substantial sum left in trust for her. She got it when she was twenty-five.'

'Ah.' Solly turned on his heel to face Lorimer, finger wagging gleefully. 'That explains why she didn't go to the Art School straight from school! Parental opposition.'

'Maybe.' Lorimer continued walking towards the park, adding, half to himself, 'Perhaps that's what she had in common with Lucy.'

But Solomon wasn't to be diverted. 'So. There was easily enough to afford an Anda Paterson.'

'And fund her favourite student's expenses,' Lorimer reminded him. 'What about the missing pictures? Perhaps the artist took them back.'

'Okay. What you're suggesting is that whoever painted them killed Janet Yarwood and knew that their presence on her wall would be a dead giveaway.'

Lorimer nodded grimly, 'Now all we need to know is what pictures they were.'

'And who signed them.'

They had turned into the gates of Kelvingrove Park and were now heading up the path that ran parallel to the river. The brown water gurgled below them. Up ahead a jogger appeared, his cotton vest soaked through. As he padded heavily over the downhill slope Lorimer's eyes roved over him. Anyone passing this way would be subject to the policeman's scrutiny, measured up against that photofit of Alison Girdley's.

'Coming up?'

They had reached the other side of the park where the curved terraced houses looked down majestically over the city. Lorimer hesitated for a moment, anxious not to play the nursemaid.

'Sure. A quick coffee would be good. Wash away the taste of the mortuary.'

Solly grimaced then his face cleared as he asked – just a shade too casually, Lorimer thought – 'And how is Dr Fergusson?'

'Oh, she looked very fetching in yellow wellies.'

Solomon refused to take up the banter.

'What more do you know about Janet Yarwood's death?'

'Well, the stab wounds were pretty extensive. Suggests a frenzy of sorts. She'd evidently put up a fight. And the strangulation was post-mortem. So your signature theory still holds up. What I am pleased about is the traces we've got from her fingernails. DNA testing is definitely on.'

'Providing you have a suspect to match.'

Lorimer nodded. They had reached Solly's front door. Inside Lorimer was pleased to see that the psychologist's flat had been restored to order. Despite the rain still battering against the bay window panes, the room overlooking the city was filled with light.

'You've been busy.'

Lorimer swept his eyes over the lounge. The place had been carefully dusted for prints and other traces during Solly's stay in hospital and had still been a mess the previous evening when they had left abruptly for Janet Yarwood's flat.

'Ah. My cleaning lady usually does everything. I'm afraid I'm not great at housekeeping.'

'Come in regularly, does she?'

Lorimer couldn't help himself sounding like an interrogating policeman. Solly grinned, catching the tone.

'Twice a week. I share her with my neighbour across the landing.'

'And she'll have her own key?'

'Yes. You're not suggesting . . . ?'

'I'm not suggesting anything. You just need to be extra careful from now on.'

'You'd be sorry to lose your criminal profiler?'

Solly chuckled as Lorimer shook his head. There had been times when he'd gladly have seen the back of this young man. But now?

They took their coffees back into the lounge and Lorimer sank into the nearest armchair, its soft leather giving a sigh. He looked around the room appraisingly. It was so different from the chaos of previous days that he had the impression he was seeing it for the first time. Solly, he was interested to see, had a fair art collection of his own. He stood up and walked over to have a closer look.

'Originals?'

'Mostly. When I can afford them.'

They were all abstracts. Could the psychologist see things in the swirls of colour the way he appeared to see into the souls of human beings? Some of them seemed to Lorimer as if huge strokes of colour had been applied with a pasting brush. And perhaps they had, he mused, surprised that the overall effects were really rather pleasing.

'Not my taste,' he began, 'but I think I could live with one or two of them.'

'That's the real test, isn't it?'

'Sorry?'

'You buy a painting because you can't bear to live without it,' he said simply.

Lorimer didn't reply. It was true enough in his own case, though he supposed there were plenty of wealthy folk who collected for investment purposes or just for the prestige of having famous signatures on their walls. His thoughts went back to Janet Yarwood. Were the missing pictures ones she couldn't live without? And if so, what had they meant to her?

'Got to go.'

He gulped the rest of his coffee and handed the beaker to Solly.

'You'll let me know if you find anything?'

'Of course. Did you think I'd let you read it in the papers?'

Solly hesitated. Now would be the time to mention his interview with that McArthur girl. The Chief Inspector seemed quite touchy on the subject of the Press. Best not say anything. Solomon held the door open, listening to Lorimer's footsteps echo down the stone stairs. Frowning, he realised there had been no follow-up to the journalist's visit. Perhaps he'd better make some enquiries of his own.

26

The reporter stood at his window looking down. Even from the seventh floor the feeling of being apart from the city was intoxicating. Now that the nights were drawing out he could see strands of cloud the colour of tallow drifting over the horizon. It was like watching white birds floating lazily home to roost at the end of another day. The open window admitted the sound of traffic below that was a dull roar like wind shaking the treetops. He rubbed sweaty palms against his best jeans, aware of his nervous excitement.

Tonight Diane was coming for a drink, though the signals they had been sending out lately hadn't fooled either of them. His heart beat fast in anticipation that the night would progress beyond their present stage of meaningful looks and, certainly in his own case, lustful thoughts. There were certain sorts of women that really turned him on. Diane was one of them. Martin glanced over his shoulder. The flat was reasonably tidy; books, newspapers and magazines had been piled into corners. Even the soapstone elephants he'd brought back from Zimbabwe were standing neatly in a row on the windowsill, nose to tail. The dimmer switch was turned down to just the right romantic light; the CD player was ready to be switched on as soon as he heard the door buzzer.

In fact, he thought smugly to himself, the room was well and truly prepared as the setting for seduction. Diane would probably see through all his efforts but he didn't care.

The door buzzer seemed louder than usual and in a few swift strides he pressed the CD play button and lifted the handset.

'Hi, it's me. I've got Davey with me. Can we come up?'

The husky voice held just a trace of apology.

'Sure. Come on up.'

Martin forced a careless tone, though he was inwardly cursing the photographer. He slammed the cupboard door open and pulled out a pack of beer. So much for the sauvignon chilling in the fridge and the dishes of Marks & Spencer nibbles.

'Hallo. Ooh, nice place you've got here.'

Diane had shed her velvet coat and handed it to Martin in one movement as she entered the living room. Ruefully, his eyes swept over her short skirt and long suede boots before he turned to say hello to Davey. The photographer's long hair hung in tangles around his face, reminding Martin for the umpteenth time of the heavenly seventies. His parents' generation. Sometimes even Davey referred to his hippy looks as a blast from the past. The leather jacket that hung on his bony frame had clearly been tailored for broader shoulders than his, if tailored was the right word to use of such a decrepit garment. Martin had once joked that his friend had invented the distressed look for clothes merely by wearing them. His precious bag of equipment that went everywhere with him was slung over one shoulder, pulling the leather jacket even further out of shape. But it was not the weight of cameras that made the photographer sway somewhat unsteadily on his feet, his glazed eyes not quite focusing.

'Whoa, you look as if you've been having fun!'

Davey smiled dreamily and raised his hand in a peace-making gesture. Martin shrugged. Maybe he wouldn't stay long. On the other hand there was a fair chance that whatever he was on would make him crash out and he'd be lumbered with him all night.

'Drinks?'

'Yes, please.'

Diane answered for both of them, Davey merely nodding his agreement. When Martin came back, a beer in one hand and a long glass of white wine in the other, Diane was curled on his favourite rug with her long dark hair tossed over one shoulder. Davey sat on the couch with a far away smile fixed to his face. Martin joined his friend, wishing it was the gorgeous gossip columnist sitting cosily next to him.

'Bin talkin' to Diane.' The photographer's speech was slurred. 'She's bin tellin' us about this Dr Bright-man.'

Martin frowned but Diane gave a careless shrug.

'Everyone knows he must be in cahoots with the cops,' she said. 'Especially after this latest murder.'

'Yeah. Another one bites the dust, hey, hey!' Davey sang, and Martin rolled his eyes to heaven. Diane caught his glance, mouthing 'Sorry'.

'What about something to eat. You hungry, mate?'

Davey was downing his beer steadily in a way that betokened regular practice.

''S'all right. Can't stay. Just came up to say hello.'

Martin grinned, his antagonism vanishing.

'We were just talking about that last murder. Davey thinks it's some weirdo,' Diane said.

'A bam. A gen-u-ine bampot.' Davey belched loudly, then put his fingers to his mouth in an expression of mock horror. 'Oops. Pardonnez-moi!' He set down his empty glass as Diane giggled, then rose slowly to his feet. 'Home time, I think.'

'C'mon then, let's see you to the lift.'

Martin tucked his hand below his friend's elbow and steered him towards the door. Was he mistaken as he glanced back, or had Diane dropped a lascivious wink? And if so, for whom was it intended?

'Safe home.'

Davey raised both hands in farewell, smiling still as the lift door closed. Martin sighed with relief. At least the guy wasn't going too far.

He turned back from the landing, light from his doorway and the strains of music beckoning. Now the evening could really begin. Diane was still sitting on the rug but Martin was pleased to see that she had taken off the suede boots. With her long legs curled under her, she reminded him of a sleepy cat settled down in front of a fire.

'More wine?'

'Mm. Yes please.'

As she held out the thin-stemmed glass, Martin caught the expression in her green eyes. It was more than sauvignon blanc she seemed to be asking for. The neck of the wine bottle was still cold against his hands as he poured.

'What about joining me up here?'

For answer, the girl uncurled herself from the floor and sank in close beside him. She raised her wine.

'Cheers!'

Martin chinked his beer mug lightly against the proffered glass.

'To us,' he said softly. 'To better acquaintance.'

Her eyes sparkled with merriment at his deliberate understatement. He watched her face intently as they sipped their drinks. Suddenly a thought came to his mind. Putting down his glass, he reached for her long hair and twisted it gently into a long cord then folded it around her neck. He kissed her startled mouth.

'Porphyria's lover,' he said.

'What?'

'"I found a thing to do, and all her hair in one long yellow string I wound her little throat about."'

'Where on earth's that from?'

'Browning's poem. "Porphyria's Lover." Didn't you do that at school?'

'No, as it happens. What did he do?'

'Strangled her.'

Diane pushed away from him suddenly.

'I'm not sure I like that. Besides, my hair's not yellow.'

Martin stroked the long thick hair back into place and looked at her gravely.

'You're beautiful.'

He kissed her again, gently at first; then, as she responded, deeper kisses followed and this time she didn't pull away. A feeling of triumph came over Martin as he probed her mouth with his tongue. She wanted him. His fingers tip-toed under her skirt and he felt her quiver under his touch. He stroked her belly, naked below the tights, guiding his fingers lower and lower until she gasped with pleasure. There was an urgency in yanking down the tights then pulling her body against his. She pressed her body closer in turn and now her fingers explored his crotch, feeling his hardness.

As he groaned softly, she whispered, 'Let's go into your bedroom.'

'No! Don't go in there!'

166

His hand shot out from the folds of her clothing as he sat up suddenly. In reply to her look of surprise, he grinned sheepishly.

'It's a tip. I don't want you to get the wrong impression.'

Diane put his hand back deliberately on her thigh.

'What sort of impression do you want me to have?'

Her throaty voice was full of invitation.

For answer, Martin unzipped and shoved off his jeans in one swift movement then pulled her under him. As the jeans landed on the floor Martin ignored the sound of a falling wineglass. In the half-light he saw the swathe of Diane's dark hair tumbling back against the couch and her eyes looked black with desire. Her knees were bent and he was aware of the sudden thought that here was no virgin for deflowering. His face contorted for a split second then he was pushing into her sweet softness, hearing himself cry out. The torrent inside him suddenly released and the cry torn from him turned to a groan.

'I'm sorry. I'm sorry. I wanted you too much.'

She was making hushing noises now and, taking his face in her hands, she kissed him as if he were a child.

'It'll be better next time.'

Her hands were still clasping his back, fixing him against her young slim body. Martin kissed her again, slowly, savouring the moment.

Next time. There was going to be a next time.

27

'Come in.'
Lorimer heard the knock and was aware of Annie Irvine hovering in his line of vision. He would finish his conversation first, though.

'Yes, sir. Certainly. Thank you. I will.'

Lorimer put down the phone as if it was a delicate piece of porcelain. He'd hoped for such a call but it was still a surprise when it finally came. So. He was to be in the running for George Phillips's job, was he? He mused for a brief moment then looked up as Annie cleared her throat.

'Right, let's be having it.'

'Sir, it's the boyfriend. I mean Sharon Millen's boyfriend. He's in the Royal Infirmary. Attempted suicide.'

Lorimer was already rising to his feet, all thoughts of promotion forgotten.

'When?'

'There's just been a call from the officer there. His mother found him in bed. Couldn't wake him up. An overdose, it looks like.'

'Tell the team I want them all in the incident room pronto.'

Lorimer whirled past her and slammed out of the room.

'Right.' Lorimer faced the officers assembled around him. 'We have already eliminated James Thomson from our inquiries. However, we cannot ignore the obvious here. You know what I'm talking about. Remorse. We've seen it lots of times before. The murder preys on their mind. They can't face what they've done and so they try to top themselves.'

There were nods all round. The officers knew the score, all right.

'But,' Lorimer continued, 'I don't want anybody jumping to conclusions. Is that clear? There may be other explanations for this incident. Until we know the facts, I want this boy and his family treated with kid gloves.'

There were glances exchanged between a few of the officers, then Alistair Wilson spoke up.

'Sir, if it *was* Thomson who did in his girlfriend, then what about the MO?'

'I'm there already, Alistair. Was the lad capable of cutting her up like that? We'll need to talk to him again. If he's in a fit state to be questioned,' he added.

Lorimer ran a hand through his hair. The team were as anxious as he was to make an arrest. But there was always the danger of an over-enthusiastic officer mucking things up. He swept his eye over the individuals he knew so well. Wilson he'd trust under any circumstances. Young Cameron had a lot to learn but Lorimer would temper his keen-as-mustard approach with plenty of basic plodding.

'We still don't know the whereabouts of Sharon Millen's murder. But let's assume for now that it took place somewhere similar to West George Lane.' He turned to Cameron. 'Anything on the buses yet?'

The DC straightened up under Lorimer's direct gaze.

'Not a thing, sir. There were several passengers who came forward but they all say the same thing. Nobody remembers the girl that night.'

'Right. Keep circulating her photo meantime. Someone's memory just might be jogged.'

'We'll go up to the Royal,' he nodded to Wilson, who merely raised his eyebrows in acquiescence. 'I want to see the boy if he's awake.'

As they dispersed to go about their various duties, the others exchanged surprised glances. But nobody voiced the opinion that they all shared. If Lorimer was going up there himself, did that mean he suspected James Thomson of his girlfriend's murder?

The Royal Infirmary sat on the Glasgow skyline overlooking the drearier part of the main Glasgow to Edinburgh motorway. Its dark spires and filthy chimneys were a reminder of earlier days when the city revelled in its industrial glory. Despite its grim exterior, however, the hospital had been thoroughly modernised and the ground-floor reception area was more like that of an airport lounge than a medical centre.

'Which ward?' Lorimer asked.

Alistair Wilson told him and they made their way towards the bank of lifts that would take them to the boy's bedside.

'He's been in theatre to have his stomach pumped,' the PC outside the room informed Lorimer. 'His mum and dad are in there with him just now.'

Lorimer waited at the door while Wilson spoke to the sister on duty. She glanced up at the Chief Inspector warily.

'The doctor says he's not to be disturbed,' she said, her lips firmly pressed together.

'Oh, we'll be very discreet, sister,' Wilson assured her, turning on his most charming smile. The nurse failed to return it.

'You'd better be,' she retorted, clearly unimpressed by any authority outside the medical world.

At a nod from his Detective Sergeant, Lorimer slipped inside the private ward. Both parents looked up as he entered. Linda Thomson had been crying. Her eyes were dark smudges where she'd rubbed away her mascara. Beside her, James's father sat holding her hand. There was a depth of pain that Lorimer could only guess at behind those expressionless eyes. He'd never known the agonies of parenthood. Or the joys, whatever they might be.

'Mr Lorimer.'

Joe Thomson started to rise but Lorimer motioned him to stay where he was.

'How is he?'

'We think he'll be all right. It wasn't paracetamol, thank God. Just aspirin.'

Lorimer nodded, taking in the boy's waxy face.

'He'll feel like he's got one hell of a hangover when he comes round,' he joked.

Linda Thomson managed a watery smile.

'Can you talk about it?' he asked gently.

Linda gave a huge sigh and nodded.

'Not in here, Mr Lorimer. Can we go outside?' Joe Thomason whispered.

'I'd rather stay,' Linda pleaded. 'In case he wakes up.'

'All right, love. We won't be long.'

He gave his wife a tremulous smile and slipped out behind Lorimer. Hospital corridors figured prominently in police investigations. Glasgow, like any other large city, had its share of violent crimes. Assault to Severe Injury often necessitated these impromptu interviews. Or, as in this case, attempted suicides.

'Mind if I smoke?' Joe asked.

'Nothing to do with me but the duty sister looks like she eats razors for breakfast,' Lorimer remarked, indicating the NO SMOKING sign. 'We could go outside, if you like?'

'Better not. Don't want to be too far away. Just in case.'

'Well, let's sit over here.'

Lorimer indicated an empty row of respectable padded chairs. Joe Thomson sat down heavily and leaned forward, head in hands for a few moments. When he sat up again, Lorimer could see that he was trembling. Also, he avoided the Chief Inspector's eye.

'You'd better tell me all about it, Mr Thomson.'

'What is there to tell? The boy was okay one day and the next he's trying to do himself in.'

'When you say he was okay, do you mean he had been behaving normally since Sharon's death?'

'What's normal? Oh, I don't know. He was very quiet. But then he's always been a quiet lad. Never any trouble at school or that. It fair broke his heart, that lassie's . . .' He hesitated then whispered the word. 'Murder.'

'And more recently?'

'Well, the wife said he'd never get over it. But he was back at school. Doing his Advanced Highers no problem.'

'Did he talk much to either of you?'

'Not really. Not what you'd call a real talk, you know. But he was studying in his room. Or listening to music most of the time. What they call music. We had no idea.'

'No idea about what, Mr Thomson?'

'Well, you know . . .' The man's eyes widened as if Lorimer had missed the point somewhere along the line. 'About blaming himself.'

'For Sharon's death?'

'Of course.'

Thomson stared at Lorimer.

'Just let me get this straight, Mr Thomson. Did James actually say he'd killed his girlfriend?'

'For Christ's sake, man, what do you think he is?' Joe Thomson exploded. 'He never saw her on any bus that night. He's been too bloody terrified to tell anybody. Him and Sharon had an argument and she stormed off in the huff . . .' The man's voice rose in indignation, then broke off. 'My God, that poor wee lassie.' His head sunk into his hands once more and Lorimer waited for the storm of emotion to pass.

'It's a hellish situation, so it is, Mr Lorimer.'

Lorimer caught the other man's eye at last.

'How do you know about this quarrel, Joe?'

'He left his mum a note. It was on her bedside cabinet. We found it when Linda called the doctor.'

'And did you give it to the officer here?'

Joe Thomson shook his head wearily. 'What was the point. We never knew if the boy was going to die or what. It didn't matter at the time.'

Lorimer gripped the man's shoulder. 'I'm sorry, Joe. But he'll be fine. He's young and he'll heal. Even emotional scars can be treated these days.'

'Aye.'

'We'd like to speak to James, though,' Lorimer added gently.

'Oh, I was expecting you to say that, Mr Lorimer. I was expecting that the minute we found him in his bed.'

'Come on, let's get back. Your wife'll wonder what's been going on.'

Linda Thomson looked up anxiously as they came in.

'It's okay. I told him. He'll speak to James when he's better.'

Lorimer hadn't agreed to these terms but he let it pass. This was simply another near-tragedy sparked off by a monster with a taste for blood. A monster in their city whose acts of brutality had been like hurling rocks into a calm pool. And the ripples were still trembling shorewards.

28

If there was one crime that Lorimer found distasteful above all others, it was the sort that offended against children. Child murder was the worst, of course. Within Glasgow's City Mortuary the usual light repartee would be silenced and even the burly technicians could be moved to tears. Identification was the worst part. Lorimer had stood behind parents at that viewing window. Screams of hysteria were less common than the profound silence of disbelief. Afterwards he'd be hard put not to show his own emotion: to be strong for those poor bereft souls who unwittingly leaned on him just because he was a policeman. Just because he was there.

Such crimes were rare, thankfully. But not so rare, these days, were cases of child molestation. With the advent of child helplines more and more cases were coming to the attention of the police. The public thought it was all new, of course, though such crimes were as old as the hills. Lorimer had been on a course south of the border in the wake of the Jamie Bulger tragedy. There he'd learned rather a lot about the history of child abuse, way back into the Dark Ages. It had gone on seemingly unchecked for centuries. Only in the nineteenth century had children begun to receive special attention, helped by enlightened reformers and indignant citizens like the great Charles Dickens. They'd come a long way since then. The European Court of Human Rights now gave definition to what a child's life should be like. Great in theory, thought Lorimer, but in practice there was still plenty of scope for improvement.

Right now he was sitting on an uncomfortable bentwood chair that creaked every time he moved. Mrs McFadden had been most solicitous when they had arrived to interview her foster son, Kevin Sweeney. Tea and fancy biscuits had been provided as she fussed about anxiously. Lorimer had chosen the bentwood to keep out of her way but also because it helped him observe the boy from an angle where he wouldn't make eye contact. That was Gail Stewart's job.

Gail had phoned from the Female and Child Unit the day before. Could he sit in on their third interview with Kevin? She had been reluctant to divulge too much, only saying that there was more to this case of abuse than met the eye.

Kevin's natural father was inside for armed robbery and his mother had done a bunk. It was thought she might be in Canada. For more than two years Kevin had drifted from one set of foster parents to another, a vulnerable and rather unstable little boy. Careful examination of his case had shown that although his current foster parents were not the most ideal of primary carers, they were apparently blameless of any acts of abuse. Kevin himself had said so, and the general belief was that the nine-year-old was telling the truth, not merely protesting their innocence under pressure.

Gail Stewart was well trained in question-and-answer technique. Lorimer had nodded his approval hearing the woman talk the child gently through the physical part of his ordeal. The preliminary interviews had served to create a rapport with Kevin; now detailed information was sought. Mrs McFadden had reported his case to the social work department. Kevin, it had transpired, claimed to have been taken away by a bad man who had 'done things to him'. The child had suffered since, his behaviour fluctuating between bouts of aggression and spells of withdrawal.

Lorimer was glad that he himself had no capacity for questioning the child. It was hard enough listening to this WPC trained in the gentle probing of areas that pained the boy so much. Now the child had to be taken through the experiences step by step in an effort to uncover the criminal behind such atrocities.

'Tell me about the van, Kevin. Can you remember if it was a big van, say as big as an ice cream van?'

WPC Stewart had removed her spectacles and her earnest young face was lit by concern. Kevin's chair was at an angle beside her. He was perched on a large cushion, his legs dangling into space. From time to time he glanced up at her face as she spoke. Was he trying to see if she had ulterior motives? wondered Lorimer.

How secure was the trust that had been built up? The boy's hands gripped the edges of his seat and he frowned now in concentration. The policeman willed him into remembering.

'It wis bigger 'n 'at.' He paused then added, 'Therr wur mair steps up intae it.'

'Were the steps at the back, Kevin?'

'Aye.'

'You said it was a white van. Now, can you remember what colour it was inside?'

All eyes were on the child's trembling lip and his downcast face.

'Ah cannae mind.'

'All right, Kevin. Just tell us what you do remember about the inside of the van.'

There was a silence broken by a murmur then, as Gail Stewart asked 'What was that, Kevin?', Lorimer realised that the boy's answer had been an unintelligible whisper. He repeated it now.

'A bed. Thir wis a bed.'

The sobs began and Kevin's foster mum slipped into the chair beside him, taking the child in her arms. His dark head was motionless against her ample bosom and Lorimer couldn't help wondering if the boy resented the belated protection of her arms. But then the sobs subsided and Mrs McFadden withdrew.

The WPC smiled encouragement as she asked, 'What was it like inside?' Her voice was casual, almost indifferent in her anxiety not to disturb the demons in his memory. Lorimer glanced at the others in the room. Gail Stewart's colleague was writing furiously in her notebook, trying at the same time to observe the boy's body language and facial expressions. The social worker sat silently beside Mrs McFadden. He was a thin, balding individual whose beady eyes reminded the detective of a hamster. The child was clearly struggling with this one and if it had not been for Gail's gentle and patient persistence, Lorimer was sure Mrs McFadden would have called a halt to proceedings by now.

'Ah'm no very sure. But Ah think it wis . . . Ah think it wis an ambulance.'

Gail shot the detective a meaningful look and Lorimer felt the hairs on his scalp tingle. It couldn't be. Hastily he riffled through his copy of the relevant notes, checking dates. My God, it could be, after all. His palms began to sweat. Kevin's molestation had occurred between the date that Lucy Haining had bought the old ambulance from Sangha and the fateful day on which it had been found a burned-out wreck.

Now Gail came and squatted in front of Kevin, taking both his hands in hers so that he looked down into her eyes.

'Kevin. It's all right to tell us about the bad man. He won't be allowed to do any bad things to you any more.'

The child's eyes looked doubtful.

'Will he go tae jyle?'

'We hope so. Is that what you'd like?'

The boy nodded. Christ, thought Lorimer, what's going through that kid's mind? His old man's in the nick and now he's going to associate that with this beast, whoever he is.

'Now take your time and tell me just what the man looked like.'

Slowly the words jerked from the boy.

'He wis big. Awfy big. Ah thocht he wis a, a doctor.'

'A doctor? Now what made you think that?'

'He had a big white jaicket on.'

'Go on. What else?'

The boy gave a shuddering sigh as further memories were dredged up from the place he didn't really want to see again. Lorimer felt the tension all around him.

'He had wee hair.'

'Wee hair? Describe it.'

'Like the back o' yer hair when ye've had the razor oan't. A slapheid.'

'All right. Now, Kevin, do you think if you saw a picture of him you would recognise the man?'

'Aye.' The word was pulled out of him reluctantly.

'Well, how would you like a trip in a police car to see some pictures?'

Kevin's eyes grew crafty.

'C'n Ah have the siren oan?'

Lorimer wanted to laugh out loud and he felt the atmosphere relax as several of the faces around him broke into wide grins.

178

'Oh, let's ask Chief Inspector Lorimer, shall we?'

Gail Stewart's expression was impish.

'I think that could be arranged, Kevin,' Lorimer said, trying to keep his tone suitably grave, but the boy had sensed the change in the room and his eyes shone with mischief that was suddenly wholesome and healthy.

An hour later Kevin left the station having been shown around the CCTV room as a reward. The boy was skipping between his foster mum and the social worker and Lorimer could almost feel his eagerness to get away to tell his pals all about it. As they reached the main door Mrs McFadden nudged him.

'Oh, aye,' said Kevin. 'Thanks very much for the ride in the car. It wis great.'

They disappeared out of the building leaving Lorimer shaking his head. How quickly kids seemed to bounce back. Even his medical examination by the police doctor hadn't been too much of an ordeal, according to WPC Stewart. Still, the process of delving into his traumatic experiences was not all over yet.

Upstairs George Phillips would soon know about this latest development. Kevin Sweeney's grubby little finger had jutted out defiantly at the photofit. Aye, he was sure. It was the same bad man.

Lorimer whistled through his teeth as he took the stairs two at a time. In his hand he held the envelope containing the photofit put together by Alison Girdley.

'It's too big a coincidence to ignore.'

Lorimer's voice betrayed his excitement. Maybe this was the break they'd been looking for. Phillips swung back in his chair, contemplating the photofit and Kevin Sweeney's statement which he held between his finger and thumb.

'The kid's been systematically abused. In an ambulance, he says. Valentine Carruthers had a record of involvement with paedophiles.' As Lorimer raised his eyebrows questioningly, Phillips added, 'Supplying rent boys in his nefarious past, you say?'

Lorimer stood up suddenly and began to pace the room.

'He dies in a burnt-out ambulance. Now this. Young Kevin has ID'd our photofit. So. What's the link?'

Phillips said nothing. Lorimer slapped his fist down on a pile of papers on his desk.

'Look,' the DCI continued, 'We've got these reports from the down-and-outs who knew Valentine Carruthers.'

'The response was pretty limited,' ventured Phillips.

'Only to be expected. Protecting their own backs. Even those who admitted knowing him didn't give much away.'

'So what do we do now?'

'I want all of these street contacts brought in for further questioning. Someone must know something.'

'You think now that a child's involved, tongues will loosen?'

The Superintendent leaned forward, elbows on the desk. Lorimer nodded, his mouth a single, grim line. He knew that Phillips could see his drift.

'What I want to do is circulate this photo among the men. Get them down to Glasgow City Mission and the regular haunts the old man visited.'

George Phillips gave a brief nod and, as Lorimer shot out of his office, added, 'And I suppose you want it done by yesterday.' But he was already speaking to a closed door.

Back in his own room, Lorimer stared at the aerial photograph on his wall. The trees and shrubs of St Mungo's Park looked so tranquil from that angle. Even the surrounding high-rise flats didn't seem such an eyesore. The red circles disturbed the picture, however. Lorimer saw beyond them to other scenes; the carnage in Janet Yarwood's home and the smell of burnt grass out at Strathmirrin where Valentine Carruthers had been so cruelly torched. A paedophile? Did the gross brutality of the killer fit in with this sort of crime? Lorimer thought of Solomon and picked up the phone.

To Solomon, Lorimer's news wasn't entirely unexpected. His own profile of the killer was not so much altered as more clearly in focus. That the man was a loner, he had never had any doubts. Loneliness often led to some striving for love and affection.

The less well-adapted members of society didn't cope with normal relationships. Paedophiles were usually, though not always, people seeking a mixture of power and affection. Some of them delighted in bizarre acts of violence. No, Solomon wasn't surprised at all.

A white man in his early thirties, reasonably articulate, almost certainly employed in a profession, maybe self-employed. A man who would appear decent and normal to his work colleagues, no doubt. Someone who even convinced himself in one half of his sick mind that he was an upright citizen. The phonetic analysis of the accent pointed to a local person. Someone on his home territory. And the mutilation? Even here the deliberate signature gave something away, like a footprint on the path as the hunter knelt to leave his false spoor. Solomon believed that there had been some trauma in his past to do with a woman. His taking of the scalps was not such an unusual way for killers to behave if they were subconsciously destroying someone. Perhaps a mother who had damaged them in some way? In fact, there was a possibility that the man they sought had a physical as well as an emotional scar. Solomon could read and understand the pattern of behaviour without in any way condoning it.

Now, as he typed in a few more details to the profile, he had a sudden thought. The missing back-up disk included this file. He sat back, colour draining from his face. If his intruder was indeed the killer, was he now in a position to double-bluff them? Or would the fact that so much of his personality was revealed tip him over the edge? Solomon switched on the printer, his fingers shaking. He realised for the first time why he had not been killed that night. The hunter wanted him alive. He needed Solomon to be there, to have someone skilled in appreciating this game of . . . what was it? Hide and seek?

But what if he tired of the game and was never caught? Solomon had a fleeting vision of Rosie Fergusson, her bright hair tied back from her laughing face.

It might indeed have been his corpse on her slab.

29

Lorimer had asked Solomon to come with them. Normally two of his experienced officers would have made the visit but Lorimer wanted to see Solomon's reaction to the Yarwood family.

A lot hinged on this visit. So far they had drawn a blank about the missing pictures in the dead woman's flat. He'd been a fool to think it would be so easy. Questioning her colleagues at the Postgraduate Centre had only revealed what a recluse the woman had been. Not exactly friendless but nobody had ever been in her flat. Lorimer was sure that that had not applied to Lucy Haining. But Lucy was dead. The neighbours had seen Janet coming and going but that was all. There had been no socialising there, either, and certainly no visits to the flat.

The School of Art's director had been marvellous, putting up with the disruption of officers questioning so many students. It had to be done, he realised, but the man's calm acceptance of the situation had impressed Lorimer. Nobody had recognised the person behind the photofit, though.

These thoughts flitted through Lorimer's mind as his blue eyes stared over the hedgerows skimming past them. Annie Irvine was driving to the house that Mrs Yarwood shared with her daughter. Her only daughter, now.

The car had swept into the countryside leaving the Glasgow suburbs behind and now they were slowing down through the conservation village of Eaglesham.

Lorimer craned his neck to see if they were still there. Yes. The playing fields where he'd played the occasional game of football stretched to his left. It had been a terrible pitch, all lumps and tussocks, even for a rugby player like himself.

They were through the village now. Lorimer glanced behind at their passenger. The psychologist's eyes seemed glued to the passing countryside, his customary smile playing around his lips. What is he really seeing, though? the Chief Inspector wondered.

'That's it up there, sir.'

Annie Irvine nodded in the direction of a cottage set against the hillside, then turned the car into a narrow track.

'The Yarwoods?' Solomon leaned forward as far as his seat belt would allow.

'Believe in keeping themselves to themselves,' Lorimer remarked as the car came to a halt.

The cottage was old. Deep-set windows told of thick walls built more than a century before. The dull grey roughcast was made even gloomier by the deep overhang of the slate roof. There was no garden to speak of, just a flat area of rough grass on two sides and a few gnarled oaks behind the house.

'Well, there's a washing out, anyway,' said Annie Irvine, pointing to a row of sheets billowing on the line to the side of the cottage.

'They'll be in all right. They know to expect us.'

Lorimer knocked on the cottage door, noting that it was painted in the same drab grey as the walls. The door opened a fraction and Lorimer could see the security chain in place.

'DCI Lorimer. Mrs Yarwood?'

He was aware of a thin face and a pair of gimlet eyes staring hard at them.

'Show me your identification.'

Lorimer had in fact held out his warrant card but now he and Annie passed them to the woman. Her outstretched claw drew them in and he could see her bent head in the shadows scrutinising them. They were thrust back suddenly and the chain fell with a dull clunk. As the door opened wider, Lorimer raised his hand to indicate his bearded companion.

'Dr Brightman from Glasgow University. He is working with us.'

As the woman stared at him, the psychologist was sharply reminded of Janet Yarwood. It was the same face, grim and unsmiling.

They were ushered into a dingy room which, from the look of

it, was seldom used. Lorimer wondered if young Annie had come across the old-fashioned habit of keeping a 'front room' for visitors. He doubted it.

'Take a seat.'

Mrs Yarwood motioned Lorimer towards a dark mauve armchair. A thin layer of dust arose as he sat on the moquette. The whole place smelled of dust and damp. Even the creamy anti-macassars were spotted with rust marks. Solomon seated himself on an upright chair by the window, facing the parlour door. Annie stood beside him, glancing at Lorimer.

'She'll be down in a minute.'

The woman sat upright on the edge of the settee, hands clasped in her lap. Her wispy white hair was pulled into a tight bun at the back of her head, accentuating the thin, sharp features. The door opened and both men rose to their feet as Janet Yarwood's sister strode in. Solomon tried not to reveal his astonishment as he quickly glanced from the young woman to the detective. Lorimer's face gave nothing away.

'Miss Yarwood? DCI Lorimer.'

The hand was taken and pumped up and down vigorously. It was hard to assess her age, thought Lorimer. She was a thick-set female with bright red hair tied back in a single plait. Her black dress covered a bulky figure that was utterly lacking in femininity.

As she grinned at them all, her expression was that of a greedy child rather than a grown woman. The detective caught himself wondering about her provenance. Was Mr Yarwood a large red-haired man?

'I understand Mr Yarwood is not at home?' Lorimer asked.

'No. *Mister* Yarwood doesn't live here any longer!'

Mrs Yarwood spat the words out as if the mention of her husband's name caused a bad taste. Janet's sister had sat next to her mother, a crafty smile on her childish face.

'Daddy was bad. He went away!'

'That's enough, Norma.'

Mrs Yarwood's rebuke failed to change her daughter's expression.

'I can give you his address,' the woman offered reluctantly.

'Yes. Thank you. We will need to talk to him.'

'Did he do her in?'

The girl bounced up and down eagerly.

'Norma, be quiet, or you'll go to your room.' Mrs Yarwood turned to Lorimer. 'I'm sorry. Norma's not quite herself these days.'

'Do you mind answering some questions about Janet?' the detective asked.

'Not at all.'

The woman's indifference struck them all. She might have been discussing the weather.

'When did you last visit your daughter?'

The ramrod back didn't budge although Lorimer noticed a tightening of her jaw.

'We were only there twice. Once when she had just moved away.'

'And the other?'

'She was ill.' Mrs Yarwood's stiff lips began to tremble. 'I made her some soup.' Her mouth closed in a tight line and Lorimer could see the struggle to suppress any emotion.

'Didn't you want to see your daughter more often?'

'This is a Godly house, Chief Inspector. I wasn't going to take Norma into a place like that!'

'A place like what, Mrs Yarwood?' Lorimer's question was smooth as steel.

'A den of iniquity! All these terrible pictures everywhere! All the terrible goings on in that – Art School! And see where it all led to? I told her. I told her she'd come to a bad end!'

'Bad end,' echoed Norma, a silly smile still fixed on her face.

'Perhaps you remember the pictures?'

'Why should I remember them? A product of Satan, that's what they were. No graven images were ever allowed in this house. She never got those ideas from me. She had a good and Godly upbringing here.'

'Did you ever meet any of Janet's friends?'

'No.' The word was spoken quietly now, her outburst suddenly over.

'Did Janet often come back here?'

The woman shook her head silently, a look of hatred in her

eyes. Was her wrath directed against her dead daughter? Lorimer wondered.

'May I ask a question, Mrs Yarwood?' Solomon cocked his head to the side in a gesture of deference. 'Did you get on well with Janet?' For a moment the woman looked as though she didn't understand the question so Solomon continued, 'Were you friends?'

'I was her *mother*.'

Solomon nodded as if she had told him a great deal in that one answer. Lorimer rose to his feet.

'I'm sorry to take up your time, ladies. Perhaps if I could have Mr Yarwood's address?'

Lorimer ignored Annie's puzzled look. He had that information already but he wanted to see the woman's reaction to the question. Mrs Yarwood stood up, hesitated for a moment, then walked out without a word. Norma sat on, her chubby hands plucking at the voluminous folds of her skirt.

'What about you, Norma?' Lorimer whispered conspiratorially, once her mother was out of earshot. 'Was Janet your friend?'

Norma nodded solemnly, the pigtail jerking up and down behind her.

'Janet's gone to the bad fire,' she whispered back, one hand cupped against her mouth.

At that moment Mrs Yarwood returned and handed Lorimer a piece of paper.

'Thank you. I may have to contact you again, I'm afraid.'

The woman shrugged slightly then led the way to the front door.

As they filed out, Lorimer looked around the room, mentally contrasting it to the city flat Janet Yarwood had chosen for her home. There were no pictures here, no photographs anywhere at all. There was just one decoration on the wall: a text with the words 'God is Love' embroidered in painstaking detail. Lorimer gave an involuntary shudder and quickened his steps to join the others out in the fresh air.

Nobody spoke until the car drew away from the cottage.

'Well!' exclaimed Annie. 'You wouldn't need a psychology degree to work out why Janet Yarwood left home!' Then, realising her gaffe, she glanced in the rear-view mirror. 'Oops! Sorry. No offence, Dr Brightman.'

Lorimer looked away, trying to hide his smile.

'None taken. And you're right. I only wonder what took her so long to make the break.'

'And I don't blame the husband either,' Annie went on, warming to her theme. 'She's not exactly a barrel of laughs to come home to, is she?'

Lorimer didn't answer, keeping his face turned towards the fields all around them as the car turned onto the main road and headed back to Glasgow. Things weren't always as simple as his young WPC made out. He was interested now to meet Janet Yarwood's father. Would he have been closer to his elder daughter?

Norman Yarwood was a stocky man in his early sixties. The red hair that Lorimer had expected was peppered with grey and thinning on top. His florid complexion was either high blood pressure or too much booze, thought Lorimer. His black suit had seen better days and was shiny along the sleeves. Despite the chilly day, the man was perspiring freely and had already taken out a white handkerchief to mop his brow.

Lorimer and Solomon had arrived at Yarwood's address shortly after their visit to his former home. Now the man was reduced to a rented room in one of the old Pollokshaws tenements. His landlady, Mrs Singh, had been none too pleased to see Lorimer's warrant card, pursing her lips in disapproval as she showed the two men to her lodger's room.

'I couldn't believe it when they told me,' Norman Yarwood began. 'I still can't.'

He sat on the edge of his bed, head bowed, twisting the handkerchief between his large red fists.

'I mean, who'd want to do something like that to Jan?'

Lorimer was seated on the only chair and Solomon stood motionless by the end of the bed, his hands clasped in front of him. Lorimer was reminded of a Rabbi come to pay his respects.

'When was the last time you saw your daughter?' the detective asked.

Norman Yarwood sighed deeply. 'Only a couple of weeks ago. We had our tea in that place in the park. You know. The art place where she worked.'

'Did you ever visit her at home?'

The man raised his head and the eyes which had threatened tears suddenly became shrewd.

'Are you trying to suggest something?'

'Mr Yarwood, we need to know if any of Janet's friends or family had visited her flat shortly before her death.'

The man nodded, then went on, 'Yes, of course I did. I didn't bother her much, mind. She had her work and it wouldn't have been fair me dropping in forever.'

'When did you last visit Garnethill?'

'Must have been about a week, maybe ten days before the last time I . . .' His voice faded and the red fists screwed the handkerchief into a ball. 'The last time I saw her,' he finished.

'Did you notice the pictures in your daughter's flat?'

Norman Yarwood gave the ghost of a smile. 'Pictures? The place was full of ruddy pictures. She never stopped working on them.' The touch of pride in the man's voice was unmistakable.

'I'm particularly interested to know if you remember the framed pictures she had hanging on her lounge walls.'

The shrewd look came back into Yarwood's eyes.

'Somebody nick them?' When no answer was given, he shrugged then frowned in concentration. 'There was the big African thing, the embroidery, the one with the donkey and –' he paused, wiping his brow again. 'There were others but I can't exactly remember where they were.'

'On the wall by the kitchen?'

Yarwood nodded. 'That's right. I remember now. They were portraits.'

'Your daughter's work?

Yarwood gave a short laugh. 'No. Not her style at all.'

'And do you know who the subjects were?'

Lorimer strove to keep the excitement out of his voice but Yarwood was fighting to control a spasm of rage.

'Oh, aye. I know who they were all right. That Lucy girl. The one who was found in the park.'

'Lucy Haining?' Solomon asked, moving across and sitting beside Norman Yarwood.

'Yes.'

'Did you ever meet Lucy?'

Lorimer sat back and folded his arms, interested to see how Solomon would proceed.

'Aye, just the once. She was a cheeky wee English get! Thought she had the right to tell me off!'

'How was that, Mr Yarwood?'

The handkerchief was applied to his face once more.

'Ach, a lot of baloney. Went on about how Janet was a liberated woman and didn't need her parents. A lot of garbage. As if I didn't know my lassie was better off away from yon . . .'

His fist smashed hard against his knee.

'So you didn't like Lucy?'

'Not much. But that's no' to say I meant her any harm. I was sorry for our Jan when her friend got killed. It fair broke her up.'

'Mr Yarwood,' Solomon said, leaning forward in order to make eye contact, 'I know it must be very painful for you but could you tell us exactly how Janet behaved after Lucy's death?'

'Will it help catch whoever did it?' the man asked, turning to face Lorimer.

'It might,' Lorimer told him.

A long sigh escaped from the man then he straightened himself and began.

'She was so happy when we left home.'

'You left at the same time?' Solomon asked.

'Oh, aye. Didn't you know? That's what it was all about. I took Janet's part when she wanted to start the Art School. Then all hell broke loose, of course.' He paused, glancing up at the policeman opposite. 'You've met my wife?' When Lorimer nodded he continued, 'Aye. Right. You'll know *why* then. Jan couldn't hack it any longer. And then when my sister died I gave all her money to my girl. She deserved it after putting up with that place all these years.'

190

'And your wife asked you to leave too?' Lorimer enquired.

'Asked?' the man laughed sourly. 'Oh, there was no asking. I was *told*.' He looked around the shabby room and waved a hand. 'See this? This is paradise on earth compared to what I had before.'

'And when Lucy died?' Solomon prompted, bringing Norman Yarwood back to the point.

'She fell to pieces. Wouldn't eat. Looked terrible, like she couldn't sleep.' His voice dropped to a conspiratorial whisper. 'I even thought she might do away with herself.'

There was a hush in the room as they digested this, then Lorimer broke the silence.

'But she carried on; painting, working with the other students?'

Yarwood shrugged. 'What else could she do?'

Lorimer drew out a piece of card from his inside pocket and placed it directly in the man's line of vision.

'Recognise him?'

Yarwood shook his head. 'No, but I've seen that picture before.'

'Oh?' Lorimer's eyebrows rose.

'*Crimewatch*.' Yarwood looked intently at Detective Chief Inspector Lorimer. 'That was you, wasn't it?'

'Yes,' Lorimer answered shortly.

'And d'you think this man – this one – killed my Jan?'

'It's a possibility.'

Lorimer briskly pocketed the picture.

'Aren't you going to ask me if I know of anybody who'd want to murder her?' said Yarwood.

Lorimer was about to reply but Solly broke in first.

'Why, do you?'

'No. But that's what they always ask, isn't it?'

'Who, Mr Yarwood?'

'Police. On the telly.' The man stood up abruptly and stuffed the handkerchief back into his jacket pocket. 'There was no one. No sane person could have had any reason to do what he did.'

Lorimer stood up and handed his card to Norman Yarwood.

'If there's anything else you want to tell us,' he said, then added, 'And we might have to talk to you again, sir.'

'Aye, but talking's no gonnae bring her back, is it?'

In two strides Norman Yarwood had reached the door and pulled it open. Lorimer and Solomon made their way out into the hall where Mrs Singh emerged from the shadows. Neither of them was surprised as the door slammed loudly behind them.

30

Art School Link in St Mungo's Murders
Exclusive by Martin Enderby

Police investigating the death of postgraduate student, Janet Yarwood, have not ruled out the possibility that her killer may also be responsible for the murders of three girls found in St Mungo's Park last year. Ms Yarwood, who was 29, had been a close associate of Lucy Haining, the second victim who was, like the others, brutally strangled and mutilated. The postgraduate student was found in her Garnethill flat on Wednesday after failing to turn up at the School of Art where she worked as a research assistant.

In a bizarre twist to the series of killings, it has been revealed that Dr Solomon Brightman of Glasgow University Psychology Department, who has been assisting police in his role as criminal profiler, was seriously assaulted in his own home only hours after interviewing Ms Yarwood. Neither Dr Brightman nor Chief Inspector William Lorimer, who is leading the murder inquiry, was available for comment. However, sources close to the investigation team indicated that a thorough questioning of students and staff at the School of Art is taking place.

Christopher Inglis, a fellow research student, told our reporter, 'We are all stunned by Janet's death. She was a quiet, hardworking artist with immense talent.' Meantime the taxi service which is a security measure for students travelling from the Postgraduate Centre at Bellahouston Park back to the Art School in the city centre has been extended for all female students travelling after dark, at the discretion of the Principal.

Leader comment page 14.

Lorimer rustled the pages furiously to see what the news editor had made of his refusal to channel information to the Press Office. As he expected there was harsh criticism of the police force and of himself in particular: 'Even with the help of a professional like Dr Brightman, the police appear no further forward in their search for this killer.'

Comparisons were made with the Yorkshire Ripper and statistics bandied about concerning the cost of mounting police operations. Lorimer's mouth was set in a grim line. At least there'd been a passing reference to that sore spot. Of course manpower cost money, and of course the Home Secretary would be under pressure to provide additional resources. Lorimer threw the paper down in disgust. It was all talk. There might be a public outcry but the Chief Constable's budget was unlikely to be stretched to provide extra manpower. The latest round of Home Office cuts had hit the force with a vengeance. The public was entitled to a continuation of the success of the Urban Policing Programme but now all areas of police work were seriously strapped for cash. Martin bloody Enderby should maybe give some space to that, thought Lorimer.

He was still on a high of fury after his telephone conversation with the reporter.

No, he wasn't about to reveal his sources.

No, he wouldn't say how he knew about Dr Brightman.

But did the Chief Inspector have any comment to make? The Chief Inspector was bloody well damned if he had but saved his expletives until he'd rung off.

How in hell's name had that reporter found out so much? What 'sources' in his investigation team had spoken to the Press? According to Alistair Wilson they were all as amazed as their Chief. Remembering Solomon's insinuations, Lorimer turned his thoughts towards the members of his team, then felt a surge of anger that he could begin to doubt them. Someone other than the student, Inglis, had spoken to Enderby, and he had to find out just who that someone was.

At least Solomon had been told to keep his mouth shut.

The psychologist was at HQ to discuss statistical data from his cross-checking of the house-to-house investigations but he listened in silence as Lorimer ranted on about the *Gazette*'s revelations.

'Wouldn't say how he knew it all! Bullshit!' Lorimer thumped the desk between them. 'You were right. Someone in here's been feeding them a line.'

Solomon stared past the Chief Inspector at a spot on the horizon. It was as if he hadn't heard a word. Disconcerted by his silence, Lorimer tried to catch the younger man's eye and failed. At last, however, Solly turned his head and looked straight at him. Lorimer took in the man's heightened colour and the way his lips parted to speak then closed helplessly. But it was the abject look of apology in his eyes that spoke volumes.

'*You?*' Lorimer exclaimed in disbelief. The psychologist nodded unhappily. Whatever Lorimer had expected, it certainly wasn't this. 'But why? How?' He broke off, then his expression hardened. 'I think you have some explaining to do.'

Solomon sighed, then spread his hands upwards in resignation.

'It seems I gave an interview to Enderby's girlfriend.'

'You *what?*'

Slowly Solomon unfolded the way he had been interviewed by Diane McArthur and the passing reference he had made to Lucy Haining.

'I'm sorry. It didn't seem like talking to the Press in quite the way you meant.'

Lorimer shook his head as if he still couldn't believe Solly's stupidity but then he suddenly leaned back, crossing his arms and gazing at the ceiling.

'Enderby's been doing his own investigating, has he?'

The policeman's voice was thoughtful. Solomon looked up, sensing the change of tone.

'His was one of the names Janet Yarwood gave me. It didn't mean much at the time. Apparently he'd been to see her at the House for an Art Lover.'

'Go on.'

The light of anger was gone from the pale blue eyes, and they had narrowed in speculation.

'He claimed the *Gazette* wanted to help mount a retrospective exhibition. At least that was his cover for talking to Janet Yarwood.'

'And what do you think?'

Solomon hesitated. 'His was one of the names on my list. Men
who might have known Lucy.'

'That was the list on your back-up disk?'

'The very one.'

Lorimer pushed back his chair and paced restlessly across the
room.

'And how did you find out that this McArthur woman was
Enderby's girlfriend?'

Solomon blushed again. 'I telephoned the *Gazette.*'

'And?'

'I was unhappy about the interview. She was too sweet and
wholesome about it all. So I checked up. There was no feature
on my work planned at all.'

Solomon sounded slightly aggrieved and Lorimer managed a thin
smile at what he presumed was the young man's vanity. Solomon's
next words dispelled this notion, however.

'The features editor at the *Gazette* seemed to think it was a mix-up
on my part. She said it wasn't Ms McArthur who'd been trying to
contact me, but Mr Enderby. She said Ms McArthur must have
been doing her boyfriend a favour. Actually,' – and here Solomon's
smile was faintly embarrassed – 'I don't think she believed I'd been
interviewed at all. I do believe she thought I was trying a bit of
self-publicity.'

Lorimer hooted derisively.

'You've got all the publicity you'll want now!'

'Yes,' Solomon assented vaguely but Lorimer could see his
mind was already elsewhere. The psychologist leaned forward
suddenly and shook his finger thoughtfully. 'But if Enderby *did*
know Lucy Haining, then maybe that's the reason for his sudden
interest in me.'

'OK, I'm with you on that,' Lorimer said, his eyes bright with
interest. A few things were beginning to make sense. 'But why would
Enderby . . . ?'

The question was left unfinished as Solomon nodded sagely.

'May I change the subject for a moment?'

He bent down to open his briefcase and extracted a sheaf of computer print-outs. Lorimer stood impatiently by his side as Solomon spread the sheets over his desk. The lines of print dazzled his eyes for a moment as Solomon ran his finger down a list of names and numbers. Suddenly he stopped in the middle of a page.

'There!'

Lorimer had scanned the list, briefly recognising the names of residents in the St Mungo's Heights house-to-house enquiries, but now he looked at the name on the list in astonishment. There, opposite an address on the seventh floor of block three, was the name: Martin Enderby.

For someone who had been anxious to speak to Lorimer so recently, Martin Enderby now seemed to be playing hard-to-get. No, he wasn't at his desk, the young man at the *Gazette* told the Chief Inspector. Sorry, there wasn't any note in today's diary to indicate where the reporter had gone. Did the Chief Inspector have his home phone number? Oh. Tried it already. Well, what about the Press Bar? The pleasant young male voice should have been reassuring but Lorimer's disquiet was intensifying. Okay, so a news reporter wasn't expected to be chained to his computer screen. Nevertheless, Lorimer had the feeling that Martin Enderby might be deliberately slipping out of his grasp.

A fruitless series of calls left WPC Annie Irvine scuttling down the corridor, her boss's wrath plainly heard from his open door.

'I want him in here *now*! And when he gets here *I* want to speak to him!'

Some time later, warrant tucked safely in his jacket pocket, Alistair Wilson led Solly down the back stairway that led to the yard, Lorimer's voice still ringing in their ears. As they hurried down, Alistair punched the swing doors aggressively. Solly glanced at the detective but his expression gave nothing away.

In the back of the Vauxhall Solly had the feeling that he was the criminal, seated as he was behind two police officers, Wilson and young Cameron, the new Detective Constable. This uncomfortable feeling was compounded by one of impending disaster. Instinctively he felt that Lorimer was haring off into yet another tangled thicket. And yet . . . how beguiling that Enderby should actually live in St Mungo's Heights. Did his flat face the park? Solly wondered.

Red lights stopped them at Charing Cross and the constable revved the engine. Wilson raised his eyes to heaven, turned and winked at Solly, a conspiratorial comment on the impatience of the young man behind the wheel. Solly tried to grin back but only managed a rueful smile. Then they were off again, the tyres squealing as the car shot forward.

Solly looked around him at the familiar landmarks as they passed by. He recognised an Asian restaurant he had visited, housed in what had once been a cinema. There was the Kelvin Hall, the Art Galleries, the Western Infirmary and now the car was swinging round towards the gates of St Mungo's Park. Solly raised his eyebrows briefly. The driver was clearly going to take a short cut through the park itself, despite the 20 mph limit. At once the tall blocks of St Mungo's Heights came into view and two pairs of eyes sought to calculate the seventh storey.

When the car screeched to a halt Solly was thrown forward on to his seat belt.

'Really, Constable!' Wilson remarked dryly, causing the youngster to colour up.

The security door only gave numbers and positions of the flats, not names, so Wilson pressed both 7L and 7R but there was no response from either. Systematically he tried the buttons for each level until he met with a response.

'Police.'

The one word provoked the deep croak of the buzzer releasing the door lock, then the three men pushed their way into the darkened hallway. It smelled of dampness but was free of the graffiti that so often decorated the walls of high-rise lobbies. The grey metal lift door shuddered open and they ascended noiselessly to the seventh floor.

Martin Enderby's front door was nondescript wood veneer with no glazing. A single Yale lock and a spyhole were the journalist's only security measures, apparently.

Wilson shook his head as the younger officer turned his shoulder suggestively towards the door.

'A wee bit of finesse, lad, if you please. It goes with the search warrant.'

The 'lad' stepped aside and Wilson drew something from an inside pocket and began to fiddle with the lock. Neither Solly nor the constable saw how it happened but there was a faint click and the door swung gently open.

At first Solly was sharply reminded of his return from hospital to the sight of his own ransacked home. Papers, books and clothes were strewn haphazardly around every room. The bedclothes lay in a heap and there were dirty dishes on any available surface as well as the floor. Cupboard doors hung open, revealing the journalist's wardrobe, and CD cases seemed to be breeding in every corner.

The lounge was slightly better. At least here most of the books were on shelves or stacked in piles. Solly moved to the window, sure what he would see.

Below him the road wound like a grey worm through the park. Miniature people and dogs were dotted over the grass, along pathways and disappearing behind clumps of laurel bushes and copses of huge dark firs. A flock of seagulls wheeled below his vision, screaming raucously then arcing out of sight. How often had he imagined a killer looking down from just such a vantage point? Again and again he had tried to enter that elusive mind, to sense the triumph of power, of ascendancy over the mere mortals scuttling below. Solly had reconstructed these crimes often within his own mind, seeing a shadowy figure drag the bloodstained corpses into the bushes; understanding the need to look down on the park where the bodies lay hidden. Solly sighed. It would have been so right, so satisfactory.

He turned back to face the room, swept his gaze over the shambles in the adjoining kitchen and shook his head sadly. What a pity.

'Right, then. Let's get started,' Wilson began.

'I fear there's little point.'

Solly's words stopped Wilson in his tracks.

'What?'

'You won't find anything here to point to a killer,' Solly went on resignedly.

Wilson gave him a kindly smile, and Solly recognised the man's sincere efforts to avoid being patronising.

'I think we'll just have a look round anyway, Dr Brightman,' the Detective Sergeant said firmly.

Solly shrugged and raised his eyebrows in acquiescence. Soon opening and shutting noises indicated that the two policemen were searching bedroom and bathroom respectively. The psychologist's eyes ran over the bookcase, automatically scanning the titles on the spines, divining the owner's predilections in literature and possibly a lot more besides.

Wilson was calling out advice on where to search but Solly didn't hear his words as his eyes swept over the books. He recognised several titles, his heart fluttering uncomfortably as he imagined what conclusion the investigating officers might draw. Psychology textbooks, criminology, pathology, they were all there. Solly's hand drew out one slim green volume and he gazed in dismay as he recognised a textbook on strangulation written by one of Rosie's colleagues at Glasgow University. The book fell open, an old envelope marking a page that was highlighted in yellow. He swallowed hard as he read the medical details describing how a victim had been strangled with a bicycle chain.

Martin sat in the interview room opposite the two detectives. The buzz he'd felt earlier that day batting questions from Chief Inspector Lorimer had disappeared. Talking on the telephone was quite a different matter from talking across this chipped Formica table. There was a cheap tin ashtray lying between them but it would remain empty. Martin didn't smoke. Briefly he wondered how many criminals had sat puffing anxiously as they sought to evade justice. His reporter's nose twitched with the scent of possible stories as he strove to assume a calmness he didn't feel and he was painfully aware of his dry throat. Why didn't they bring him some coffee? Didn't they always do that on TV? Well, they couldn't keep him in here, he was sure of that. Wasn't he?

Lorimer had refused to talk to the psychologist on his return to

Headquarters, choosing instead to listen to his detective sergeant's report. Things seemed to be falling into place now. He looked across at Enderby, taking in the pale yellow shirt and brightly patterned tie, seeing the long limbs stretched under the table, arms crossed in defiance of his authority. They often began like that, Lorimer knew.

'Mr Enderby,' he began, a politeness in his tone that they both knew was simply a veneer. 'I believe you visited Miss Janet Yarwood in the last few days?' Lorimer rustled some papers. 'February 27th, to be exact.'

Martin Enderby stared mulishly at the Chief Inspector. He might not answer any of his questions, Lorimer knew from bitter experience. Would he demand the presence of a lawyer? Sometimes the interview tape was peppered with *No comment.* Lorimer was relieved when Enderby decided to reply.

'I did pay a visit, yes.'

'Why was that, Mr Enderby?'

'I'm an investigative journalist. I was investigating the St Mungo's Murders.'

'And you interviewed Miss Yarwood?'

'Yes. She was a friend of Lucy Haining. I thought she might give me some angle on the dead student. We talked about the possibility of an exhibition of Lucy's jewellery.'

'I see.' Lorimer's voice sounded as though in fact he saw a great deal more. 'Were you yourself acquainted with Miss Haining at all?'

Martin appeared suddenly disconcerted, not by the implications of the question but by the blue gaze that fixed on him so powerfully.

'Me? I'd never even heard of her until she was dead.'

'What did you study at university, sir?' Wilson was questioning him now, his face a polite mask, the voice almost deferential.

'Well, journalism, of course.'

'Not psychology, then?'

'As a matter of fact I started out with psychology but I switched courses at the end of my first year.'

'Stood you in good stead, did it?' Lorimer asked.

'Yes, it did. It still does. A bit of insight into human behaviour always helps,' Martin retorted.

'*That* will be why you have so many books on the subject.' Lorimer spoke lightly, as if he'd suddenly solved a problem, but the tone wasn't lost on any of them. Martin didn't reply, so Lorimer continued, 'Pathology too. You take a special interest in how to strangle people?'

They saw a pulse in the journalist's throat begin to throb with anger.

'Now, look here –'

'No,' the voice cut in,' *you* look here, Mr Enderby. Investigative journalism is one thing but it seems to me that you had a great deal of knowledge about the St Mungo's Murders that didn't come from the police Press Officer.'

'Of course I had!' Martin thumped his fists on the table as he leaned forward. 'I read up every bloody thing I could find on the subject. Good journalists do, you know!'

'Really.'

Lorimer's tone indicated that he was unconvinced.

'Yes, really!' Martin ran his hand through his fair hair. 'You don't think *I* had anything to do with the murders?'

His exclamation was met with silence. Lorimer was writing something down and the detective sergeant looked across at Martin, his bland gaze never wavering. The enormity of the situation seemed to be settling on the journalist and he looked around him in panic. Now both men sat staring intently at him. Martin took a deep breath.

'Are there any traces?' he asked.

'Sir?' the detective sergeant feigned puzzlement.

'Traces. You know. To test for DNA.'

'Why do you ask?'

The Chief Inspector had his fingertips together under his chin but his stare never faltered.

'Because if you have, then you can do tests on me right now! I have done nothing wrong whatsoever and you have an obligation to eliminate me from your, your, *enquiries.*'

Enderby loaded the word with meaning. Lorimer wondered if

he'd make anything of it. The Press Association might have them up for harassment.

'I take it you had a warrant to search my flat?'

'Of course, sir,' Wilson replied, smiling a thin-lipped smile. 'I see housework's not your strong point.'

'That's hardly a chargeable offence!'

'No, sir, it's not.'

'You gave a brief statement during our house-to-house enquiry, did you not?' asked Lorimer.

'Yes. There wasn't anything to say. I saw nothing until your guys had the scene of crime cordoned off.'

'Good view from your window?'

'Yes, actually. Though I don't spend a lot of time standing looking out. I've usually got better things to do.'

'Where were you on the nights of October 21st, 25th and November 3rd, Mr Enderby?'

The man's face became quite blank for a moment. Was he considering what he had said in his statement to the police that winter night on his doorstep? Everyone in the flats would have talked about it when they'd met up in the lift, Lorimer was willing to bet. They'd maybe even have compared the questions asked, wondered if the police thought the murderer was being harboured by a neighbour. Speculation always ran rife. And sometimes to the advantage of the police.

Lorimer's blue eyes were still turned on him.

'I'm sorry, I can't remember off-hand. I'd need to check last year's diary. No. Wait a minute. The third girl. I was at a club with friends the night before . . . well, the night it happened. We got the news first thing and my piece was in the earliest edition.'

Lorimer folded his arms and regarded the journalist speculatively. He'd rattled his cage all right. But he didn't need Solomon Brightman to tell him he wasn't sitting across the table from a multiple killer. Certain things had fitted nicely but Enderby seemed to be speaking the truth. Lorimer was pretty experienced at hearing the truth. Also, he doubted whether that fair hair flopping over his forehead could have grown from a cropped cut in a mere four months. Perhaps he'd send him to the doc for testing all the same. See if any fibres or traces matched.

'Excuse us a moment.'

Lorimer motioned Wilson to follow him and they left the journalist alone except for the uniformed officer standing sentinel at the doorway.

'I can't hold him, he's not being cautioned,' Lorimer said. 'But at least he's co-operative about the forensics. I'd like to have a mouth swab and a blood test done. Bastard knows too damned much for my liking. Nosied into something he should have left alone.'

'Dr Brightman said right off we hadn't found the killer,' remarked Wilson casually.

'Oh? Did he give a reason?'

'Said Enderby was totally disorganised. We're looking for Mr Neat-and-Tidy, according to Brightman.' Wilson paused then asked, 'So, what's to do? Tell him to clear off or give him the kind of fright that'll make him want to cover the ladies' page in future?'

Lorimer glanced at his watch.

'Let's have a think about this over coffee, shall we?' Lorimer smiled at his colleague, indicating the way upstairs to his office. There was plenty of time before he needed to be home preparing for George Phillips's big night. He'd let the journalist sweat for a while in the interview room then politely ask his co-operation in a series of tests. To eliminate him from their enquiries. Tomorrow they'd stick a certain young DC on his tail for a while, just to see the company he kept. They weren't finished with this one yet.

31

If he couldn't get any more on Brightman and the murders, then he could switch his attention to police methods, thought Martin viciously. He felt soiled by the contact with the interrogation room, with the specimens he'd had to give the Police Surgeon and, yes, if he was honest, he felt downright shit scared. Nothing in his journalistic life, however seedy, had prepared him for the personal experience of being a suspect in such a crime. In his worst nightmares, Martin could never have imagined the reality of being imprisoned in that ill-lit room, a police guard barring his escape while the power of these officers took decisions out of his hands. He even wondered if he'd be cautioned, charged, put in a cell and left to rot. The mind played strange illogical tricks when fear took over. Latterly there had been co-operation of sorts between the police Press Office and the newsdesk in covering stories. But now, Martin's editor had snarled at him, he'd alienated the lot of them. And what had he got to show for it? Jangled nerves, a splitting headache and an assignment to cover some Glasgow councillors on the fiddle.

The journalist kicked his chair against the desk and loped out of the open-plan office, ignoring the raised eyebrows that glanced his way. He took the lift down to the ground floor and strode out into the street. Automatically he turned left and swung into the Press Bar. He might as well face the jibes sooner than later.

'Hi, man. They let you out then, did they?'

Davey was leaning back in his chair. It looked as if he had been craning his neck to see the television mounted on the wall. The All Blacks tour was on and Scotland's players were facing their turn for annihilation.

'Get the man a beer, Eddie,' Paul from the sports desk was grinning over his shoulder, 'he's got a bad taste to wash away.'

'Cheers, Paul.'

Martin sank down beside the photographer and waited for Eddie the barman to bring his drink. Davey was regarding him quizzically.

'You all right, man?'

Martin nodded and swallowed. Did he really look as shaken as he felt? A swift glance around reassured him that Diane at least wasn't there to witness his humiliation.

'What did they ask you?'

Davey was watching the rugby but threw the question over his shoulder. Martin took the beer from Paul and swigged it down thirstily before he replied.

'Easier to say what they didn't ask. Wanted to know about my *hair*, of all things. Christ, what goes on with these guys? Seems they have plenty of traces to test for matches or something. But to think they thought that *I* had something to do with these girls.'

He drank again, looking down into the glass to avoid anyone's eyes.

'What exactly have they got, really? I mean that fire must've finished it all off.' Davey's voice was scornful. 'Oh come on boys, that was pathetic,' he added as yet another scrum collapsed.

'Well, I wasn't exactly taken into Chief Inspector Lorimer's confidence,' Martin began, 'but it's obvious they've got something.' Davey nodded, swinging back and forward in his chair. Martin went on, 'If you ask me, the fact that I live in St Mungo's Heights was the main reason they had me in. And the fact that I'd been doing a bit of sleuthing on my own.'

'Oh yeah? Sherlock Enderby? Nah. Doesn't sound right.'

Davey's grin suddenly seemed to defuse the whole situation and for the first time that day Martin managed to raise a smile. The photographer finished his beer and slowly whirled round in his chair.

'Tell you what, Marts. How about we go to the Ashoka for a carry out and take it back to your place?' Martin shrugged as Davey added, 'Can't bear to watch the sight of blood any more. You know what a sensitive soul I am.' A roar of disgust had gone up from the Press men watching the rugby. Scotland were being well and truly trounced.

'Okay. A tandoori might just settle my guts.'

'Right, then.'

Davey clapped him on the shoulder and they set off for the car park in the next street where Martin had left his car.

A pungent aroma met them as they pushed open the doors of the Ashoka and headed for the carry out counter. There was already a buzz of voices in the restaurant; Friday-night diners straight from work. Davey and Martin had been in this celebrated curry house plenty of times and knew the menus backwards.

'How're you doin', Ali?' Davey addressed the Indian behind the counter.

'Hallo, there. How are you?' The man's Glasgow accent was as thick as Davey's own, not a trace of the Orient in his voice.

Eventually, weighed down with two chicken curries, fried rice and naan bread, the two men set off for St Mungo's Heights. It had started to rain and the rush-hour traffic was becoming heavier. Still, thought Martin, it was the end of a shitty day and he still had Diane to look forward to. The thought of her slim body cheered him up immensely.

Martin parked in the space by the shrubbery. He had reversed in, ready for the journey across town later on. Davey was already out and heaving his bag of cameras after him.

'C'mon, that smell's gettin' round my heart, as my granny would have said.'

Martin pushed his key into the lock and made for the lifts. Once inside the flat, he ignored the mess on the floor, headed straight for the kitchen and returned with two huge platters and a couple of forks. Davey sank into the sofa, pushing aside the empty McEwans cans with his boot as Martin spilled the curries carefully onto the plates.

'Right. Doon heid, up paws, thank God we've jaws,' the journalist intoned the old Scots Grace with relish.

This would wipe the taste of that interview room well and truly from his mouth.

32

'Have you seen my cufflinks?'
    'Which ones?'
    'The silver ones. You know. The square Rennie Mackintosh ones you gave me.'
    'Oh, those. In your top drawer.'
    Maggie paused, the eyeliner brush held in mid-air, as she regarded her husband's reflection in the mirror. He was still a good-looking man, she thought to herself. Lorimer's dress shirt was open, revealing a lean and desirable body. His thick hair, still damp from the shower, fell boyishly to one side. Maggie suppressed a sigh. It was so unfair that some men improved with age whereas almost every woman struggled in vain to keep some vestige of her youthful looks.
    With renewed determination and a steady hand she outlined her eyes. The magazines all urged you to keep looking good for your man, she thought, with the veiled threat that he'd trade you in for a younger model if you didn't keep up to date. Maggie normally dismissed this as a cynical marketing ploy on the part of the cosmetics companies but tonight, as she glanced at Lorimer who was concentrating on putting his cufflinks in the right way round, Maggie wondered if *she* would still be around on *his* sixtieth.
    Her new black spangled jacket lay on the bed. It had cost a packet but she wouldn't let her conscience spoil the evening. Shaking her curls as if to dismiss the thoughts that irritated her like so many bad imps, she then sprayed herself liberally in a mist of Chanel No. 5. She would enjoy this party tonight.
    'Ready?'
    Lorimer stood behind her, checking his bow tie in the dressing table mirror.

'And waiting,' she replied then stood up and extended her arm towards him.

Lorimer met her eyes, smiled then took her hand and kissed her fingertips.

'Your carriage awaits, ma'am.'

Maggie scooped up the glittering jacket and smiled back, warmed by the approval in his blue gaze. A whole night together! This was going to be fun.

The hotel was crowded when they arrived. Maggie slipped off to the ladies room to renew her lipstick and Lorimer stood gazing into the groups of black-suited policemen, finally locating the huge figure of George himself. The Superintendent was laughing uproariously at something as Lorimer approached.

'Ah, Bill, come and have a drink.'

They pushed their way through to the bar without difficulty. The guest of honour parted the waves of dinner jackets like Moses, thought Lorimer, and grinned at the big man towering over the bar. George Phillips might have his faults but he certainly made his presence felt.

'Thanks,' said Lorimer, raising his glass. 'Good health.' And as an afterthought: 'Happy birthday.'

George chuckled. 'Happy retirement, you mean!'

The Detective Superintendent swallowed his malt thoughtfully then looked over Lorimer's shoulder, gazing into the middle distance.

'Where do they go? Sixty years!' His eyes returned to his DCI and crinkled into a smile. 'Still there's life in the old dog yet. And,' he added, 'I won't be out of your hair entirely.'

'Oh?'

'Wait and see. Got a few surprises up my sleeve.'

Lorimer raised his eyebrows as though this were news to him but rumours had filtered down that George was likely to chair a new advisory panel into Drug Related Crime, the Chief Constable's pet that gobbled up so much of their budget. That was fair enough but he just hoped that George would remember their stretched resources when it came down to murder inquiries.

'Happy birthday, George!'

There was Maggie shimmering in that new evening outfit, kissing the big man on both cheeks.

'Maggie! Ah, the sight of you does an old man's heart good!'

Maggie giggled while Lorimer scrutinised her. She did look good, he thought, eyeing the black silk hugging his wife's curves. There was a sparkle about her that wasn't just an illusion created by the spangly blazer. It made Lorimer feel suddenly reckless.

'How about a bottle of champagne?'

Maggie looked momentarily surprised then nodded. 'Great idea. After all, you've got plenty to celebrate.' She turned to George and twinkled mischievously at him.

'Ah, yes. Freedom. Slippers by the fire. I'll think of you all when I'm hacking my way around the golf course.'

'Quite right, too,' Lorimer heard Maggie declare as he turned back to the bar to order a bottle of Möet.

As he raised the fluted glass to his lips, Lorimer couldn't help wishing that they were celebrating more than George Phillips's retirement. He'd have bought a crate of the stuff to toast their success in finding the St Mungo's killer. He was never very far away from Lorimer's thoughts. Somewhere on the edge of his mind hovered a shadowy figure with cropped dark hair swinging a silver bicycle chain. The voice on the *Crimewatch* tape played over and over in his mind. 'Can you guess . . .'

'Can you guess where George is going on holiday?' Maggie's voice broke into his thoughts.

'Where?'

'The Algarve, of course. All those golf courses.' She put her head to one side. 'We've never been there.'

'Would you want to go?'

'Not to play golf, but . . .'

Her voice drifted off and her eyes grew dreamy, no doubt picturing white Moorish houses smothered with purple bougain-villaea, thought Lorimer.

'Just to have a holiday,' she finished lamely.

Lorimer poured more champagne into their glasses then grinned wickedly.

'On one condition,' he said.

'What?'

'That you pack *this* into your suitcase.'

He gave a gentle tug on the strap of her dress, feeling the weight of her breasts underneath. Maggie raised her glass in a salute.

Just at that moment there came a series of thumps and the Master of Ceremonies bawled out the command for dinner. Lorimer was glad that he and Maggie were not at the top table with George, who had included the Chief Constable and the Lady Provost among his guests. The Lorimers were at table two, he knew, with four other couples. He saw Alistair Wilson and his wife Betty, a professional cook who was as plump and cheery as he was slim and debonair. Also at the table was DCI Mitchison, an officer from George's previous Division. Lorimer had come across Mitchison a couple of times at police seminars. He was one of these men who always did things by the book, Lorimer remembered. He didn't drink and could be relied upon to bang on about delegating authority. Lorimer had taken an instant dislike to the man, who also had a much younger blonde in tow. They were already standing behind their seats as Lorimer ushered Maggie forward, squinting at the place cards and hoping he wouldn't be next to the unknown blonde. He noticed, however, with surprise and not a little pleasure, that Ms Rosaleen Fergusson's name was to his right. Good old Rosie! So long as she didn't put the diners off with any professional anecdotes! Lorimer grinned then wondered who would be partnering the lovely pathologist this evening.

He didn't have long to find out. He heard the wolf whistles first. Then Rosie appeared dressed in an outrageously short, white, strapless number, her hair caught up in a Grecian knot. With her was Dr Solomon Brightman. Introductions were made, ladies ushered into their seats, and Lorimer heard himself make polite small talk with Betty Wilson on his left, who was already enthusing over the menu.

All conversations were hushed as the Selkirk Grace was given by the Chief Constable and Lorimer had a moment to reflect. Solly and Rosie. Well, well. He caught the pathologist's eye and made a discreet thumbs-up sign.

The meal passed in a pleasant haze of passable wine, good food and better company than a Detective Chief Inspector usually enjoys. On the opposite side of the table his wife and Solly were in animated conversation; meanwhile Rosie was telling Alistair Wilson about her visits to Rwanda. Betty was explaining the use of herbs in cookery to the couple on her left, leaving Lorimer's mind free to wander.

It wandered through St Mungo's Park in the back of an old ambulance. The driver wore gloves, just as Alison Girdley had described. Was there anyone in the passenger seat? Lorimer drank the rest of his glass of Vouvray and tried hard to imagine a female beside the cropped-haired driver. A live female wearing a blonde wig. Kanekelon. Japanese hair fibre.

He looked appraisingly at the women around the table. Mitchison's companion had swept her platinum locks into a huge wave at the side. More artifice than art, thought Lorimer, comparing the young woman with Rosie's elegance. Who would ever have imagined that these slim hands with their pearly painted nails could wield such an effective scalpel? Appearance and reality. Belatedly he wondered what DCI Mitchison's young friend did for a living.

The driver had stopped now and come round to open the rear doors. Lorimer fast-forwarded the scenes in his mind. There would have been the need for a hose, or a scrub-down of some kind. No trace of bloodstains had been found in the burnt-out ambulance. It would have been cleaned up thoroughly. To rid it of evidence and to prepare for his predations on other innocents. Little boys. There was no doubt now that the paedophile who had lured children into his 'van' was also an accomplished killer. He'd offered them sweeties. And threats. Wee Kevin Sweeney had painted a picture of a menacing creature who also had the power to beguile. Had he beguiled Lucy? And Janet Yarwood, who had loved the younger artist? At some point Lucy had become involved with this man and his predilection for little boys. That she had known all about it and used her knowledge as blackmail was one theory Lorimer was anxious to prove. The large sums of cash paid into her account had been spent lavishly on gold, silver and precious stones. Lorimer and Solly had built up a picture of the red-haired art student whose determination to succeed in the world of jewellery design had cost her dearly in the end. He cast his mind back to the exotic arm

213

bangles and shining collars that were to be exhibited posthumously at the degree show. The spoils of blackmail.

'Don't you think so, Bill?'

Rosie was smiling at him, quite aware of his discomfiture. She knew fine he'd been away in a dream.

'Just run that past me again, Rosie?'

Lorimer wasn't quite as sober as he'd have liked but his wits weren't totally scattered yet.

'The double-doctor system. We have twice the work but twice the advantages when it comes into court.'

'Undoubtedly.'

Lorimer picked up on the thread of conversation, a perennial topic for Scottish pathologists who, like so many other professionals this side of the border, were convinced of the superiority of their system.

The wine waiter came between them, replenishing glasses, and when he'd gone Lorimer found to his relief that Rosie had renewed her conversation with her other dinner guests. Lorimer laid down his knife and fork. He'd hardly touched the sirloin steak. Perhaps the champagne had spoiled his appetite. And all that wine, a small voice reminded him.

'Excuse me, is Detective Inspector Lorimer here?'

All eyes at table two turned to the red-coated MC who stood holding a piece of hotel notepaper.

'I'm Chief Inspector Lorimer.'

'A phone call for you, sir.'

The paper was delivered and the MC marched away, duty done.

'Excuse me, won't be a moment.'

Lorimer got up, smiled reassuringly at Maggie, and threaded his way through the tables to the hotel lobby. There was only a number on the paper. Lorimer recognised a South Side code but beyond that it was unfamiliar. The call was answered by Norman Yarwood. His voice was pitched higher than Lorimer remembered, a sure sign of nerves.

'There's something I've found.'

'Oh? What would that be, then?'

Lorimer tried to keep his manner light but already he could feel the tension gripping his chest as Norman Yarwood revealed his new information. He'd been going through Janet's things, sorting them out. That's when he'd found the photograph of Lucy. It had been taken in Janet's flat. And in the background, he'd noticed, were the missing pictures.

'I don't suppose you know who . . . ?'

Lorimer's face twisted into a grimace as he heard the reply. Once more he imagined the back of the killer's dark head. For a moment he'd hoped to catch a glimpse of the face.

'Yes. Well, thank you Mr Yarwood. I'm most grateful for this information. Could you bring the photograph down to Head-quarters first thing tomorrow?'

Lorimer nodded into the receiver as the man gave him his assurance, apologising yet again for any inconvenience. As Lorimer rang off he thought about the big red-haired man in his Pollokshaws bedsit sifting through the few reminders of his talented daughter. His anger at the delay in finding this nugget of gold suddenly evaporated. How would he feel if it had been his own daughter?

Lorimer stood quite still for a moment. There was no flash of light or sense of euphoria. Just the terrible clarity that comes to a mind sharpened by excessive alcohol. He knew with an unshakeable certainty that the killer of this man's child was very close to being brought to justice.

'Bill?'

Maggie was by his side, looking anxious.

'It's okay. Just some information. Let's go and see if there's any pudding left.'

He laced Maggie's fingers through his and stumbled slightly as they moved towards the doorway, smiling an apology. She shook her head despairingly. Whatever had called her husband away was not as trivial as he was making out, not from the deep furrows etched around his brow.

The pudding had indeed been served, a pink mousse topped with a single out-of-season raspberry. Lorimer wolfed down the mousse, his appetite suddenly restored, and began to chat to his fellow dinner guests.

Solly wondered why Lorimer had suddenly become the life and soul of their table. Obviously it had something to do with that phone call. But what? Lorimer gave no sign that he intended taking the psychologist into his confidence and seemed content instead to push the party along.

The meal long past, the speeches thankfully over, Lorimer watched the Superintendent rip paper off a stack of gifts and hold each item aloft amid much clapping and a few ribald comments. There were the usual 'proper' retirement presents, including several boxes of Edinburgh crystal, but other less conventional tokens had also crept in. China mugs with lewd comments, potions promising to improve everything from George's golf swing to his sex life and, last of all, wrapped in shiny silver paper, a 'See-you-Jimmy' hat.

There were cries of 'Put it on, George!' and the Superintendent made a great play of smoothing down the false red wig topped with its tartan tammy. Roars of laughter rang out as George gave a wiggle and sketched a pas de bas. Then the hat was tossed around the crowd. Lorimer pulled it on and gave a bow, then it was snatched off and passed to the desk sergeant who swept it on over his military crew cut.

'Suits you!'

'Better'n that suede head!'

Jeers rang out as the sergeant capered around. Lorimer was watching the antics with everyone else when for some strange reason the whole tableau seemed to freeze. The red wig blurred in front of his eyes and for a moment there was ringing in his ears. Then the vision cleared and Lorimer searched around for the dark-bearded face of Solomon. The psychologist was watching him intently. Lorimer jerked his head in the direction of the hotel lounge and the two men withdrew unnoticed from the fun and games.

'Your phone call?' Solly's query was eager but polite.

Lorimer shook his head, still dazed by the revelation.

'It's not that. Though I've got some crucial new information. I've just seen our killer.'

'Through there?'

Solly's jaw dropped in astonishment as he pointed back towards the reception hall.

'In here,' Lorimer tapped his head. 'Christ! I've been looking down the wrong end of the bloody telescope! All this time we've assumed that our man answers to the description the Girdley girl gave us. But it's the wrong way round!'

'I'm sorry. I don't follow you.'

'Kanekelon!'

'What?'

'Japanese hair fibre. A wig. A bloody See-you-Jimmy!'

Solly shook his head. It sounded like the ravings of a drunk man. But there was a chilling sanity in the policeman's expression.

'Don't you see?' Lorimer's excitement was mounting. 'The short cropped hair. That was how he appeared to his victims. And in the dark. It's not a disguise.'

'I still don't see . . .'

'He wears a wig! I mean *all the time*. That's the disguise . . . his normal everyday appearance. Not the other way around. Don't ask me why. Maybe it's – what's that disease called? The one that the princess in Monaco had?'

'Alopecia,' Solly answered automatically, then added, 'How can you be sure?' One look at Lorimer's face was all the answer he needed. 'Oh, dear God,' Solly breathed at last.

It was as if the profile that had been theory for so long had become embodied and sat there between them. Solly felt weak. There always had to have been a reason for the savagery behind the killings. Even the most calculating of murderers would never have committed such butchery unless a deep force had driven him on. The lack of hair. The scalpings. Some strange vengeance.

'Come on.'

Lorimer was standing up now, smoothing down his dinner jacket.

'Where?'

'HQ. Get another warrant. Those traces won't have been analysed yet. It'll take at least another couple of days. But I can't wait that long. I want him in custody now.'

'Enderby?'

Lorimer nodded, recalling Enderby's fair hair flopping over his forehead. His heart began to pound. They'd interviewed him and let him go. Where was Enderby now?

33

There was barely time for a garbled explanation to Rosie before the two men left the hotel in the first available taxi. The street gleamed wet under the sodium lights as the black cab curved effortlessly around in the direction of police headquarters. Maggie Lorimer was left gaping in disbelief as the blonde pathologist took her arm and led her back to the party.

If the desk sergeant was surprised to see Detective Chief Inspector Lorimer in full evening clothes, accompanied by Solomon Brightman, he didn't show it. Expecting the unexpected had long since become part of the job.

Lorimer took the stairs two at a time, Solomon almost running in his wake to keep up.

'What do you propose?'

Solly looked uncertain.

'Get another warrant. Shouldn't take more than a couple of hours even at this time. The Deputy Fiscal will be glad to have his night brightened up, I'm sure,' Lorimer grinned.

Solly nodded, remembering the last time Lorimer had waited for a warrant to search that flat in Garnethill. There was always a Fiscal and a Sheriff on duty through the night. Crime didn't keep office hours.

'There's not much point going back to George's bash, now. Anyway,' he added, 'Maggie'd kill me. She was really looking forward to an uninterrupted night out.'

Solly thought of the woman's face as they had hustled off from the hotel. Sheer disbelief might well turn to disappointed anger. Would Rosie be like that? he wondered. Rosie Fergusson, who spent her working life, scalpel in hand, out in the wilds of Rwanda or Glasgow parks. What might it be like being married to her? Solly's mind wandered over the prospect. Her laughing smile and that deliciously short white dress chased his thoughts from the squeamish side of her profession to how he might have spent the rest of the night. His sympathies went out to Maggie Lorimer.

The phone never seemed to be out of Lorimer's hand for the next hour as the team was rallied yet again for the search to come. St Mungo's Heights had, of course, been tried. There was nobody at the other end of the phones. That disembodied voice on the tape was not going to make itself heard again.

'Pity,' Lorimer remarked. 'The voice match would have made helpful evidence. Mind you, it took fifteen months of painstaking work to analyse the voice of the Yorkshire Ripper tape. And at the end of the day it wasn't him at all.'

The *Gazette* security man was sorry, he couldn't help. Nobody was left in the building. Where was Enderby?

'Diane McArthur?'

'Could be. Have we got a number?'

Solomon blushed and produced her card from his wallet.

'Of course, your book interview.'

Lorimer didn't glance at the psychologist but the sarcasm cut like a knife.

The phone rang on and on. Just as Lorimer was about to hang up, the ringing tone stopped and he waited for the ubiquitous answering machine to roll out its message. He was wrong.

'Please, who is it?' A girl's voice whispered. Lorimer stiffened. This wasn't a woman disturbed from slumber. She sounded ill.

'Chief Inspector Lorimer. Miss McArthur?'

'Oh, please help me. Please, somebody help me.'

'Is Martin Enderby . . . ?'

'He's gone.'

There was a pause and Lorimer heard the weak sobs as the girl tried to control herself.

'What happened?'

'He . . . I think he's hurt . . . the knife . . .' There was another pause and Lorimer could hear a choked sob. 'Please, could somebody help me?'

'Miss McArthur, I'm sending officers over right away. Just stay there. Can you open the door when they arrive?' Lorimer's voice was gentle and reassuring.

'I think so. I don't know.'

The voice faltered again and Lorimer immediately imagined blood loss of some kind weakening the girl.

'Help's on its way. Won't be long. I'm going to ring off now but if you need to talk to me ring this number.'

There was a lengthy interval during which Lorimer gave Diane his number and she, in her weakened state, found pen and paper and took it down. He then took only a split second to kill the phone and redial. Solly listened as Lorimer barked orders. Diane McArthur wouldn't be alone for long.

At last the warrant arrived at HQ and the two men bundled out to the waiting Rover. The radio would keep them in contact with the woman DC who had been mustered to assist the young journalist.

Diane McArthur was being helped into an ambulance as Lorimer and the psychologist approached her West End maisonette. Her head and shoulders were covered by a blanket and a WPC had her arms round her.

'Chief Inspector,' the WPC began.

Lorimer stepped up into the ambulance with the two women.

'Just a couple of minutes.'

He sat opposite Diane while Solomon stood outside. Diane McArthur raised her white face and slowly pulled off the blanket. Her long dark hair had been hacked off leaving a jagged, spiky mess and there was a deep wound running down one side of her neck.

'Martin Enderby?' Lorimer enquired.

Diane's eyes widened in horror and she jerked her head up painfully.

'No! Martin tried to stop him. He just went berserk.'

'Then who?'

'Davey.'

'Where are they now?' he demanded.

'I don't know. They went in Martin's car. He had that knife.' Her voice tailed off into gasping sobs.

'When was this?'

'About half an hour before you phoned, I think.'

Lorimer made a swift calculation. That call had been made nearly an hour ago. They could be anywhere in the city by now. Or out of it.

'Where have they gone, Diane? Think. Where could they be?'

Her sobs were apparently ignored by Lorimer who leaned over the girl, persistent in obtaining this information from her. She swallowed hard.

'I don't know. I told your policewoman. He, he told Martin to put his bag in the car.'

'What bag?'

'His cameras and stuff.' She paused tearfully. 'He never went anywhere without them.'

'Then what? Try to remember exactly what he said.'

The girl's face worked for a few moments then she shook her head.

'All I can remember is Martin telling him to leave me alone, then he was being forced out of the house. I don't remember. Honestly. I think I must have passed out.'

Lorimer nodded. It made sense. The girl had sounded ghastly when he had made that call. She'd surely have made it to a phone sooner if she'd been able to.

In a flash he was out of the ambulance and motioning to the attendant that he was free to go to the hospital. Solomon followed him back to the Rover where orders were given over the radio.

Lorimer looked around him into the darkness. It was now well after three in the morning, that barren time when the soul is at its lowest ebb, the streets deserted save for the police presence. It was a respectable neighbourhood, this. The row of yuppie maisonettes faced a red sandstone church built in the Victorian tradition of mock Gothic vaults and slender spires. Beside him, Solomon shivered. They hadn't stopped to take their coats from George Phillips's party. The warmth and fun of the Superintendent's big night seemed days rather than hours ago.

'Are you going in?' Solomon indicated Diane's house.

'No. Let the boys do it. No need for me there. Besides, looks like we'll have other fish to fry.' He frowned, seeing Solly shiver again. 'You want to go on home? I could get you a squad car.'

Solomon shook his head. Lorimer knew that many of his questions and theories had been answered but the psychologist might still feel an overwhelming need to confront the man whose shadow had fallen over so many lives.

He had a warrant in his pocket. A warrant he'd been going to use to search Enderby's flat once more. He'd just have to bend the rules a little.

The car swept up to the black tower that was St Mungo's Heights. Lorimer was suddenly aware of his incongruous evening clothes as uniformed officers swarmed over the place.

Davey Baird's room was exactly as Solomon had said it would be. To the casual, untrained eye, it was the epitome of minimalist chic. The floor was a bare sweep of pale, polished beech, the only warm colour in the room. Metal lamps hung in rows from the grey ceiling. A steel stereo system dominated one corner. The sofa was black leather with a silken throw the colour of pewter draped over the back, the shades of white and grey echoing the black and white photographs on the wall in their clip frames. He caught Solomon looking at the pictures, then at Lorimer. They were studies of redskin warriors. Lorimer's eyes widened and saw the psychologist give a fleeting smile of satisfaction. He continued his examination. The room appeared to be waiting for a long-absent presence to return. There were no signs of the usual clutter of everyday living: no papers lying on the dark ash table, only a lump of porous rock and a white porcelain bowl that gleamed like a ghost in the subdued lamplight.

They knew without looking that the uncurtained window gave a panoramic view of St Mungo's Park. They had already been so close. Lorimer moved into the hall and Solomon followed him through to where they knew the bedroom would be. This, unlike Martin Enderby's bedroom six floors below, was split into two rooms. The tiny bedroom held little other than a cabin bed and a set of drawers with a sliding wardrobe against one wall. It was predictably neat. Lorimer pushed open the connecting door. The other room was totally dark. There was the click of a light switch then the room was swathed in eerie red light.

'His darkroom,' Lorimer nodded, and both men slowly entered the photographer's inner sanctum. Several large machines dominated the floor space.

'Oh, my God!'

Solomon's hand flew to his mouth in horror as the sight met their eyes. On a glass shelf above a sink were small heaps of hair. The congealed blood had left brown stains that looked like varnish carelessly spilled on the glass.

For a few moments they stood transfixed by what they saw. Lorimer's gorge rose as he looked from left to right. Black, auburn, blonde and grey. Four bloodied scalps. A mental image of the wreck of humanity he had seen fixed itself in his brain and he struggled to remember the thin, gaunt face of Janet Yarwood.

Lorimer broke the silence with a long sigh.

'In here, boys.'

He spoke softly as if they were in the presence of unhappy spirits that might somehow be frightened away. The scene-of-crime officer hovered outside in the hall and Lorimer nodded towards the darkroom. The painstaking work of fingerprinting would now begin.

Lorimer stood at the window gazing out over the city lights that twinkled so innocently in the distance.

'They'll find it all here,' he said, almost to himself. 'Even traces of kanekelon.'

Solomon looked at the detective. Standing there in his evening clothes Lorimer seemed in no hurry now to be off and apprehend the killer. Instead a quiet calm had taken over.

'Shouldn't we be doing something?' he asked.

Lorimer turned with a weary smile. 'Oh, I think we'll be doing plenty before long. Once we know where they've gone.'

Solomon didn't speak but he chewed his lips anxiously. Then Lorimer's radio crackled into life and suddenly the Chief Inspector was alert. The tinny voice on the radio came through clearly.

'Got him, sir. The car's been spotted in Paisley Road, turning up towards Bellahouston Park.'

'The House for an Art Lover?' Solomon interrupted.

Lorimer and he exchanged glances briefly.

'Scramble air support. We need them to home in on the park. We have reason to believe he may have gone in there.'

'The road by the ski slopes,' added Solomon.

'Hear that? Good. We're going that way now. Should be there within ten minutes.'

34

Martin Enderby felt the pain in his right knee as he tried to keep the Peugeot at a steady speed. That stab had come as he'd tried to wrest the knife from Davey's hands. The knife from Diane's kitchen. Then, as he'd fallen to the floor yelling, he'd seen that awful slashing and hacking. Diane's screams still echoed in his brain.

Events had happened so quickly that he'd had no time to think. Sweat had made his jersey damp under the armpits and he was desperate to urinate. He tried not to look at the man on his left. The man he'd once thought of as a talented, funny guy. The man he'd assumed was his friend.

His thoughts went back to their meal together, how Davey had leaned his long body back in his armchair. The yellow stains of curry were all that had been left in the foil containers.

'See that inspector,' Davey had begun, 'did he say if he'd found anything in here?'

Martin had opened his eyes in surprise then. 'Jesus Christ, how could he find anything here? I've got nothing to do with that girl.'

'Which girl?' Davey had taunted.

'What do you mean "which girl"? I only wrote about the other poor cows. Janet Yarwood was the only one I ever set eyes on alive.'

'Oh, yeah. The postgrad student.' Davey had lit up a cigarette, inhaling sharply. 'She give you much info, did she?'

Martin had frowned then, hating to be reminded how he'd wormed his way into the woman's office on the pretence that the *Gazette* were setting up a retrospective show for Lucy Haining. How obvious it was that the poor bitch had been grieving for a lost love. Martin had hardened himself at the time but now his sense of shame was compounded by a dread of this man at his side. He remembered the fatal turn of their conversation so well.

'She did tell me about Lucy. Said she'd got in with a bad crowd. Usual story. She'd been involved in some money-making scam to fund her art work.' Martin had paused and stared at his friend. 'I forgot to tell you. Janet Yarwood asked if I knew you. Since I was on the *Gazette*. Said she knew your work or something.'

Davey had laughed at that.

'What it is to be famous, eh?'

Recalling his reaction, Martin shuddered. These words had a different meaning now. He'd tried so hard to remember the dead woman's exact words. What had she said? 'I've got a couple of Davey Bairds at home.' Martin saw again in his mind's eye the waif-like frame and that face full of misery; but she had brightened up as she'd said that.

He'd wondered why Davey was so interested.

'So what photos did she have of yours, anyway? Were they from that exhibition at the Collins Gallery?'

'Yeah, probably. Don't remember.'

At this, Martin had been puzzled. He'd told the photographer about his visit to the House for an Art Lover. Yet Davey had never made any mention of his photos. Of course, he'd probably sold so many prints, it would be hard to keep track. That had been his conclusion at the time. Then he'd glanced at the insouciant faces of the two boys in his own signed print.

'Where d'you get the models, Dave?'

The question had been asked casually but the other man's reaction had been explosive.

'Where the hell d'you think? I *pay* for them. OK? You journos are so bloody nosy!'

'Sorry I spoke.' Martin had held up his hands in a gesture of peace. 'I'm going off to get changed. Seeing my lady tonight.' Then, as Davey had made no move to leave, he'd added, 'How about sticking the kettle on? I could do with a cup of something after that curry.'

'Sure thing.' Davey had smiled a thin-lipped smile. 'Can you give me a lift there too? I need something I left at Diane's the other night.'

Martin recalled his curiosity being aroused. What was going on? As far as he knew, Davey Baird had never set foot in Diane's flat. He'd decided to take him along, though, grudgingly. Then they'd arrived and the nightmare had begun.

They'd been driving around for what seemed like hours and he was gritting his teeth thinking of Diane and that gash along her throat. What if she was dead? Martin shuddered. They had driven through St Mungo's Park, Martin picturing himself as another corpse below the bushes. But he had been told to drive on, through the city, up past the Art School, down a rutted lane, on and on weaving in and out of the dark places of Glasgow. From time to time he'd glanced at the petrol gauge, hoping that they'd run out of fuel somewhere in the city centre and then maybe he could make a break for it. But the needle was steady at a quarter full, only dropping slightly as the journey continued.

Now the road ahead was clear of traffic, the rain on the windscreen only a fine mist.

He should do something heroic, Martin thought, flip the car over, seize that Sabatier kitchen knife that Davey held in his fist. Anything at all to escape. But his stomach churned weakly and he just drove on, concentrating on the lane markings.

They passed under the gantry near Ibrox Park.

'Left.'

The word snapped out. It didn't sound like Davey Baird at all. It was a nightmare where everything was distorted. In his dream Davey had turned into the St Mungo's killer. Surely he'd wake up any moment and see Diane safe and sound by his side.

The traffic lights were green and they sailed through.

'Right at the gates.'

Martin risked a glance then looked swiftly away. The black-handled knife gleamed under a passing street lamp. He slowed the red car down and read the two signs. The ski slopes, or . . .

'Right.'

Martin drove slowly around the curving driveway that took him up that familiar road. Guiltily, he recalled the last time he had been up this trail. His interview with Janet Yarwood.

'In here.'

Martin brought the Peugeot to a halt and cut the engine. For a moment he thought of leaving the lights on. A signal of some kind for help. But Davey leaned over and snapped them off.

'Keys.'

Martin handed them over, fingers trembling.

'Keep that seat belt on till I come round.'

The car door opened and Martin was facing that blade again.

'Out.'

For one mad moment the journalist feigned a stumble and lunged out at the man with the knife. He screamed as the blade slashed his wrist bone.

'Get to hell, Marty.' Davey Baird was a crouching shadow as Martin sank to his knees with the pain. 'Get up. Walk.'

The blade came close to his throat and Martin eased himself up away from its lethal point. Davey motioned ahead of them into the darkness.

'Down there, and don't make a sound or you'll get more of this.'

The knife jabbed through the wool of his jersey, forcing Martin into a stumbling walk. The curry he'd eaten hours before tasted sour in his mouth.

The path, if there was one, was in total darkness and Martin had the sensation of going deeper and deeper into some valley. The House for an Art Lover lay behind them now, screening them from view. His breath fogged the darkness as he strained to make out the ground which suddenly became stony. Steps. There were steps. He must count them. But there were only four. An archway loomed above him and, as he ducked his head, he felt the knife in his back once more.

The car slewed off onto the expressway and Solomon felt pinned back against his seat as the driver risked his own licence to speed to the park. The helicopter had been scrambled and was on its way. The heat-sensitive device could track their quarry on the ground,

Solomon knew. One way or another, this one wouldn't get away. But would the journalist escape unharmed? The dark shapes of trees and bushes burst into colour against the full beams of the headlights as they turned off into Pollokshields. The car squealed around a bend then slowed down to enter the narrower paths leading up to the Rennie Mackintosh house.

'It's a dead end at the car park,' Solomon advised.

'Right. Alert all units.'

Lorimer began to speak into the radio again, issuing instructions.

The trees lining the driveway loomed towards them and then the shape of the house came plainly into sight. There were no lights on anywhere but there was a solitary car parked at the far end of the car park.

The Chief Inspector and the uniformed driver opened the doors of the Rover, motioning to Solomon to leave them open. No noise. That was understood. The rain had stopped and only the sound of dripping branches could be heard as they stood peering into the darkness.

'It's Enderby's, all right.'

A torch was swept over the red Peugeot's registration and briefly into the interior. The three men stood listening. Not a sound.

'Get onto the radio. Tell air support our exact location,' Lorimer whispered.

His glance flicked over Solomon, who had leaned against the red car. Where on earth had they gone? With the darkness for cover and hours until dawn the whole park was a threat. He recalled St Mungo's Park in the wake of the three bloodied corpses and the surveillance exercise there. Would the dogs be circling this perimeter yet? Suddenly a faint noise made him look up. The light from the helicopter was a swiftly moving star in the distance.

Another sound from the driveway alerted them to the approach of other cars. They'd killed their lights and were like grey shadows coming through the trees. Soon the whole area was filled with uniformed officers. Lorimer's call for mutual aid had alerted numerous other Divisions. Briefly he wondered if any of them had been called away from George's party. But despite the numbers, there was no immediate move to scour the park.

'Why aren't they making a move?' Solomon was indignant.

'Air support.' Lorimer pointed upwards. 'They'll use the tracking device to follow anyone moving across the park. The infrared picks them out. We'll just have to hope that there is still a moving target.' Solomon glanced at the Chief Inspector, as if sifting his words for meaning.

Catching his look, Lorimer gave a crooked smile. 'Oh, yes, Dr Brightman. These men are armed.'

They looked up as the twin-engined Eurocopter banked above them, its lights flooding an area as big as the football pitch at nearby Ibrox. Lorimer returned to the car, leaning forward to hear the radio controller's report. So far there was no movement in the park. The beams from the helicopter swept over the wet grass, illuminating the lawns for a second, then the darkness seemed blacker than ever.

Martin was on his knees under some sort of wall. His hands had been forced behind him and tied with a chain that cut into the flesh. He wanted to cry out but his throat was dry and, anyway, who would hear him? Davey Baird sat above him on the steps, still clutching the Sabatier. For a while he had simply stared at him. What the hell was going through his mind?

'Want to know why I did it, Marty?'

The voice didn't sound familiar in the dark. It was the sneer of a badly acted villain in some cheap drama. Somehow that gave Martin a glimmer of hope. It would come to an end. It wasn't real.

'No?' the voice continued. 'Well, I'm going to tell you anyway. Remember the wee hairdresser? That first one? I didn't know her from Adam. She just turned up when I needed her. And the third one? The schoolgirl? All that rubbish about a number seven bus. She never even caught one. Had a spat with the boyfriend and hitched a lift home in an off-duty ambulance. Only the nice ambulance driver turned out to be me.' He laughed softly. 'I had them hopping all right. Thought they'd got another Yorkshire Ripper. St Mungo's murderer. Oh, Marty, what a help you were in keeping that jackanory going. And all along the only one who needed to be done in was that bitch, Lucy.'

Martin cringed at the venom in the voice.

'Got so bloody greedy. Was going to spill a whole can of worms if I didn't keep her in funds. Then that stupid old fool. Knew about the ambulance, of course. Had his own kicks in there often enough.'

Martin moved his hands in their metal bond, feeling the blood from his wrist slippery on the chain links. The photographer's blonde hair fell over his face as he jerked him up.

'Oh, no you don't, Marty. I haven't finished with you yet.'

The boot went into his stomach and Martin buckled in a deep groan.

'Shit! Bloody helicopters.'

Davey pulled away, letting the journalist fall back onto stony grass. Bright, searching beams picked out the sunken hollow and Martin was suddenly on his own. Davey had vanished into the darkness.

Once the moving target had been sighted, the police spread out in all directions, leaving Lorimer and Solomon with just three officers by the cars. The helicopter pilot kept up a running commentary.

'Out by the walled garden. No, he's turned back. Must be locked. No sign of another person.'

Solomon and Lorimer exchanged looks. Was Martin Enderby already another victim?

Lorimer knew the team of men would be tracking the killer now, following the voice above on their radios. The sound of the chopper drowned his thoughts as it wheeled overhead once more, circling an area not too far from the main building. Was he heading their way?

This is a Celtic place, full of sacrifice. Full of blood. The stones form his cross. The sacrifice has to be made.

The figure in the dark seizes his victim and raises the knife high.

A burst of sound resonates into the air and a beam floods the place with light.

He drops the victim and the dark returns.

He has the knife. He is on another level, up and away from this sunken garden and its Celtic knot. Away.

His feet are drumming on the wet turf. The light above points its long finger towards him and he cries out in a whimper as if it pains his eyes.

Keep running. No one can get to you now. The darkness will cover you. Keep to the darkness. The knife feels strong and powerful. A weapon of destruction. Like the chain.

Lorimer was aware of a movement to his left. Turning, he caught a glimpse of a shadowy figure whose pale hair gleamed in the light from the chopper. Then he was gone. Lorimer was after him like a shot, feet thudding over the wet grass, slipping and sliding until they found the path below. There he was, heading for the nearest patch of trees. With his breath coming in short bursts, Lorimer hammered after him.

The man looked round once and suddenly Lorimer was flinging himself at the running feet in an old-fashioned rugby tackle. Lorimer grabbed the hand brandishing the knife. The killer struggled under his grip then cried out in pain as Lorimer jerked his arm backwards, squeezing tighter and tighter, until the weapon fell dully to the ground.

Other footsteps thumped over the path and Lorimer glanced up, relieved to see PC Matt Boyd.

'Right, you!'

Boyd dropped quickly to his knees by Lorimer's side, handcuffs out and ready. With a click they were on and the constable yanked the killer to his feet. Lorimer straightened himself up, wiping mud from his dress trousers. Under the helicopter's dazzling lights the Sabatier glinted on the wet grass. Lorimer bent to pick it up gingerly, folding it inside a handkerchief.

Light illuminated the face between them. Lorimer saw the dirty yellow hair and the wild staring eyes. Then the head was drooping and sullen, all fight gone out of him. Lorimer became aware of other uniformed figures closing in on them. He nodded to Matt Boyd then watched as his men marched back towards the car park, Baird a dark shadow in their midst. The noise of the chopper's blades receded into the night. Taking a deep breath of fresh night air, Lorimer began the climb back up to the waiting cars.

Very little was said as the officers put the man into the back of the waiting car. Lorimer stared at the man in shocked disbelief. How the hell could such a slight figure have wreaked such havoc? Still, there was one more thing left to do.

'Give me a moment, please,' Lorimer said.

The uniformed officer beside Davey Baird slid off his seat to make way for the Chief Inspector. Baird was handcuffed, so it was not too difficult to take hold of the blond wig and pull it from the scalp of the photographer. The resin gave way to reveal the skinhead below. Lorimer nodded to himself as he saw the scars lacing the man's scalp. Old scars. Solomon would find the last pieces of his own missing jigsaw there, he was certain. He tossed the wig onto the man's lap but as he turned to go Davey snarled at him suddenly and spat. The gob of spittle ran down Lorimer's dinner jacket like a slowly moving slug. The two men locked eyes for an instant.

Then the door was slammed and Solomon was standing by his side, watching the car take the road to Headquarters.

'Sir, we've found him!'

Lorimer turned to see two officers with a tall man limping between them. An ambulance had already been called. Martin looked up as he saw the Chief Inspector. All traces of his earlier humiliation were gone.

'Diane, is she . . . ?'

'She's all right, son. She's all right.'

Then, as the journalist broke down and wept, Lorimer patted him on the back and let him be led away to a waiting squad car.

'Well, that's it,' Lorimer breathed deeply, feeling the night air cold and fresh in his lungs.

Solomon watched as the officers gathered again in the car park. 'Now, what?' he asked.

Lorimer heaved a deep sigh.

'The interview room. See what this bastard has to say. Get it done. Then, home. Bed. For an hour or two at least.' He smiled at the psychologist who shuddered. Every nerve in Soloman's body was trembling but Lorimer stood, hands clasped in front of him, calm and unruffled. For once, Solomon tried to make sense of the man's body language but failed.

'How do you feel?' he asked outright.

'Feel? Bloody glad that it's over. Relief, frankly. That's it, barring the paperwork. All over. All that investigating. We'll have the reports to conclude. Then it's up to the courts.'

'What do you think he'll get?' Solomon queried as they walked together towards the Rover.

'Forever, if justice is done. Lock him up and throw away the key.' Lorimer shrugged. 'Maybe he'll plead insanity. Fancy yourself as an expert witness?'

His eyes gleamed in the Rover's headlamps, and Solomon looked to see if Chief Inspector Lorimer was really as unaffected by this result as he made out. But the blue eyes were unfathomable, following the progress of a certain police vehicle as it disappeared between the trees.

35

The High Court of Justiciary in Glasgow stood in an area of the city poised between life and death. On one side the City Mortuary hugged the new Court buildings while on the other, Paddy's Market displayed its wares as people drifted in and out, picking over the discards of other people's lives. Looking across at this, as if from an aloof distance, stood a Spiritualist Church housed in a plain shop-front.

Within the precincts of the Court, life and death were very much to the fore. Lorimer was sitting towards the rear of the court. He'd arrived early. Gazing around at the now familiar modern courtroom he took in the details of the place. The room was brightly lit from a multitude of concealed ceiling lights. Wooden wall panels were punctuated by three columns either side with circles of greenish frosted glass that glowed from the picture lights behind them. They reminded Lorimer of the works of Rennie Mackintosh. There was a frieze of Celtic inlay, dark olive in colour, at picture-rail height. The whole effect was pleasing to the eye, so long as the Court remained empty. The moment the black-gowned figures entered, however, Lorimer's attention was immediately transferred.

The trial had lasted seven weeks so far but today, he'd been advised by Iain MacKenzie, sentencing would certainly take place. It was months since Baird had been taken into custody. He'd been questioned countless times about his part in the paedophile ring. But there had been no more names given.

The killer had spent the whole summer in Barlinnie after his initial appearance before the Court, a summer now long past as the days grew darker once more. Even Lorimer's Portuguese holiday with his wife was only a warm memory now.

Baird had pleaded not guilty.

His solicitor had evidently spent plenty of time and trouble obtaining evidence to show that David Baird of 3/13 St Mungo's Heights, Glasgow, had been of unsound mind whilst perpetrating the acts of which he stood accused. Several dates had already been fixed for trial. Postponements had included days when the accused was unfit to appear due to illness, or when the defending advocate had some detail that required more careful scrutiny prior to trial. Lorimer had seen it all before. The time-wasting of the law courts was legendary. That it was the same south of the border, and probably the world over, was little consolation. Days had turned into weeks, Lorimer only attending at specific occasions, as the Fiscal kept him informed of proceedings. There were times when he thought he knew Iain MacKenzie's voice better than Maggie's.

Lorimer had not been cited as a witness. There was a morass of statements from his officers who had stood already in the witness box, stony-faced and answering questions in clipped monotones for the most part. He'd been proud of their disciplined manners towards the cross-questioning, especially of DC Cameron who had been rigid with nerves.

Matt Boyd's commendation had more than made up for his disappointment that the case had not after all been drug-related. In the witness box he'd stood ramrod straight, never once referring to his notebook.

Solomon had surprised him, too. The psychologist had been, if anything, more professional than all the others. It was almost as if he'd been detached from the whole affair. Even when he had described his own attack, there had been the usual considered pauses and an air of seeming indifference to the fate of the accused.

The background reports and the trial itself had thrown up so many aspects of the murderer's past. Solomon's profile had been uncanny in its accuracy. And there had been answers to other questions Lorimer had been unable to work out. How had Baird made his way from Strathmirrin without an accomplice? In the end, as so often, it was a simple explanation. A bicycle. Obvious, really, once he'd pieced it all together.

The murder weapon should have given him a clue, of course. The man rode his bike all over the city, it seemed. It also explained why the ambulance had never been seen in the vicinity of St Mungo's Heights. It had never been there. Baird had kept his bike in the old ambulance. Kevin Sweeney remembered that later. Other small boys interviewed by Gail Stewart confirmed this.

Norman Yarwood's visit to HQ on the day following Baird's arrest had also been most satisfying. Lorimer had shown Solly the file that contained the witness statements taken at St Mungo's Heights all those months before. Any long-running murder inquiry was logged into their computer system and Lorimer had pointed the cursor at the name, highlighting it. Davey Baird. Thirteenth floor, St Mungo's Heights. Occupation: photographer. He remembered Solly's astonished face as he'd told him.

'Yarwood found a photo of Lucy Haining taken in Janet's flat. The missing pictures were in the background. They weren't paintings at all.' Lorimer had paused to let his words sink in. 'They were black and white portrait photographs. Of Lucy.'

Solly had nodded sagely. 'And he'd taken them down after . . .'

'Exactly. Janet Yarwood must have become suspicious or he wouldn't have had to kill her too. Those photographs told too much for his liking; that he'd known Lucy and had met Valentine through her classes.'

'And his name would be on my list. The one on the disk.'

'Janet Yarwood must have told him. She never realised that she'd signed her own death warrant. But he knew you'd have his name by that time.'

'So he paid me a visit.'

Lorimer had nodded. 'But he didn't need to do you in. A quick slug and you were out of the way while he found that disk. Anyway, you must be pretty pleased that he fitted your own profile.'

'Indeed.' Solomon had agreed. 'Baird was motivated by the effects of his abuse as a child. The redskin warrior was lurking underneath all the time.'

'Don't forget the other motive, though,' Lorimer had warned him. 'It was being blackmailed by Lucy that drove him to want to kill her in the first place.' He'd shaken his head wearily, thinking of the meaningless sacrifice of those other young lives.

'It seems we were both right,' he'd added. But looking back

at them now he knew neither he nor Solomon had taken any satisfaction from his words.

Since then all the missing pieces had been put into place.

Now the summing up was to begin and the jury would have to decide on a verdict. Lorimer had no doubt what they would choose. He listened as the prosecuting counsel began his address to the jury. It was a harrowing litany of evil; murder, mutilation and child abuse. Lorimer noticed with approval how the advocate paused to let his words sink in as he outlined each item in the catalogue of crimes. He wasn't ramming it down their throats. He didn't have to.

Forensic evidence had shown clearly that Baird had indeed killed and mutilated the four young women. The pathologist's testimony showed that the traces of blood from their scalps matched those found among the photographer's camera equipment. The traces of DNA had also conclusively linked Baird with the deaths of all four women and Valentine Carruthers.

Now the defence would begin its summation. Lorimer uncrossed his legs and sat up straight. These seats were not designed for the comfort of a long-legged policeman. Lorimer's lip curled in distaste for what he was about to hear.

The advocate chosen to defend Davey Baird was an older man, much experienced in the ways of murder trials. Lorimer had encountered him before. He began slowly and gravely. But Lorimer noticed that he avoided looking at the defendant. There was the usual stuff about an unfortunate background. Baird's mother had been a convicted drug user. There was no mention of a father. The child had drifted in and out of care but not before the mother had taken a knife to the boy. It had happened while she'd been under the influence of hallucinogenic drugs. The pictures held up earlier had been close-ups of Baird's damaged scalp.

The advocate was banging on about the psychological damage done by a mother. But into Lorimer's mind came the image of another mother, stiff and unbending, standing beside that bleak cottage door. Now the man was relating background reports that had shown how Baird had been subjected to sexual abuse at the hands of his carers. He clearly wanted the jury to take account of all this when they made their decision.

There was a clearing of throats and a rustling of papers as the Court prepared to hear His Lordship's charging of the jury.

The judge reiterated the gravity of the case, not dwelling on the horrors but nonetheless spelling out the catalogue of crimes.

Not a snowball's, thought Lorimer, glancing at the jury. He noted the faces pale with stress and fatigue after all these weeks. One man put his hand under an older woman's arm as they rose to consider their verdict. All eyes in the Court were on them as they made their way to the jury room.

Lorimer looked at the red digital clock on the side of the bench. There was plenty of time before lunch. It would all be over soon.

As they filed back into the Court, not one of them looked at Davey Baird, flanked by the two police officers in the dock.

'Guilty, my lord.'

The words rang out in Court.

Lorimer stared at Baird's back. He had reeled as if he'd been struck a blow. He made to sit down but the two officers had him on his feet again and then there was silence as the Court waited for His Lordship to speak. There was no kindliness about the judge's demeanour now.

Lorimer could see the back of Baird's head, the scars more evident now because he knew they were there. The killer's eyes would be fixed on His Lordship's, needing to know his fate.

'David Baird, you have been found guilty of the following crimes . . .'

Lorimer listened to the familiar litany of the man's atrocities. One after another of his crimes was awarded custodial sentences and Lorimer counted them up rapidly. The man would never see the light of day again, if the sums really added up. But things could change, as Chief Inspector Lorimer knew. With the overcrowding in prisons reaching crisis point, there was a tendency towards early release. There could be remission then rehabilitation followed by community involvement and even a spell in the open prison system, all laudable things in themselves but not for the likes of the St Mungo's murderer. At least he hoped not.

The last Lorimer saw of Davey Baird was his descent from the dock. His head hung down as he looked towards his feet. Again Lorimer was struck by his slight frame. Who would have thought, looking at such a poor creature, that he'd be capable of all that bloodshed?

Lorimer stood as the judge left the Court then gathered up his raincoat. There were other crimes waiting to be solved, other prisoners awaiting trial, but he would be unlikely to see anything like this one again in his career. Still, you never knew. And the shades of fate cast long shadows.

Epilogue

RETROSPECTIVE DRAWS IN THE CROWDS

The opening of TIMES PAST at Glasgow School of Art is by any standards a huge success. This retrospective exhibition of the work of two talented young artists seeks to show the world the unfulfilled promise of each before their untimely deaths. Janet Yarwood's sensitive paintings of children were hailed by many as a new dimension in portraiture. Her protégé, Lucy Haining, demonstrated Yarwood's influence in her own child drawings, the striking luminosity of the eyes being a particular feature. Haining's jewellery was also on show, including her final-year portfolio, which, of course, she never had the opportunity to present. The exhibition was officially opened by Mr Norman Yarwood, who expressed his delight at the recognition given to his daughter and her pupil. Glasgow School of Art will host the exhibition until the end of this month, when it will be taken on tour to art colleges throughout Scotland and England.

Review by Jayne Morganti

BOOKS

Offender profiling is not by any means a new topic written about by our eminent psychologists. Nevertheless, a recent publication by Glasgow University Press has taken the scientific world by storm. Dr Solomon Brightman, whose expertise was used in the investigation into the notorious St Mungo's Murders, has revealed some astonishing new techniques in what is still a fairly young branch of psychology. Using the case as a model, Dr Brightman puts forward theories about criminal behaviour that seek to promote a holistic approach to criminal investigation. Alternative Methods *uses statistical studies of over three hundred urban murders in recent times and deals with the patterns of criminal behaviour that reveal deep-seated psychophysical motives. The book has already met with some controversy from the establishment, notably from Dr Gifford Gillespie, who accused the author of 'Seeking sensationalism at the expense of scientific rationale'. Channel 4's* Science Now *will feature the two psychologists in a debate that promises to be lively. See Reviewer's Choice page 22 for details.*

NEW FACES

Detective Chief Inspector Mark Mitchison has been promoted to Superintendent following the retirement last year of Divisional Commander, Superintendent George Phillips. Superintendent Mitchison has declared his intention to pull all senior officers into a new management strategy in the light of the latest round of Home Office budget cuts.

KILLER WINS MAJOR AWARD
Exclusive by Jack Pettigrew, Home Affairs Correspondent

The Special Unit, HM Prison, Shotts, has been the focus recently for a series of artistic and literary works by its inmates. The latest of these to gain public renown is David Baird, the St Mungo's murderer. Baird's photography was already well established in the Glasgow art world but won increased notoriety during and after his trial.

Since his imprisonment, Baird has been encouraged by the regime at Shotts to continue his creative work. Sales of his existing work have risen dramatically, and now the one-time freelance photographer for the Gazette *has added considerably to his prestige by winning* The Times' *annual award for best photographer of the year. Prison officers are reported as saying that they are impressed by the prisoner's behaviour in the year he has spent in Shotts, one officer even going as far to claim that Baird is a model prisoner. This can only augur well for Baird's solicitor who has now lodged the appeal against his sentence. If Baird were to serve the full sentence, he would never be eligible for release. It would then be at the discretion of the Home Secretary to offer any hope of eventual change in his sentence. With the Government's current white paper on rehabilitation of offenders under discussion by Parliament, the timing of Baird's award may prove to be fortuitous for the man who claimed insanity as a defence for multiple killing and mutilation of young girls.*

Leader Comment page 12.

Light was flooding down from the stained glass above him as Lorimer approached the familiar sweep of stone steps. He'd been coming to Kelvingrove Art Galleries and Museum since boyhood when he'd first revelled in the dinosaur skeletons and cases full of stuffed animals. Eventually that same small boy had found the paintings and he'd been looking at them ever since.

As he turned an angle of the staircase, Lorimer gave a cursory glance towards the people's choice of paintings ranked row upon row against the varnished panelling. It was a place full of contrasts, he mused, considering the brightness of the modern glass work followed by these dark corridors: just like the Rembrandt he had come to visit.

Lorimer slowed down as he entered the room. The natural light gave warmth to these walls and each painting glowed within its heavily gilded frame.

This was the one.

He sat down on the bench, sensing a stillness within himself as he looked at the painting. Everything else was forgotten as he took in the rich browns and reds, the elegant brushwork, that quality of light on helmet and eye; the chiaroscuro that was the artist's trademark. He knew it so well and yet it never failed to amaze him. How many people had sat, as he did now, seeing Rembrandt's *Man in Armour*? How many more would marvel at the artist's genius in years – no, centuries – to come?

As Lorimer continued to gaze he felt almost invisible before the work of the great master. It was as if his own life suddenly lacked any significance. Perhaps he'd make superintendent some day, perhaps not. Did it matter very much? One day he'd be gone. Other feet would always find their way to this bench; other eyes drink in this masterpiece. Lorimer's gaze took in the face in the painting. Was it only great art that endured or was there something in the human spirit that survived this frantic tilt at life?

His thoughts were broken as he felt a thump on the bench beside him. From the corner of his eye Lorimer could see a child of about seven perched on the bench, swinging his legs. Noticing the boy's sticky hands clutching the edge of the seat and his sweetie-reddened mouth, he moved instinctively aside. The boy didn't seem to notice, absorbed in his own study of the Rembrandt.

'Hey, mister,' the child asked, turning to Lorimer. 'Is he a sojer?'

Hiding a smile, Lorimer replied, 'That's right, son. He's called *Man in Armour.*'

The wee boy looked back at the picture, considering.

'And did he kill anyone, like?'

Lorimer's eyebrows shot up, then he followed the child's gaze to the grave face of the knight. What was the boy seeing? The shield? The knight staring towards a shadowy sword clutched in one gauntlet-clad hand? He was only an artist's model, Lorimer knew; some fellow got up in cloak and armour for Rembrandt's studio. He could tell the child all this and more besides. Yet no one knew who the man in the armour really was.

'Here, Billy. What have I told you about talking to strangers? No offence, pal.'

A young woman in jeans and cropped top was pulling the child off the bench and making an apologetic face at Lorimer. He watched them as they made their way towards the door, the child protesting as he was escorted firmly from the room. As Billy turned for one last wistful look at the famous painting, Lorimer was painfully reminded of another small boy who had talked to a stranger and another man who had dressed up to play a part.

Lorimer stood up to leave but turned back to look at the helmeted figure, feeling suddenly cheered by the wee boy's fleeting interest in his favourite painting.

Billy, he felt sure, would be back.

Acknowledgements

I would like to thank the following for their time and help in researching this novel: Strathclyde Police, particularly Superintendent Ronnie Beattie and former Superintendent Val Grysbek, PC Kirsty McCartney and PC Mairi McMillan of the Female and Child Unit, Greenock, and the Street Liaison Group, Cranhill; Professor Peter Vanezis and the staff at the University of Glasgow Department of Forensic Medicine, particularly Dr Black and Dr Cassidy; the late Mr Fenton Maxwell, Supervisor, and the staff at Glasgow City Mortuary; Dr W. Rodgers, former head of Forensic Science, Pitt Street, Glasgow; the staff of the High Court of Judiciary, Glasgow; James Freeman, Iain Wilson and Ian Hossack of the *Herald* newspaper, Glasgow; Ian Johnston, Director of Postgraduate Studies, Glasgow School of Art; Eric Thorburn, photographer; Sturrocks Wigs, Glasgow; James Margey, hair stylist.